D0396843

SWANN'S WAR

— A NOVEL —

MICHAEL OREN

DZANC
BOOKS

2580 Craig Rd.
Ann Arbor, MI 48103
www.dzancbooks.org

Library of Congress Cataloging-in-Publication Data Available Upon Request

ISBN: 9781950539604
First US edition: October 2022
Interior text design by Michelle Dotter
Cover by Dorothy Carico Smith
Author photo by Joshua Fleisher

This book is a work of fiction. Any references to historical events, real people,
or real places are used fictitiously. Other names, characters, places, and events
are products of the author's imagination, and any resemblance to actual events
or places or persons, living or dead, is entirely coincidental.

Printed in the United States of America

10   9   8   7   6   5   4   3   2   1

For Pola Miller (1928-2015)

With belated gratitude

FOURTH CLIFF

The Emplacement

P.O.W. Camp

Cranberry Bogs

The Moors

Flotsam Bar

Shipyard

Docks

General Store

The Town

First Congregational Church

Falmouth Ferry

McQueen's Boarding House

Police Station

Lighthouse

Prologue: May, 1944

Just after sunrise, in a Mercury coupe painted black and white to look like one of the squad cars from the coast, Captain Swann patrolled. The route began in town, still locked up at this hour, the storefronts dark, and continued along the docks rising slightly with the tide. A few begrudging streetlamps, a moss-mottled stone for the fishermen lost at sea. From there, the vehicle crawled up a bluff to an intersection lorded over by the First Congregational Church, and then turned north, past the general store and Old Man Gainor's shipyard and finally the Flotsam Bar. Beyond lay only landscape, crusty and gnarled. Twenty miles off the shores of Massachusetts, this was the island its original inhabitants called Hockomok—The Devil's Place—but whose Puritan settlers renamed Fort Wheelock and later, less belligerently, Fourth Cliff.

Picking up speed, the coupe passed by a few faux-rustic summer houses, most of them boarded up for the duration, and the skeletons of skiffs washed up by storms. The cranberry bogs and the prison camp with its Quonset huts and wire. And then, as incongruous as a cinderblock plopped on a holiday table, the emplacement. Three rectangular bunkers, the biggest one in the middle and sprouting a long, black barrel pointing eastward. That and the flagpole set in a ring of symmetrical stones was the only evidence that this was a military site. A lone cannon guarding an entire nation from enemy ships that had all but disappeared.

The road turned from pavement to sand. The end came abruptly, after some scraggly dunes, on a scarp overlooking a beach. Little more than a shingle really, it proffered neither sand nor shade, only pebbles and sharp-edged shells. The ocean was gray and still too cold for swimming; its whitecapped waves rose and fell uninvitingly. Captain Swann stepped out of the car, hand on holster, and gazed down at the shore.

This was where they used to drive on his motorcycle and lay naked on a boho blanket. They made love here that last August night and were still commingled at dawn. Entwined between the gull screeches and the salty smell of their bodies, the sizzling of surf between stones. Here they wept, or at least she did, her tears tinged with rage.

Atop one of the island's four cliffs—whether the second or third was widely debated—the police captain lingered. Not for much longer, though. Soon, the boats would be setting out to sea only to return at twilight brimming with cod, bluefish, herring, and scup. The weighing and filleting would then begin and the bargaining with the buyers who arrived on the last of the three daily ferries from Falmouth. Another day in a world utterly cut off from the real one, boring, unchanging, and seemingly at peace.

With a tip of a hat brim, the captain returned to the patrol car and steered it back toward town. The main task now was to figure out how to pass the next eight hours. Filling out forms for requisitions not needed, reports for a stolen bicycle or an unpaid bar tab, never anything graver. Hogan, the well-meaning but half-witted patrolman, screwing up in yet another exasperating way. But other than that, nothing. Just thinking, remembering, and wrestling with loss.

The Mercury arrived back in town with the sun lodged firmly in the sky. The stores, many of them selling tackle, were open and boats were nestling the dock. But something was different. The way the fishermen gathered, not gabbing or bragging or smoking their tenth Old Gold of the morning, but murmuring anxiously to one another. They scarcely looked up as the captain parked and exited the coupe. Their eyes were fixed on a net hauled up and tangled around a by-catch too large to be a fish, even a shark.

"'Bout time," the captain heard one of the trawlers hiss.

They were an elderly bunch, some visibly sick, others not by trade fishermen at all. The real ones, the healthy ones, were off fighting the war in Europe and the Pacific or stationed stateside far from Fourth Cliff.

The captain edged closer to the net and heard another of the old trawlermen spit, "Black Bass," a vicious nickname. But this was no moment for argument, only for concentration. Assessing the evidence.

Inside the net was a man in a khaki uniform, a shoulder patch visible through the mesh.

"All right, who knows who this is?" Swann asked, and then after a pause, "Was."

But the fishermen only gawped. Most had never addressed the captain before, at least not officially, and were clearly unimpressed by the rank. Nothing seemed to command their respect, neither the black leather jacket or the eight-point cap, not the duty belt with its handcuffs and Colt. There was little time to worry about it, though, with a foreigner dead and dripping on a Fourth Cliff dock.

"I do," one of them finally volunteered. By far the youngest, the Devereux boy, working until his number came up. "I do," he repeated to the captain, Mary Beth Swann. "Ma'am."

PART ONE

1.

FRANCESCO ALBERTINI, THAT WAS THE NAME SHE WROTE IN HER onionskin notepad, and the cause of death, *drowning*. Identification was simple. The crews of the trawlers he often worked on knew him, as did the dockhands and merchants. They remembered a rangy, snaggle-toothed man in his twenties but still acne-scarred, a sadness stamped in his expression. Yet he stopped to help old ladies carry groceries and had a buoyant "Buongiorno" for everyone.

If all that didn't suffice, there was his shoulder patch testifying to his status as one of the ninety or so Italian prisoners of war interned on Fourth Cliff Island. Captured in America's battles overseas, first in North Africa and then in Sicily and now Italy itself, the POWs were shipped stateside and kept separate from their German allies, who were considered more belligerent. Rather than being penned up all day behind barbed wire, the Italians were left mostly on their own and allowed—encouraged—to go out and work. For the shorthanded fishermen, shopkeepers, and farmers who hired them for minimal wages, the Italians were a lifeline.

But nobody threw one to Francesco. Most of the Italians were farm or city boys who could easily hurt themselves fly fishing. Mary Beth could almost picture him tripping over some hawser and tumbling off the pier. No one would have heard his cries, not over the chugging of engines. The accident was regrettable, certainly, but hardly suspicious.

The body was cut loose and laid out on the dock. Mary Beth forced herself to kneel next to it, trying not to look at the face, the tongue bulging purple, the eyes already plucked out by crabs. She could not show any squeamishness, not with half the town looking on. Resisting the urge to play with her wedding band—an old nervous habit—she plumbed the pockets for effects.

There weren't many, only small change, a St. Christopher's medal, and a wilted photograph. Stuffing these into her jacket, she asked one of the tackle store owners to go and fetch Doc Cunningham. From another, with a pickup truck, she requested that the body be brought back to the camp for burial. Then, pushing the cap up her forehead, wiping her hands on her pants, she rose and returned to the coupe.

Driving to the station, her queasiness thickened. It wasn't just the memory of the dead man's face, puffy and pale, and the smell, but a nagging sense that she'd missed something. It gnawed at her while she completed the report at her desk. It haunted her at noontime, killing her appetite. She stared through the filmy glass on the door, reminded again that the name *Captain Swann* stenciled there referred to somebody else.

Her eyes fell to the photograph drying on her desk blotter. It showed a much older woman, black-clad and plump, and two little girls in braids. The three of them seemed to stare back at the police captain, as if in judgment.

What was there to write, really? That a young farm boy, suddenly shipped out to war and imprisoned in some faraway land, died not in his own bed surrounded by family but in a frigid ocean alone? And, even if she filed a report, who would read her it? She had no superior officer that she knew of, no one back on the coast who cared a feather what went on and didn't on humdrum Fourth Cliff, especially not in wartime.

The only power on the island was Old Man Gainor, the owner of the shipyard and Fourth Cliff's de facto mayor. He oversaw the upkeep of the docks and roads and the pay of anyone who needed to be paid, police included. Yet his true authority was a mystery to Mary Beth, who could count on one hand the times she'd seen him, much less spoken to him. Absent some dire emergency, the old man kept to himself. He'd read her report, possibly, but doubtfully do anything about it.

Mary Beth scribbled it out anyway, afraid she misspelled Albertini. Signing the form, she sighed and tried not to look again at the photograph. A car crunched on the coquina drive outside. Straightening behind her desk, Mary Beth nodded as Dr. Horace Cunningham gimped in.

"You might have been hasty," he wheezed.

He sat, or rather crumbled, into a chair opposite her and lit up a Chesterfield. Years of smoking had stained not only his fingers but his teeth. His skin was sallow and his blonde hair thinning and limp. The cuffs of his tailored shirt had frayed.

"Hasty? How?"

Cunningham puffed. "I took the liberty of examining the body."

"And?"

"Before burial, I asked that it be brought to my office."

His office was in reality a two-room apartment over the Fourth Cliff's only diner, not exactly the Ritz. That was where this Dartmouth-trained practitioner, a Back Bay grandee, languished after an incident some years ago with a disgruntled patient in Newport. Luckily for him, the islanders needed his services—the occasional stitch or baby delivery. Otherwise, they ignored him. Mary Beth, too, sensing in Cunningham something alien, even to an outlander like herself, preferred to keep her distance. It took something unusual—a post-mortem on a waterlogged corpse—to engage him.

"You examined the prisoner, yes?" Unusually high even in casual talk, Cunningham's voice crescendoed. His eyes, a diluted blue, grew dark. "I'm not blaming you, of course, what with the net and all those clodhoppers watching."

"But?"

"What made you think he drowned?"

Silence gripped the station, broken only by the crackle of tobacco.

"The tongue," Cunningham said. "Stuck out and swollen. And the red marks on the cheeks, easily mistaken for pimples. Look a little lower, under the collar, and you would have seen the welts."

"He struggled."

The eyes were now midnight, the voice for once deep. "He was strangled."

"You mean…murdered?"

"Unless he garrotted himself. Not easy," the doctor exhaled. "Tried it once myself."

"And you're positive." Already she was twisting the ring.

"Just to make sure, I took a syringe and drew a sample. While I'm no coroner, I know a dry lung when I see one."

This was said with a triumphal puff, followed by the screech of the doctor's chair. "I think, Captain Swann, you have a case on your hands. Your first, correct?" A smile followed, almost lipless, and far from sympathetic. "I wonder," he said while leaving, "what would Archie do?"

*   *   *

Alone again, Mary Beth looked around the station. There wasn't much to observe. Two radios, a Philco cathedral she listened to those nights when nothing happened, which was virtually always, and a two-way Motorola hooked up to the coupe in case of emergen-

cies, which they never had. An electric fan not yet necessary in this
still-cool May, perched on military-style file cabinets that she knew
stood mostly empty. Two blinded windows and walls with the island's usual bric-a-brac—a spindled ship wheel, an unnamed whaler's
portrait, a mounted three-foot cusk—along with a map of Fourth
Cliff. The locals likened it to a fishhook, but to Mary Beth it was
saxophone-shaped: thick and curved at the point of the town, wide at
one end and tapered at the other. Printed some years before, the map
was missing both the emplacement and the prisoner-of-war camp,
though both had been penciled in.

The station was a rickety affair, always in danger of blowing away
in some gale. If so, the desk, alone, would remain. Fashioned from
sturdy black ash, it sat on lion's paws and housed coffin-like drawers
and a blotter of seafoam green. On this, Mary Beth laid her head,
chin first, and considered her bleak situation. She tried, sweetly painful though it was, to remember just how it was she got there.

How could she have known, that Saturday in the Commons five
years before, that her entire life was about to change? How could she
remotely have anticipated the earthquake about to take place as she
sat by the pond and ate her ham and cheese lunch, gulping so as not
to be late?

Like any rookie, she had to prove herself, but ten times more so
as a woman. This meant chasing after streetwalkers and urchins in a
calf-length skirt, an ill-fitting kepi, and shoes made for shopkeepers. It
meant putting up with pinches and wisecracks even from other police.
"Wanna see my billy club?" they'd taunt her, and "Can I cop a feel?"
Nothing protected her, not the badge or her formidable build or even
her father, a third-generation Boyle in uniform. There weren't many
women in the BPD back then, and fewer still made it through their
initial assignments. She would survive, though. She'd prove her worth
to all of them, her father foremost. Someday, she'd even make sergeant.

The last thing she anticipated, crumbling her lunch bag, was to hear someone suggest, "You might want to wash that down," and to look up into a blinding penumbra. Mary Beth squinted, she blinked, and only then detected the figure of a young man, not too tall or broad-shouldered but solid nevertheless, holding out a Coke. A breaker of brown hair and teeth, a whiteness not often seen in her working-class Southie neighborhood. Though pushing thirty, his looks remained boyish, his nose pugged and chin cleft. His manner was easy enough for a student's, but the way he carried himself, relaxed yet subtly on guard, and his hard-baked tan told her he, too, was a cop.

Still, she was not the type to talk with strangers, especially on duty. But it was hot outside, a piece of crust was stuck in her throat, and there was something in the feminine figure of that bottle, pierced by a single straw, that made her reach out and accept it. That kept her from shifting too far on the bench as the young man sat down and introduced himself. So she learned his name, which, in view of the swans plying the Public Garden pond, made her laugh, and that he was indeed a policeman, which didn't. He talked about the weekend training with his Marine reserve unit, the game he took in at Fenway, and the maritime world he policed. Mostly, though, he asked questions—what life was like for her on the force, the challenges she encountered. More shocking than his inquiries were her heartfelt answers. She felt like a little girl in church again, confessing.

And she appreciated the way he looked at her. Not at her body or even at her face, black Irish pale and keenly pretty, but directly into the green of her eyes. Dinner that night was almost assumed, as was Sunday brunch the next morning, before he returned to work.

Five years and an eon ago, with so much upheaval in between. Her father's anguish at her Protestant wedding, her relocation to a place which, from his perspective, might have been Timbuctoo. And then the islanders who, though accustomed to summer vacationers, could be cold to those "washashores" who stayed on. Especially the Bostonians with accents stripped of most r's and squeezed through the nose, who said "frappe" when they meant milkshake and "tonic" even for a Coke. And to Fourth Cliff's first-ever policewoman, the locals could be downright hostile. Who did she think she was, they seemed to carp, this city slicker looking down on everyone, a stranger who just happened to marry their captain?

For Archie Swann was more than just the law for them. Descended from the earliest settlers, the sea and its supplicants in his blood, he understood the island as few could. Knew all the names and every strand and inlet. The only child of a father who died of polio and a mother of heartbreak shortly thereafter, he was unofficially adopted by all of Fourth Cliff. The people respected him and he, in turn, cared for them, guarded them as best he could from the ocean's myriad hazards, and comforted them in their hour of loss. They put up with his crisscrossing the dunes on his beloved Harley and forgave him for coming home with a Beantown brat. It didn't mean, though, that they had to like her.

Mary Beth remembered all this, with her chin still pinioned on the blotter. She recalled the love, the companionship, the sex, and then, of course, the war, which erased all that. And she recalled her anger. But refused to give in to it, not tonight, with a murderer lurking. Instead, she remained at her desk, wishing she had a drink and a cigarette, both of which she'd given up for that straight-laced husband of hers.

The distant surf crashed, a foghorn yowled, and her eyes fell once again to the photograph. An old woman in black with two braided girls—Francesco's mother and sisters, she supposed. They would eventually learn of his death and ask why there had been no justice. Why had there been no law?

She asked herself all the same questions, along with the one raised by Cunningham. She posed it out loud as if someone were beside her in the station—to the whaler's portrait and the mounted fish. "What would Archie have done?"

2.

Motive.

That's what Archie or any competent officer would seek first. The reason why one human being would take another's life, in this case with extraordinary violence. The need to avoid being caught for the crime and to make it seem like an accident. But who in Fourth Cliff would want to kill Francesco?

Mary Beth combed her mind. The victim was Italian, a nationality not universally adored in America. Sinatra and DiMaggio notwithstanding, many people, including her own father, considered them either untrustworthy or slavishly loyal, oversexed or effeminate, underworld types or publicity hounds. Incapable of following orders, they nevertheless marched when commanded by the Pope or Il Duce. Wops, greaseballs, dagos—all were flung around interchangeably in her old Irish neighborhood. Italians thought twice before detouring down her street.

And what bubbled over in South Boston stewed just below Fourth Cliff's surface. Those affable islanders with their ayuhs and chowdah, their rantum scoots and nor'easters, harbored entire armadas of hate. For black people, first, then Jews—not that they knew any—followed by "fahners" from any number of Mediterranean or

Eastern European countries, especially Roman Catholics—"Papists," the locals called them—like the Italians. For more than three years, Italy had been at war with the United States. Francesco was not merely an alien but an enemy alien, in certain circumstances, justifiably shot on sight.

These and other thoughts swarmed through Mary Beth's mind during the rest of the day and into the night, most of which she spent pacing the station's floor. Dawn broke as she lifted her head from the blotter and saw that it was too late to go home. Instead, she made herself a bitter cup of Postum, poured in some "armored heifer"— canned milk—and a teaspoon of rationed sugar. Mug in hand, she returned to the desk and began rifling its drawers for a pocket mirror, half-hoping she wouldn't find one and have to grapple with the knots in her cropped-short hair and the circles under her eyes. She had not put on a speck of makeup since high school, not even on her wedding day. The blue of her uniform was more than enough color for one woman, Mary Beth declared.

Her search was interrupted by the *brrring brring* of a bicycle bell. A cringeworthy sound on all other mornings, on this one it was birdsong.

A moment later, Officer Hogan ambled in. A man of maybe twenty-five with a long, pinched nose, eyes slightly crooked, and teeth so bucked that her father would have said they could eat cob corn through a picket fence. Too dumb for the draft—so people claimed—but not for the Fourth Cliff police. His duties were minimal, cycling about and assisting lost children, retrieving a cat from a tree. Anything more urgent, such as the fisherman who nearly bled out from a wolfish bite, and Hogan could freeze or faint. Though armed with a pistol, Mary Beth doubted he'd ever fired it or even if the old weapon worked.

"Morning, Captain," he chimed, as if oblivious to the state of emergency.

"Lemuel."

"You should see what the *Minerva* pulled in."

Mary Beth braced herself. "Not another one…"

"Mackerels. An entire hull of 'em. The look on Shattuck's face. Grinning from here to Swampscott."

She couldn't decide whether to berate or embrace him. Harmless and loyal, Hogan never questioned the few instructions she gave or her decision to appoint herself captain. Mary Beth had merely to straighten his high-peaked hat, a leftover from the 1920s, and tighten his shoulder strap and tie so that he at least looked the part. The bicycle would *brrring* and off he'd go on a beat that nobody knew or even cared about, until reporting for duty again the next morning.

Only today was different. "You heard about the prisoner, yes, Lemuel?"

Hogan lowered his head. "Francesco."

"You knew his name." Mary Beth was genuinely surprised. Hogan had trouble remembering many things, such as the north from the south side of the island, the Atlantic from the coast.

"He was always so friendly. Always saluting me and calling me amico. Or something like that."

"Then you know that your amico was killed yesterday. Killed, not drowned. And I have to find out by who."

The eyes knotted, the jaw sagged. Hogan nodded as though comprehending.

"And you, Lemuel, all I ask is that you stay on the lookout for anything unusual. Anything suspicious."

"Anything suspicious. Got it, Captain."

"And report it immediately to me."

"To you, yes, right away."

Hogan turned to exit the station, but halted at the door. "Francesco promised to take me for real spaghetti, in the North End, after the war," he said, though not necessarily to her. "I guess that's not going to happen."

Mary Beth waited for the bicycle crunch to fade before getting up from her desk and retrieving her duty belt, complete with handcuffs and Colt. She brushed off the eight-point cap she'd worn since the day she'd thrown out the kepi and the calf-length skirt, replacing it with midnight blue pants. She punched into Archie's old black leather jacket, which fit her just fine. Its epaulets sported the H-shaped captain bars that first looked like gateways to freedom but now seemed to lock her in. Her five-star badge, once a shield, had come to feel like a target.

*   *   *

The coupe followed its usual early morning route, beginning in town and then heading cross-island, past the shipyard and the Flotsam Bar and through the row of cranberry bogs. Apart from fishing and catering to vacationers, this was Fourth Cliff's only industry. With a high-water table and unlimited supply of sand—both needed to produce profitable crops—cranberry farming thrived. The only challenge was the paucity of manual laborers, as most of the locals were too proud or too old to stoop to the hard, wet work of harvesting. But that problem was solved abundantly enough and at minimal cost by the Italians.

The patrol car swung into their camp, a collection of Quonset huts hastily erected and then sealed off with wire. Four guard towers, one at each corner, loomed over the prisoners. The wire had rusted and snapped in most places, and the towers were manned solely by gulls. Apart from the Ballard brothers, both veterans of the Great War, who showed up in their doughboy uniforms once daily to deliver food and essentials, nobody supervised the place. Nobody took roll call or kept track of the prisoners' whereabouts. There was no need.

In their distinctive khakis, the Italians couldn't just board the ferry from Falmouth, and the coast was too distant to swim. And while one of the fishing boats or some pleasure craft could be shanghaied, that danger was deemed absurd. These were not German POWs, but Italians—peace-loving paisanos, most local people believed, who'd been only too happy to surrender, as allergic to war as landlubbers were to seasickness.

Mary Beth knew better, though. While many of the inmates were indeed sick of war and wanted only to reunite with their mamas and bambinos and whatever, some still itched for a fight. And though the majority had celebrated Il Duce's demise the previous year, openly toasting his overthrow, others quietly seethed. Some rejoiced at Mussolini's rescue by Nazi commandos and prayed for his triumphal return.

But those few fascists were nowhere evident as Mary Beth emerged from the coupe. All she saw was khaki-clad men loitering and smoking with lowered heads, kicking the sand. True, there had been deaths in the camp before, mostly from fevers, but nothing like this. Nothing like what had happened to Francesco, who was apparently well-liked, even beloved.

"A very good, very good, how do you say? Anima." Lorenzo, widely considered the camp spokesman, told her. Or rather sang, his voice modulating up and down like an aria. "Soul. He never hurt a fly."

Mary Beth scribbled something in her notepad. "No enemies? Nobody who wanted him dead?"

Lorenzo's head, large compared to the rest of him, completely bald and bony, shook several times. His hands wiped imaginary mist from the air. "No. No. No. Francesco was very…" Again, he turned to consult with men behind him, only to turn back to her shrugging. "Popolare."

These men, Lorenzo included, were so unlike the Italians she'd known—street-wise, sure of themselves, and large. The prisoners, by contrast, were sheepish and innocent-looking and seemed half her size. That's what war and poverty had done to them, Mary Beth reckoned. All except for one. He stood apart from the rest, a dapper-looking man with a pencil moustache and a jacket draped over his shoulders, at whom Lorenzo kept glancing. Out of fear or need for approval, Mary Beth couldn't tell which.

That man remained in sight as she followed Lorenzo around the camp. Though she passed it almost daily, she'd never been inside and was surprised to find it so homey. The Quonset huts housed neatly made bunks and potbelly stoves, each with an even ziggurat of wood. Walls decorated with modest black-and-white pinups, photos of volcanoes and bays, and makeshift crosses—all, no doubt, violations, but she wouldn't trouble someone over that.

Later, in a garlic-scented mess hall, she was greeted by the bug-eyed, white-smocked cook who alone among the prisoners had some meat on his bones. He smiled effusively, florid cheeks reddening, as he lifted a wooden spoon toward Mary Beth's mouth.

"Per favore! Per favore!" he begged her. His bug eyes appeared to bulge.

Mary Beth hesitated, then sipped. The tomato sauce was unlike any she'd ever tasted, with a seasoning totally unknown. "What in the Sam Hill is this?"

She turned first to the cook and then to Lorenzo, who seemed at a loss for the translation. He had to make do with the Italian. "Origano."

Throughout, the moustachioed man kept staring at her. Mary Beth tried to ignore him, not let him get under her skin. Beneath her jacket, though, she'd begun to sweat, and her fingers kept brushing her holster. She was about to turn and confront him when the mess hall's bell started clanging.

Lorenzo, the cook, even the hostile-looking prisoner all turned and walked outside. Mary Beth followed and found herself on the rim of a funeral. Francesco's, of course, but without the priest who came once monthly to hold Mass and take confession, only a squad of pallbearers carrying an unadorned coffin to an open grave next to several whitewashed markers. Different inmates took turns speaking, and though Mary Beth couldn't understand them, she detected the anguish in their tone. The same sorrow inflected the song they sang, to the accompaniment of wooden flutes and an upside-down bagpipe, with a single word—montanara—she thought she recognized. They were singing still as each mourner tossed a shovelful of dirt and crossed himself. Only one of them declined.

∗   ∗   ∗

Was Francesco the victim of a fight between the prisoners themselves and, if so, what was the nature—personal, political? Hardly the contentious type, had he merely been a bystander, or had he somehow provoked his own death? In that case, any of the prisoners could have killed him, even Lorenzo. For wasn't he the type you'd find in any prison—short yet commandeering, smiling and singing to you even as he shoved you in the deep? A quarryman back in Umbria, she learned, capable of breaking rocks. And that other inmate, the one with the moustache. Mary Beth could almost imagine him with a piano wire strung between his palms, slicing through the victim's windpipe.

But then another question beset her. If this was an Italian-on-Italian crime, why should anyone care? For all their warmth, not so long ago, these men wouldn't have thought twice about shooting any Americans. Archie, too. Would one less POW really matter, Mary Beth wondered? Chalk it up to the war.

These were the thoughts that accompanied Mary Beth from the camp. But another nagged her. Irrespective of his status, Francesco was a human being, and by all accounts a decent one. And no less than any resident, the Italians were her responsibility. Most compelling of all, though, was the realization this case had become her litmus. Failing to solve it would make her a laughingstock, confirm all those whispers behind her back.

The prisoners were also leaving, climbing onto the back of the trucks that took them to the cranberry bogs or to the waterfront. Back in her car as well, Mary Beth considered driving further north to the beach, but convinced herself not to go there. Not today, with real police work to do. And what good would it do anyway? The memories, the bitterness, the regrets about not having put her foot down or even a gun to his head and told him, "To hell with your call to duty, your duty is to stay here with me." The remorse she felt for remaining tight-lipped just as she'd been raised, as she'd learned to stay those first brutal years on the force.

She wouldn't go to the beach today, but what, then, was her next stop? The investigation had scarcely begun and already she felt stumped. Should she return to the docks and grill some other fishermen or interview Old Man Gainor at his yard? Perhaps the pastor of First Congregational knew something, or Minnie at the Flotsam Bar? She could almost hear the fishermen cackling again, calling her Black Bass.

Mary Beth hit the brakes. TDust enveloped the car. Which was just as well, she thought. No one would see her slamming the steering wheel or hear her curse. Feeling smothered, suddenly, she stepped out into a brisk day clear enough to pick out a row of figures aligned beneath a flagpole. M1 rifles and olive-green fatigues. She got back into the coupe and drove.

* * *

If the emplacement had a number or even a name, Mary Beth didn't know it. Neither did anyone else on the island, for that matter, and perhaps not even the soldiers themselves. There were six of them, four privates, a non-com, and an officer. Together, they manned the three concrete installations consisting of living quarters to one side and an ammo magazine on the other, and between them a squat, trapezoidal bunker with a gun. A six-inch naval cannon, this was supposed to guard Forth Cliff and, behind it, the continental United States, from Nazi invasion or at least an enemy sub.

Though one had recently been sunk off the shores of Nantucket, the threat of U-boats had largely faded. This left the crew inside with next to nothing to do, which was fine for the sergeant and his men. When not on watch or cleaning the barrel, they could take their jeep for a spin into town, date some lonely local or catch the ferry for Boston's shadier sides. The days could be spent reading *Yank* or smoking Lucky Strikes. Nobody really cared, after the morning inspection.

This had just begun as Mary Beth pulled up and Sergeant Herbert Perl saluted her. She wasn't sure if she was to return the gesture or, if so, whether she fully remembered how, and instead merely touched her cap brim. The men remained at attention.

"Sergeant."

"Cap'n."

The salute was followed by a smile that was genuine enough, even if inflated by frequency. Perl was always smiling, at least in the few times she'd seen him before, a happy man in his early twenties hailing from a faraway place known as Brooklyn. Lean, light-footed, his hair already receding beneath his garrison hat, and a nose best described as squirrely. Mary Beth knew the type, had seen them passing through Chelsea and Dorchester, the Jewish neighborhoods with their corner groceries and furniture stores and outside of each of them some stout, bald man with a ten-cent cigar just sitting there smiling. A content people, it seemed to her. A mystery why so many others, her father included, resented or feared them or both.

"I suppose you know what happened yesterday. The POW."

The sergeant's smile turned sad. "Yeah. Dabrowski heard some people talking about it, last night at the bar."

One of the soldiers, still rigid and presenting arms, nodded from behind his rifle. Mary Beth took out her notepad and scribbled while Perl yammered on. Understanding him, though, wasn't easy. While both the Italians and the locals disliked ending words with consonants—bar, for them, was bar-a or baah—the sergeant dwelt on them. Talking became tawking and night was noight. Still, she managed to get his drift. Simply that the emplacement was strictly off limits to the prisoners and, coming within range of it, they could easily get shot in the gut. None of them came near, fortunately, and in town, none of them fraternized.

"Look like a nice enough bunch of fellas, though. Like some guys I know from Bensonhurst."

She didn't even try writing Bensonhurst. Instead, she paused for a moment as if to digest some facts while also getting a sense of the surroundings. The magazine with its heavy metal door, behind which were stacked enough explosives to devastate half the island. The bivouac bunker with the warning WATCH YOUR GI HEAD painted over its entrance. And the cannon jutting out of the casemate and over a cliff—one of the four—and the breakers frothing below. No sign of danger, of course, only a string of troop ships lumbering northward before steaming east toward Britain.

"You'd let me know, won't you, sergeant, if you'd seen anything unusual." She brought her face closer to his. "If any of your men here showed signs of being in a fight or some other struggle. Any grudges you know of."

Perl smiled at her. She was beginning to see the variety in them.

The smile of greeting and of bittersweet loss, the smile of being posted here, in maritime paradise, while your friends are slogging through hell. The smile that turned grin-like, fleetingly, before disappearing into a crimp as someone shouted "Ten-hut!"

Now even the sergeant stiffened. Mary Beth, alone, remained at ease, yet even she braced herself as the lieutenant approached. Unlike Perl and the men, he did not drink at the Flotsam Bar or grab a bite at the dockside diner. He seemed never to leave the base. All she knew was from the scuttlebutt around town, his rank, and illustrious name.

"I trust my sergeant here has been helpful to you, Captain," Lieutenant Aldrich Colburn said, striding toward her.

"Oh, yes." Her chin took in the squad. "They all have."

"Pleased to hear." He stood close to her—she could smell his Pepsodent breath—and towered above her head, which was unusual for the taller-than-average woman.

"The people of Fourth Cliff have been so hospitable to my men and me, so supportive, the least we can do is cooperate with their police."

He was handsome. Not merely good-looking in the Archie sense, but in Cary Grant and Laurence Olivier's league, a heartthrob. Raisin-haired and mesa-chinned with eyes like polished jasper. And suave. The son of Beacon Hill bluebloods, so she'd heard, well-connected muckamucks who pulled whatever strings necessary to get their son assigned as far from the fighting as possible. His many requests for transfer to a combat zone were denied at the highest level.

"And I appreciate it, Lieutenant. Officer to officer." She reddened slightly, aware that while hers was an assumed rank, his bars were earned in a course.

He smiled at her—it came across more like a frown–as Mary Beth took in his spit-shined boots and the buffed silver eagle on his cap. Unlike his soldiers, dressed in simple battle fatigues, he wore his full insignia, complete with a tan tie and the crossed-cannon pin of the Coast Artillery Corps. He bore his own weapon as well. In place of Perl's .45 pistol, the lieutenant packed a carbine that he shouldered muzzle-down, warlike.

Mary Beth continued. "About the murder…"

"You're sure about that now? Murder?"

"Afraid so. And I intend to find out by who."

"By whom is immaterial, I'd say, if the perpetrator is another POW." From his breast pocket, Colburn removed a pair of aviator sunglasses, held them up and blew on their lenses before donning them. Even then, she could feel his eyes pierce.

"Understand, I have nothing against Italians," he said. "Private Falcone here can vouch for that." Another ramrod soldier, thick-necked and burly, frowned. "But as for the prisoners, I have only contempt. If they want to kill one another, then let them."

Mary Beth was speechless. "Well, a job's a job," she managed, and added, "You have a good morning, Lieutenant." She thought about saluting but managed merely a two-fingered tap on her hat brim, turned, and retreated to her car. Wincing into its rearview mirror as she left, she saw Colburn marching up and down the line of four soldiers, inspecting and haranguing them. Close behind, Herbert Perl smiled.

*   *   *

A fellow prisoner or perhaps one of the GIs, somebody strong, somebody angry. Those were the only possibilities Mary Beth could think of at this stage, with no solid evidence for either. With each passing day, the chances of finding the perpetrator diminished—that much she knew about homicides—and she'd already run out of suspects.

She drove back to town and had lunch at the diner that had

neither name nor menu. The choice was usually between burgers and tuna, with chowder invariably thrown in. The pies came in one flavor, cranberry. But the coffee tasted less like chicory than most and the company was equally genuine.

Here she could see the real Fourth Cliff, or at least what was left of it. The young men who once crewed the trawlers and raked the cranberry bogs, who hauled the fish crates and repaired the docks, were all snatched up by the war. So, too, were most of the tourists, along with the innkeepers and victualers who provisioned them. The female population had also dwindled, many escaping to jobs in the Navy yards on the coast and to marriages with sailors on leave. This left the old and the unwell, the 4F's and the underage, and a few essential service people such as the island's only fireman, Bob Culliver, his red truck parked behind the church. Trudy, the woman who waited on her, was an arthritic widow, and Pascal, owner and short-order cook, was missing two fingers on his right hand. Most of the customers who drifted in that morning—humpbacked, half-blind—had enough difficulty dragging their own bodies around, much less that of a dead man.

Mary Beth had begun to question whether Francesco had been killed on or near the docks as she first surmised, but perhaps had been strangled elsewhere. His corpse could have been pushed off a pier or even tossed into the surf on an entirely different part of Fourth Cliff and carried by the current into the net. He could even have been thrown overboard from one of the island's many craft. The possibilities were limitless, she conceded, as she took another loop through town, searching for witnesses. No one knew or had seen anything, not the shop owners nor the fisherman arriving late with their catch. No one had a clue, least of all Mary Beth.

By sundown, footsore and frustrated, she quit. Departing town, passing by the Flotsam Bar, she braked suddenly and performed a

U-turn. The coupe had no problem finding a parking space. The lot was empty.

From the outside, it looked like little more than a shack with a sputtering Schlitz sign, and inside the joint was hardly upscale. A jumble of wobbly tables, struggling lights, and a dartboard. And yet it was here, in that magical interval between Depression and war, that mainlanders mingled with mariners and the floor rocked with jitterbugging saddle shoes. In the wanton decade between Prohibition and rationing, the liquor flowed and rarely a night passed without at least one of the patrons leaving horizontally. The occasional fistfight broke out, usually over baseball, but more often trysts were arranged and consummated in the dunes out back.

All that was gone, replaced by creaking floorboards and air as silent as it was stale. There was no music, no sound at all except for the deep-throated laughter that greeted Mary Beth as she entered. "My God, Swann, I've seen prettier shipwrecks."

She groaned onto one of the stools and planted her elbows on the bar. "Just what I need right now, compliments."

Leaning into the light, she looked the barmaid over. Big-jawed and steely-eyed, Minnie Beaudet was hardly what they called a looker. Her nose was flattened as if by a fist and her figure was as round as a funnel. Her curly-ringed hair was rust-colored. Yet, there was no suppressing the sweetness of her face or the warmth of her pudgy fingers as they brushed Mary Beth's wrist.

"What is it, sister?"

The captain told her, down to the depressing details, most of which Minnie already knew. There were few things she didn't know about Fourth Cliff—who was cheating on who, which fishermen were cutting their competitor's lines, and what secrets needed to be kept. Her ears were always open and her painted mouth sealed.

"But who?" Mary Beth asked her glass as Minnie filled it with her usual, Moxie tonic. "The dandy at the camp, the one the inmates are clearly scared of, or loyal to, or both? Or this Colburn character, the lieutenant? He hates the Italians, sure, but he hates getting dirty even more."

Minnie lit a Viceroy and sent up a corkscrew of smoke. "Criminy, girl, use your noggin." She wrapped Mary Beth tenderly on the head. "Don't just think infighting or prejudice, think heartbreak. Think love."

With vacuous eyes, Mary Beth glared at the bar owner. Minnie, smirking, spelled it out for her. "Who on the island has had a son or a husband killed in the war? Who would want to get even? Or whose wife or girlfriend was this Francesco kid romancing? Maybe he was a Casanova."

"A crime of passion…"

"Passion," Minnie pouted. "You remember what that is, don't you?"

Mary Beth didn't answer. A refugee from Montpelier, Vermont, from the Cape and the Vineyard, too, where they didn't exactly take to her type, Minnie arrived on Fourth Cliff shortly before Mary Beth and quickly became her best friend. Her only friend. Yet she wasn't always so supportive. Jealous of Archie at first, furious at him for leaving but also disappointed in Mary Beth for not insisting that he stay, Minnie seemed to enjoy having Mary Beth all to herself.

"You sure I can't put something stiffer in that?" Minnie nodded at the Moxie. "A little courage?"

"Thank you, I really should go…"

The pudgy fingers returned to Mary Beth's wrist and clasped it. "You don't have to, you know. Here there's no need to be tough."

Mary Beth touched those fingers once, lightly, and rose from the stool. "You know what they're saying about me, Minnie. I've got to solve this thing quick."

Behind them, through the weather-beaten door, two aged salts stomped in. With their mangy beards and yellow sou'westers, they looked like storybook whalers. But didn't stop them from scowling at Mary Beth and griping out loud, "Black Bass."

"Ignore them." Minnie glared at her. "All of them. Just as long as you know who and what you are," she stated. "The rest is bullshit."

*   *   *

The coupe crept along the potholed trail snaking through the moraine, though thickets of bayberry, rockrose, and boneset. The tires kicked up dusty concertinas before reaching a tiny promontory where Mary Beth parked and got out. She could hear the waves bursting on the boulders below, feel the spray moistening her cheeks. Breathing in the brine, she said to no one, "Honey, I'm home."

She could hardly remember the last time she'd been here—two days ago?—and the place looked strange to her. The keeper's lodge where she usually slept, the adjacent shed with its storm warning signs, sacks of de-icing salt, and a tarp-covered Harley Davidson. She remembered the sound the motorcycle made when Archie spurred it across the dunes, that loud, throaty growl, and cringed at the thought she might never hear it again. She was exhausted to her bones. Yet rather than plop down in the lodge, she lumbered toward the red-striped lighthouse twenty yards away and limped up its spiral stairs.

The kerosene lamp at the top cast the faintest reminder of the blinding beam that once swung here, guiding oil-laden whalers through the shoals. Still, it sufficed to illuminate her life. Or what had once been her life. The old brass telescope they used for sighting humpbacks and the windup gramophone they danced to. The mattress on which they'd often made love like newlyweds, preferring it to their four-poster bed. On the circular wall, tacked to a large corkboard, was the Sox's 1942 schedule and two four-by-six photos of

Archie. One showed him smiling in his black leather jacket and captain's bars, a hand cantilevered on his gun. In the second he beamed, Major Swann in his still-crisp fatigues, just before shipping out. The first she'd always cherish. The second she could have burned.

Next to the board she'd taped a map of the South Pacific, most of it blue but studded with pushpins, each one stuck in an island. Pestilent places totally unlike Dorothy Lamour's paradise in *Her Jungle Love* or even Joan Crawford's in *Rain*. Utterly alien to Fourth Cliff. New Georgia, New Britain, Makin and Tarawa—the archipelago of battles that Archie had survived so far, the chain of his limitless chances to die, all of them senseless.

Yes, senseless. As a policeman and a captain, with no one to replace him but his wife and a slow-witted patrolman, he could easily have received a deferment. But no, not the brave captain of the Fourth Cliff police, not the major in a Marine Corps reserve unit being mobilized. No war could be waged without him.

"How could I tell them to go and fight while I stayed here? I'd never be able to look at myself again." He'd said this while combing his hair in the pocket mirror nailed up next to the Sox schedule, the one he consulted after each of their afternoon breaks on the mattress. "Tell me, Daddy, what did you do during the great World War II?" he asked, affecting a little boy's voice. "Well, son," he murmured. "I caught drunks and ate chowder."

Mary Beth said nothing. Having tried for several years to give him a child—the son that might have kept him at home—she felt less within her rights. And raised alone by a hard-headed father, she knew that cops didn't cry, especially if they were women. Instead, she put on her uniform and laced up her shoes and tried her best to act as if nothing was changing.

Only that last night, as they lay on the pebbly beach, naked on the boo blanket beneath the shadow of the cliff, did she dare reveal her wound.

"Why are you deserting me, Archie?"

"How could I desert my men?"

"They can fight without you. They can die. I'm not sure I can live."

But Archie just laughed his schoolboy laugh and flashed his alabaster teeth. Like the moonlit sea, his eyes glistened. "Don't be silly, Mairzy Doats"—his latest nickname for her, which she hated— "You're a lot stronger than you think. Stronger than I am, even."

"Then you listen to me, Archibald Swann," she said and held his lanky body close to her broader one. "You come home to me or else."

"Else what?" Again, that laugh.

"Else I leap from the lighthouse and dash myself on the rocks. And you'll have no one to blame but yourself."

Two years had passed, and she still had not expressed all the anger she felt, the hurt. Her letters bore no hint of it. How could they, when they finally caught up to him in some godforsaken jungle, wet and feverish and surrounded by danger? How could they convey anything but love? Especially when his letters, the few that irregularly reached her, increasingly revealed his pain?

The last she had received almost three weeks before. Postmarked Talasea, an island so small she couldn't find it in any atlas, the location of its pushpin only guessed. For days, she'd carried the mud-stained note folded in her jacket pocket, taking it out repeatedly to read.

March 23, 1944

Dearest Muffy Buns,

It rains here. That's all it does. Hard rain, soft rain, drizzles and downpours, but rarely a speck of sky. And in the few times it shows, the sun is so strong it can sheer your skin off. So we're wet all the time, whether from the showers or our own sweat, and our toes are starting to rot. Who'd ever think I'd miss the Japanese? Who'd ever think I'd long for nothing more than a single moment with you in our lighthouse, snuggled against the storm?

Not much of a leatherneck anymore, am I? I suppose I should apologize for thinking only of myself out here and not giving more thought to you and what you're going through. At least I have plenty of company, if not from my courageous men, then surely from the slugs and mosquitos. Still, loneliness comes in all forms, I guess, and who's to say whose is deepest?

With all that, I know that you're holding up just fine. Remember I told you how strong you are? A regular Rinty Monaghan. Nobody can ever defeat you, not that anybody in Fourth Cliff would try.

I love you with all my soul, M.B., and with every inch of my waterlogged body. From somewhere in the bush, in a lean-to in the middle of nowhere, I send you a thousand kisses.

Your adoring husband,
Archie
PS: Say hello to Hogan for me and remember to oil the Harley

Mary Beth didn't let the hurt out, not in her letters or anywhere else someone could see it. Instead, she cut off her long black hair— goodbye Victory rolls, hello Prince Valiant—and assumed her husband's uniform and rank. It wasn't official, of course. There wasn't a single woman police captain in the entire country yet, only an honorary one, Francis Lee, an old New Hampshire lady who specialized in forensics. But no one protested her decision, not even Lemuel Hogan, who Mary Beth passed over. The island needed a police force, if for no other reason than to keep drunken sailors off the docks, and the police force needed a chief. Yet few people showed her respect. The often-asked question, "What would Archie do?" was just as frequently followed by the threat, "Just wait 'til Archie gets home."

But Archie wasn't returning any time soon, and in his place came the Italians. They arrived from places no one had ever heard of— from El Alamein, Taranto, and Licata—looking scared and hungry and haunted. It was difficult to hate them, even if they were the enemy, and even tougher to refuse the hands they lent to the labor-starved island. They didn't drink much, didn't cavort, and for the most part kept a low profile. They didn't get strangled to death and end up eyeless in nets. Or at least, they were not supposed to.

Alone in the lighthouse which no longer shone on the shoals, by the flicker of a hurricane lamp, Mary Beth removed her duty belt. She took off her cap and jacket as well and glanced at herself in the mirror. Her features, once precisely cut—thin nose, sculptured lips— had acquired a hard, almost industrial quality. The eyes in which her father said gleamed Irish glens had hardened into hazel. Not much of a beauty for Archie to come home to, nor much of a bruiser for some murderer to fear. Perhaps she was only what those fishermen called her. Black Bass. Scaly, toothy, and big-mouthed, a bottom-hugger that changed its sex in adulthood. A predator which, despite its transformations, always ended up caught.

PART TWO

3.

More than the gold star in the window or the grass which had not yet been cut this spring, there was something about the house itself that shouted mourning. Perhaps it was the sagging porch or the mailbox overflowing with letters. Or the aged Newfoundland sulking in the weeds.

Exiting the coupe, Mary Beth removed her cap and locked her gun in the trunk. She forded the lawn, pausing only to pet the dog, and climbed the creaking porch. She wasn't surprised when it took not one but three sets of low-key knocks for the door finally to crack open.

"Pardon me, ma'am," she began, smiling sadly, "barging in like this. Especially now. I was just wondering if I could have a word with you."

From a single eye peering out, the door swung to reveal a face almost as common on the island as kelp. Once comely, no doubt, but now worry-cured, hair reduced to crinkles. Dentures that left a depression around the mouth. Eyes the murky blue of sea glass. In her gaze, though, Sarah Hall retained a glint of her youth, as well as its hard-bitten intelligence. She knew why Mary Beth had come.

"Don't bother wiping your shoes."

Mary Beth entered a typical Fourth Cliff living room. Rag rugs and embroidered epigrams, a china cabinet arrayed with crockery—earthenware and pewter, anything *but* china—and a long-cold Franklin stove. And a rocking chair in which he sat motionless, Sarah's husband, Bill.

"Hello, how are you today?" Mary Beth began. If she'd had her gun, she could have shot herself. The answer was clear from the unswept floor to the hollowness of Bill's expression. Shoulders, chin, breastbone—everything about him drooped, like a melted candle stub. How was he? The slouching man barely shrugged.

"Forgive me for not coming around sooner, to check in and all. I guess folks assume you'd rather be left alone." Mary Beth was babbling again, unsure of what to say to a pair of grieving parents. Even less sure how to begin interrogating a man about the murder of a person whose countrymen had killed his son.

The young man's photo was framed on a wall from which all other decorations had been removed. Though black and white, one could almost see the color in Christopher Hall's cheeks—a wind-buffed red—and the royal blue of his eyes. His hair was rippled dunes. In his uniform with its corporal's stripes and Fifth Army patch, he looked much older than eighteen and, from the way he beamed, seemed destined to live to one hundred. But that fate was preempted by another awaiting him on Italy's Anzio beach, just as he exited the landing craft. A single burst of machine gun fire literally cut him in half.

The news left the island in shock. Some two dozen residents were serving then, several, like Archie, overseas, and a couple had been wounded, but none had died. Not that tragedy was unknown to those who fished in fickle seas, and not that flus and fevers didn't take their yearly toll. But Christopher's death was different. Distant, impossible to envision, and unspeakably brutal.

Ever since then, for the past three months, no one saw the Halls, not even in church. In charge of shipping the best of each day's catch to the fish markets in Provincetown and Boston, Bill no longer showed up for work, and Sarah phoned her orders into the general store. People left baskets on the porch and Reverend Miller stopped by, but otherwise the Halls were phantoms.

"We're old island stock," Bill explained without being asked. "We keep our feelings inside."

He, too, knew the reason for her visit. Word in Fourth Cliff, like its salty air, penetrated everything, even this cloistered home. "Truth is, Mr. Hall, it's not your feelings I'm questioning. It's your whereabouts earlier this week. It's whether you knew a man named Francesco Albertini."

Hall's face was as cold as the stove. If incensed by Mary Beth's question, he kept his voice dispassionate. "We were here, of course, Sarah and me. We're always here." But when it came to Francesco's name, the old longshoreman seemed to stumble. His dewy eyes narrowed and his nominal lips shrunk. The rocking chair shifted, almost imperceptibly. "Heard of him," he said, "and heard what happened to him, and I only wish it'd happen to them all."

"Now, William…"

A raised hand silenced his wife. "I only wish I could find the man who did it," he went on flatly, "and thank him."

Mary Beth, standing with her notepad and pencil ready, did not even pretend to write.

"They took our boy, officer. A person who never did harm to nobody. Who only wanted to live." His chin, lifting slightly, indicated the photograph on the wall. His voice for the first time cracked. "They broke him, our beautiful boy. Christopher."

The rocker teetered now, the floorboards creaked, and from the stern look on Sarah's face, Mary Beth understood it was time to leave. With a twist of her wedding band, she muttered, "My deepest condolences. If there's anything you ever need…."

Before she could finish the sentence, though, the door was opened and Mary Beth found herself outside. She again plied through the lawn. She retrieved her cap from the front seat of the coupe and her Colt from the trunk and prepared to drive back to town. But her mind was already racing.

Though diminished by grief, Bill Hall remained a big man, muscle-bound from years of cracking ice and lifting it in fish crates. It would be quick work for him to wrap his hands or a length of rope around the neck of a much-weaker victim, to squeeze the life out of him, and toss his body into the sea. And the man certainly had motive. The only problem was his alibi, which much of the island would corroborate, as would, of course, Sarah. Yet mightn't she have blessed the deed or even put her husband up to it?

Mary Beth pondered these facts as she drove the unpaved track from the Halls' house and linked up with the island's main road that stretched from the first cliff at the northern end to the fourth in the extreme south. She returned to town, parked outside the diner, and grabbed a piece of cranberry pie.

Like everything else in this case so far, her next destination was a mystery to her. She was almost grateful when, returning to the car, she found a handwritten note on its windshield.

In black ink and flowery letters, the note contained Francesco's name. Alongside it was that of Abigail Pitt, separated by a single space. But even that was filled, by a small, blood-red heart.

*   *   *

An inn, a lodge, some people went so far as to call it a hotel, but at the end of the day Mrs. McQueen's was a boarding house. Eight rooms with a common kitchen and bathrooms, clean sheets, and comfortable enough beds. And secrecy. Located just outside of town on the road leading south, the establishment was within a healthy man's walking distance to the docks and but not far enough to discourage a woman in skirts from meeting him there. The fact that all of them had to pass before the First Congregational Church, its spire rising sentinel-like over the intersection, discouraged no one.

Nor were the townspeople especially disturbed by Mrs. McQueen's own reputation for trysts. Traditionally prim, culturally repressed, they rarely alluded to sexual matters or even acknowledged their existence. Love, at least in its carnal sense, was a private affair and as long it remained so nobody protested. If Reverend Miller cared what went on barely stone's throw from his chapel, he never let on in his sermons.

No less discreet was the proprietress of the place, the unflappable Abigail Pitt. Not related in any way to Mrs. McQueen, no more than were the Mitchells from whom her grandmother purchased the place earlier in the century, Abigail was known for efficiency, honesty, and tact. What people did behind closed doors was their business, even if those doors were hers. And not all of her rooms held lovers. Traveling salesmen, weekend boaters stranded by squalls, and mainland families on a weekend break also frequented her establishment. Abigail didn't ask. The walls, cut from stout birch, were thick and soundproof, much like those she raised around herself.

Which didn't prevent the townspeople from sensing something amiss in the Pitt household. Adultery and assignations were never discussed, but the same discretion wasn't paid to marital difficulties, which had long been on display at McQueen's. Orson Pitt, an ox of a man, a crabber with a taste for bourbon and the occasional brawl, was not known to spare his wife a slap or two whenever he felt she merited them. And even when she didn't. These grew more frequent in recent years—not only slaps, but jabs and punches, the effects of which no amount of makeup could hide. Not a formidable woman, small-boned and brittle, she nevertheless possessed the fortitude in-grained in virtually all of Fourth Cliff's women: the ability to put up with endless disappointment, even abuse, from their husbands, and plug on.

No one complained when Orson was called into service, least of all Abigail. Posted as a weapons instructor in Camp Carson, Colo-rado, he was not in any danger but was far enough away to cease threatening her. She scarcely replied to his letters when they came. Instead, for the first time in anyone's memory, Abigail Pitt could be seen smiling at the general store, happily relinquishing her ration stamps, or at the diner, briskly crumbling crackers into her soup. At Evensong, her reedy voice could be heard above the other parishio-ners', trilling.

But maybe, Mary Beth speculated, the reason for Abigail's sud-den contentment was not only the absence of Orson in her life, but the presence of another. What if, as the note on her windshield in-timated, that other was the late POW? In which case, it stood to reason, the keeper of McQueen's would be devastated.

But she wasn't. Mary Beth realized that the moment she entered the gray-shingled two-story and found Abigail dusting a counter. Though dressed in overalls with rollers in her hair and a polka-dotted kerchief over that, her simple beauty showed through. A face be-fitting a porcelain statue's—bitty nose, puckered mouth, eyes like glazed enamel.

Seeing Mary Beth, Abigail stopped working and beamed. "Cap-tain Swann," she declared with a shake of her feather duster. "What a wonderful surprise!"

"Delightful seeing you, too, Missus Pitt." Missus, not Abigail, even though Mary Beth, at twenty-eight, was older. Better to keep this professional, she thought. Better to treat Abigail as an interested party, if not quite a suspect herself. "And a pleasure to see you keeping this place in tiptop shape even with your husband away."

The tiny nose scrunched up toward one Delft eye and her pursed mouth compressed. "Well, even when he was, he wasn't much around." She managed a wink. "If you get my meaning."

Mary Beth did, but didn't wink back. Rather, she focused on Abigail's expression. Luminous, true, but how much of that light was artificial? Were her spirits really high, or just propped up to seem so, especially after the events of this week?

Only one way to discern, Mary Beth concluded. "Francesco Albertini—you've heard of him?"

Abigail went back to dusting. "The poor man they found in the net."

"The poor man," Mary Beth added, "who was strangled."

The feathers ceased rustling, but only momentarily. "No. I didn't."

"Didn't?"

"Know him."

"Never came around here at all? Never stayed in one of your rooms, even for an afternoon?"

Abigail stiffened. She patted her kerchief and the rollers beneath and between her pouty lips inserted a cigarette. Flatly, she asked, "Am I being accused of something?"

"Of loneliness, perhaps," Mary Beth offered. She played with the dome-shaped counter bell. "What many of us here are guilty of, I suppose. And the victim they say was a decent man, nice-looking, maybe romantic. The perfect cure for a case of the home front blues."

Sucking hard on her cigarette, once, twice, Abigail stubbed it out and snapped, "You've got nerve, Mary Beth. You can pin those bars on your collar and call yourself captain, but that doesn't give you the right to come in here and falsely accuse someone. Especially a woman with a husband in uniform. Archie would be ashamed."

"Archie would be curious, just like I am, whether that husband in uniform is keeping tabs on you here. Whether he might have some friends, big guys like him, looking out for you." *Ding* went the bell as Mary Beth fingered it, punctuating her point. "For him."

"Pshaw," laughed Abigail Pitt. She was back to being ceramic again, a smile fired into her face. Breakable. "Orson has nothing to worry about with me. Never had and never will. And anyway," she giggled, "what man would ever take an interest in me?"

*   *   *

Not Francesco Albertini, Mary Beth concluded as she fled the boarding house. If she had been romantically involved with him, Abigail scarcely seemed disturbed by his death. Not unless she was totally unfeeling, made not of porcelain but stone.

The day outside was hot, surprisingly so for the first day of June, and the sun was blinding. Squinting, Mary Beth tried to clear her mind. No, she concluded, Abigail had unlikely been Francesco's lover, but even she had, so what? With so many women on their own and thousands of miles from their menfolk, wasn't it natural for them to seek comfort elsewhere? And what better place to find it than with ninety young men, Europeans to boot, bound to be repatriated well before the GIs returned?

But she couldn't be entirely sure, not of the Abigail's affair with an Italian, and certainly not of Orson ordering revenge for it. She didn't even know who wrote that note stuck on her windshield, though the floral script and the crimson heart suggested a feminine hand. Mary Beth was still stumped. The fishermen had other words for it: foundered, beached, marooned. And turning at the intersection, she could've added another. Capsized.

Penetrating her open window, the *brring brrring* of patrolman Hogan's approaching bicycle made her brake.

"Captain. Captain," he gasped, out of breath and sweating. But Mary Beth was in no mood for his babbling.

"What now?" she practically barked at him. "I haven't got all day." Only quickly to atone. "Sorry, Lemuel. How are you?"

Slack-jawed, with his teeth protruding and his eyes more criss-crossed than usual, he had trouble gathering the words. "Cranberry," was all he managed, and "bog."

"Cranberry bog, that's what you said, right?" She was struggling to maintain her patience. "Just come out and tell me, Lemuel, which bog, where?"

"McKee's. Go. Now."

"But why, Lemuel? What did the farmer tell you?"

He stuttered, he spat. Spittle ran down his chin. Many sounds came out of his mouth, but Mary Beth understood only two of them. *Body* and *dead*.

4.

It was floating face down, limbs splayed. Another POW, to judge from his uniform and the green-and-white ITALY patch on its shoulder. A man roughly the same age and height as Francesco, but somewhat slighter and blonde. And though water-soaked, there was never a question of whether or not he'd drowned. Deep red in the October harvesting season, now, in June, the cranberries were still a pale pink. The crimson clouds around the body were not from the fruit, then, but seeping from the dead man's back.

Removing her leather jacket, rolling up her sleeves, Mary Beth waded into the bog. With the muck and swamp odor, it was hard to imagine that this was the source of that sweet jiggly sauce that accompanied every Thanksgiving turkey. Few families would ever know where the cranberries came from. Far more would care, presumably, knowing they'd been nourished in blood.

There was a great deal of it as Mary Beth surveyed the scene. While there was no hope of garnering clues, not in the knee-high water, clearly the man had been assaulted and bled out in the bog. Yet there was no sign of struggle, no other tears in his uniform, not a button or seam undone. He had, she surmised, been attacked from behind, most likely by someone he never heard coming and, even if he did, maybe wouldn't have feared. The perpetrator had snuck up on him and dealt him several mortal blows. The rest of them—at least twelve she could count—were purely for insurance, for spite perhaps or even for fun.

She rifled the victim's pockets but found nothing, no photos this time or IDs. But a name was supplied by the farmer, Wallace McKee, who just then arrived from town. Parking his Model T pickup, he splashed into the bog in his rubber boots and overalls and helped drag the body onto land. This erased whatever evidence Mary Beth might have found on the bank, but at least she learned something about the deceased.

A responsible worker, Antonio De Luca had shown up early each morning to check on the vines, shooing off the rabbits and crows. Like Francesco Albertini, he was an amiable man, well-liked by his fellow prisoners and courteous to the people in town. After the war, Antonio said, he was determined to stay in America. Now, most definitely, he would.

All this she heard from Wallace McKee, a man just beyond middle aged but already humped and half-toothless. Yet he could still hoist the body as if it were a bushel basket and lay it in the back of his truck. Farmer McKee, the people called him. A man as renowned for his simplicity and his equally simple, childless wife as he was for his generosity, always showing up at funerals and July Fourth picnics with the freshest bounty from his bog. Not the type to repeatedly stab his own worker, and certainly not in the back. Yet, Mary Beth wondered, how much did she really know about the man? How much, indeed, about anyone on this tight-lipped island?

"You say he came here every day, same hour?" Mary Beth interrogated McKee or tried to.

"Ayuh."

"Always alone?"

"Ayuh." He looked at her with eyes as pallid as unripe cranberries and rubbed his stubbled chin.

"And you said you don't know if Antonio had enemies? Anybody who'd want to do him harm?"

"Ayuh."

"Yes or no?"

"Ayuh."

She smacked her pencil on her open pad and jabbed the stub behind her ear. She could live here the rest of her life, Mary Beth realized, and never understand these islanders. Exasperating, sphinx-like. A wonder *they* weren't murdered.

She asked McKee to drive to Doc Cunningham's office, just above the diner, and ask for a death certificate and postmortem. The truck puttered away, leaving Mary Beth alone with the buzz of the season's first bees. She tried to picture the scene: Antonio De Luca laboring over the stems, facing south. His killer came from the north, quietly, a person who'd had some practice. A man of some strength and skill with a blade, knowing where to plunge. But how did he get here? How did he escape?

She searched the ground beneath the banks, hoping to find something the perpetrator might have dropped—a cigarette butt, a chewing gum wrapper. Squatting low, she separated the weeds with her pencil. Nothing. Nor could she hope to find anything on the path, scored with Model T tracks. But behind them loomed another tread, unlike any she'd seen. About six inches wide, about the same as her own Mercury's tires, but with alternating bars and vertical stripes. Nearby she also found half a footprint, a man-sized boot with a cross-hatched sole.

No sooner had she found this evidence when it began to vanish, erased by a sudden downpour. If only she had a camera! Only then she remembered something she'd seen once in Fourth Cliff's cemetery, tourists seeking out the oldest stones and tracing their inscriptions on paper. Tearing an onionskin sheet from her notepad, she carefully covered the impressions. Then, retrieving the stub from the back of her ear, hastily, Mary Beth rubbed.

*   *   *

She got back into the coupe, turned on the wipers, and drove on. The cranberry bogs were near the island's northern tip, just before the POW camp and the U.S. Army emplacement. In the first, Mary Beth saw little activity—the inmates were off at work—and in the second, no sign of anyone, not even a sentry. The flag hung lifelessly in the rain. She reached the point where the pavement turned to sand, the path that led through the dunes to second or third cliff and the beach where she and Archie made love. Rather than continuing, though, she swung the car around and sped once again, this time in the direction of town.

She needed time to think. The first murder could be chalked up to a crime of passion or vengeance, a singular affair, but not the next. One killing is an incident, but two is a wave. Yet what did they have in common? The victims, first, and the violence, and the need to have the bodies discovered. The assassin was sending a message of sorts, a way of saying "I'm here." But who, then, was *I*?

If not a bereaved parent or a scorned lover, what person or persons wanted the Italians dead? A hate-filled fisherman or some drunken GIs ferrying over from the coast? Wallace McKee or some other farmer acting out of some misplaced patriotism? Again, she considered the possibility that this was an internal squabble between different factions in the camp, fascists versus the resistance. "If they want to kill one another," the words of Lieutenant Colburn came back to her, "then let them." But what if the homicides had nothing to do with politics? What if, Mary Beth for the first time considered and her grip stiffened on the wheel, the murderer was merely depraved?

Back and forth, keeping to the wiper's beat, her mind vacillated. She thought of Archie soaked and lonely in the jungle, inconceivably far from home and constantly endangered. She thought of her father as well, his laughter the day she told him she was joining the force. The townspeople whispering viciously behind her back. In the misted windshield she saw the cord twisting around Francesco's neck and the knife plunged into Antonio's back and heard their gasps for help.

"Help!"

Mary Beth jammed on the brakes. The coupe skid on the wet pavement and fishtailed ninety degrees before halting. She burst from the car, certain she had hit someone, adding manslaughter to the list of murders. But the person was unharmed, at least physically, and still standing in the middle of the road, still hollering for help.

"Alva, calm down, it's me."

With shaky hands, she cupped the woman's shoulders, but Alva just shrugged them off.

"You have to help us, Mary Beth! He's out there somewhere. Help!"

Every village has its idiot, Mary Beth had heard, but Alva Fitch was far from dumb. Deranged, unquestionably, and better-off institutionalized, she was once a typical islander, diligent, churchgoing, content with serving her family. This consisted of a husband and two sons, all fishermen, and she gained a reputation for shoring up those women who found life as fishermen's wives—the intermittent poverty, the loneliness, the fear—unbearable. Alva was also known for her powers of observation, to see through the shiniest exteriors to the darkest truths within, even to tell the future.

Alva might have grown old that way on Fourth Cliff, become one of its equivalents to a dowager, respected and prim. But the Great Hurricane of '38 destroyed all that, just as it did for hundreds of New Englanders. Caught in the open sea, the Fitches' bodies were never recovered, and neither was Alva's mind. She began wandering the streets, even in winter, searching for them, receiving handouts but refusing to abandon the house where, any minute, she insisted, her husband and sons would return.

Every village had one, but not every town had Alva, a person who had lost her wits but never her wisdom. Nor did she lose her clairvoyance. On the contrary, it only quickened, enabling her to predict that the hairline-cracked hull would soon disintegrate or the rattle in some skipper's throat would metastasize. For these reasons, the people of Fourth Cliff put up with her and at times even cherished her. Craziness was a meager price for prophecy.

And now Alva Fitch was out in the rain, soaking wet and shrieking.

"*Him,*" she bellowed. "He's here!"

"Him?" Mary Beth pressed her. "Who's him?" She put her face so close to Alva's she could see the grain of her features, her ember eyes. Her hair was sodden hemp.

"You know, the killer."

Killer, not killers, Mary Beth noted. Him, not her. "And where's here?"

Alva smiled with teeth that seemed made of driftwood. "Here?" she laughed or rather warbled. "On the island, of course!"

Meaning he was a native to the place, Mary Beth wondered, or just passing through? And if a stranger, was he still lurking around?

"And he'll do it again, I know. 'Less you stop him."

"But how? Who?" Mary Beth's hands were still shaking, now with frustration. They clasped Alva's shoulders again. "Where!"

Alva smiled at her. With rain dripping from her eyebrows and running down her withered cheeks, she brought her mouth close to Mary Beth's ear. Her breath smelled of brine. "Watch out for the last cliff," she warned.

*   *   *

"Watch out for the last cliff," Mary Beth huffed. Where did Alva think she was, in some Boris Karlov movie? Just what she needed in the middle of this madness. A madwoman?

Back at the station, hanging her wet cap and jacket on the ship wheel nailed to its wall, she collapsed behind the black ash desk and leaned her elbows on the blotter. The Philco cathedral was tuned to *It's Maritime*, with tales of adventure at sea, and the two-way Motorola crackled with no one on the other line. The setting sun hurled spear-like shadows through the blinds.

Watch out for the last cliff. Perhaps it meant nothing. Still Mary Beth stared at the map. There was the fat fishhook of the island, yellowed with age but still accurate. The main road, the docks, and the church were all indicated, with the POW and army camps penciled in. A crowding of contour lines showed the location of each of the four cliffs, from the first on a bluff overlooking the town. That was where Francesco Albertini was found, though he might have been murdered elsewhere, while Antonio De Luca met his death in a cranberry bog, smack between the second and the third cliffs. Though there was some debate about which was which, there was none about the last, the fourth.

It lay at the extreme southern tip and long served as a landmark for mariners. A vertical drop into a spumy sea, it rose at the end of a marsh of mud and scree inaccessible to everyday vehicles. So imposing, so remote, no wonder the entire island was named for it.

The fourth cliff was where the killer would eventually strike, if Alva were to be believed. But what if she were speaking metaphorically, the cliffs being not physical but mental obstacles—Mary Beth's own massifs of doubt? What if she meant external factors, people who would arrive and interfere with her investigation, pushing her over the edge? Or what if there were no meaning at all to the old woman's raving? What if, like so much of what had happened in the last few days, her words were simply insane?

*   *   *

Eight in the evening, and the town was already asleep. Mary Beth walked from the station to the intersection and down through the empty streets. Streetlamps sputtered, barely illuminating the storefronts and the docks, the memorial stone engraved most recently with the names of Alva's loved ones. One hand on the grip of her Colt, she strode toward the one light that shone, though weakly, directly over the diner.

Horace Cunningham's office consisted of a single room equipped with half-empty cabinets, a rust-stained sink, and an examination table that could have been fifty years old. The smells of fried burgers and stale cigarettes almost overwhelmed the stench of chemicals and the whiff of decomposition already rising from the body laid out under a pillar of light.

Entering the room, Mary Beth gasped. She'd dealt with dead people before, most of them homeless, but apart from Archie, she had never seen a man fully naked. And this man, Antonio De Luca, was beautiful. Finely featured with feminine lips and whorls of black hair inherited perhaps from the Romans. And well-endowed, to the best of her minimal knowledge.

"Quite the specimen, I agree," the doctor, appearing behind her suddenly, made her both jump and redden. "Truly a tragedy."

Mary Beth cleared her throat. "What can you tell me other than the fact he was murdered?"

"Massacred was more like it." The tone of his unusually high voice dipped somewhat, as it did, she'd noticed, when discussing homicide. "Multiple perforations, though any one of them would have sufficed."

He lit a Chesterfield and inhaled so deeply she thought the smoke was ingested. But out it came in jets from his nostrils and rose languidly into the light. In the scrim, his skin looked even more lack-luster, his eyes a watery blue. Back in Boston, she would have found him sinister, a creep to be avoided at all costs. Here on Fourth Cliff, with few others to choose from, Cunningham was an ally.

He puffed again and said, "Come, help me flip him over."

Mary Beth swallowed—not audibly, she hoped—and watched while the doctor hooked his hands under Antonio's armpits before she finally grabbed his calves. Slender, the cadaver was easily turned. Mary Beth gasped.

From nape to coccyx, his back was furrowed with punctures—far more than she had counted in the bog. Clearly a monster had done this, though it remained to be seen with what.

"Good question." Shooting his threadbare cuffs, Cunningham took up a scalpel. He inserted it inside one of the wounds, a spindle-shaped slit tapered at both ends, and plied it open. "A knife, but I doubt it's the kitchen type. Roughly seven, seven and half inches long, with a double-edged blade that bulges slightly in the middle. Also here."

He pointed at the bruise marks surrounding the deepest gash. "It seems it had a hilt. And something more. Something I can't quite fathom yet." The tip of the scalpel bounced on four small holes just beneath the left shoulder blade. "Something sharp—a hand rake, per-haps—that he used to push the body forward after the first fatal stab."

Mary Beth jotted all of this in her notepad, while Cunningham ponderously smoked.

"Seems you've got quite the case on your hands, Captain Swann," he observed. For once, she noticed, he hadn't mentioned Archie.

"And it seems I've got quite the coroner."

Into an enamel tray once used for forceps, Cunningham stamped out a butt. "Shame I didn't study pathology," he said shrilly. "The pa-tients never complain."

5.

The next day, June 4, a Sunday, found most of Fourth Cliff in church. Mary Beth lingered in the center of town, fast by the fishermen's memorial, listening to the bells. Salvaged from long-dismantled ships and still stamped with their names, the bells sounded at special occasions—eight rings for an islander's death, sixteen to welcome in the New Year. And on holidays, of course, and Sundays, when the peals were followed by the hum of organ music and the drone of Reverend Miller's sermon. A lapsed Catholic and certainly no Congregationalist, Mary Beth didn't attend. Nor did she join that other group of worshippers dedicated to the god of Fenway Park and its apostles—Catfish Metkovich and Skeeter Newsome, Johnny Peacock and Pinky Woods. Some diehard fans stayed at home, ears to their radios, as the Sox played a double-header with Detroit.

Not much for religion or baseball, Mary Beth remained alone most Sundays. She'd come to relish the solitude, especially this morning, with rumors circulating of invasions. Armies were gathering in England, preparing to land in France, but also in the Pacific. Another island, another battle, this one even larger. And Archie in the middle of it. She pictured him wading through the water and smoke, blood and fire, and felt her insides wilt. No amount of tolling, no Ted Williams homers over the left field wall, could restore them.

Later, before the parishioners exited and noticed her, she again drove north to the POW camp. Mary Beth expected to find another funeral underway, or at least a mass conducted by some visiting priest, but instead she encountered a riot.

News had reached the camp of Rome's liberation from the Nazis. While the people of Fourth Cliff either prayed or cheered, American soldiers were streaming through the eternal city's streets. For the most part, the prisoners seemed to be celebrating. Outside the Quonset huts, they kicked and leapt with arms folded behind their backs while an accordionist joyously squeezed. Others passed around wine bottles, which were also no doubt prohibited, and smoked black market cigars. But elsewhere, between the bunks, fistfights had broken out, accompanied by words Mary Beth could tell were profane.

In the eye of his melee, she stood perplexed until Lorenzo approached her.

"Roma e libera!" he sang to her and offered her a swig.

She declined and instead leaned down to shout in the little man's ear. "What about the funeral? What about Antonio De Luca?"

Lorenzo rubbed the bones of his face and his hairless pate. "Povero Antonio, we bury him this morning." With the bottle in his right hand, he crossed himself with the left, then scratched in the vicinity of his fly. "But see, signora Capitana, everybody happy. Roma, la nostra capitale, Roma!"

"And them?" She gestured in the direction of the huts.

His smile went straight to scowl. "Not everybody so happy, you see. Fottuti idioti. Some are sad." His voice dropped so low Mary Beth could barely hear him. "Some still like Il Duce, il pezzo di merda." Lorenzo spat and folded a forearm in the crook of his elbow.

Mary Beth fingered her holster and thought about intervening, but then held back. As much as she detested the fascists, it was not her place to step in. But she was frustrated by her inability to question the prisoners and find out more about Antonio. Not just who would want him dead, but who would mutilate his body. One of the revellers, perhaps, or the brawlers. Or the haughty man with the pencil moustache whom Mary Beth recognized from her last time in the camp. The suspicious type, cold and distant, who stood apart from the both the festivities and the fights and seemed to be scrutinizing her again.

She turned to confront him, but he was already striding toward her, a linen jacket trailing cape-like from his shoulders. "Enjoying our festivities, Captain?" he asked.

"Is that what they are?"

"Violence and joy—it's an ancient Italian custom. Recall our gladiatorial games."

She didn't but neither did she let on. Instead, she studied the man's face, a web of contradictions. Fox-featured yet refined, raven-haired but creamy-skinned, ice-blue eyes that nevertheless radiated warmth. The pencil moustache that reminded her either of Clark Gable or of Claude Rains as the corrupt police chief in *Casablanca*.

"Why don't you join them?"

"The merrymakers?"

Actually, she was thinking more of the mischief makers, those on the side of Mussolini, but all she said was, "Why not?"

"Too early," he answered.

Mary Beth felt flummoxed. Seemed she understood nothing about the Italians, and less than that about this man who wore his khakis like formal attire and spoke slightly accented but otherwise perfect English.

"Call me sentimental, but I am what you'd call a patriot. Yes, an Italian patriot who loves his country dearly and cannot bear to see it debased."

He said this matter-of-factly, with no expression, which was also an expression of sorts.

"Debased?"

"By promiscuous men such as Francesco Albertini. Forgive my bluntness—in your line of work, I'm sure you're accustomed to it—but our little Romeo was satisfying not one but several of your island's lonely hearts. And Antonio De Luca, believed by all you Americans to be an upstanding young man, hardworking, was also a crackerjack smuggler. In league with some of your island's less scrupulous fishermen. Beneath the cranberries De Luca packed were hidden the very best contraband goods, everything from silk stockings to Scotch."

Mary Beth took this all in, keeping a straight face yet marking every detail. "And you? You're an angel, no doubt. A regular immaculate conception."

The man laughed, finally, dryly. "An angel, no, but a guardian nevertheless. Pardon my rudeness. Paolo Varrone." He clicked his work boots and bowed. "Formally, a graduate of your M.I.T. and chief architect of Milan, and more recently, *connello* in the Royal Italian Army, veteran of the Ethiopian and North African campaigns, Sicily and Lazio, and for the past five months an uninvited guest of yours on Fourth Cliff."

She could only reply with her name.

"I know who *you* are, Captain Swann. And I know you are determined to find the murderer, as you should. But I am no less determined to prepare my country for the future, to rebuild and revitalize her, all the while preserving what little remains of her honor. That cannot be done by men who bring us nothing but disgrace."

She eyed him suspiciously, lips pursed. "Determined?"

He laughed again, this time boisterously. "Not determined enough to kill anyone, I assure you Captain Swann, but enough not to mourn their deaths."

She still couldn't shake some doubt. Sufficiently large to strangle or stab someone, the prisoner had also detailed his motives. Yet, inside, Mary Beth already believed his innocence. Perhaps because, strangely, this man was the first person in Fourth Cliff who had answered her questions, even her accusations, without reservation. When he called her *Captain Swann*, she didn't feel he was mocking her. He seemed somehow drawn to her, and she was disturbed to realize it wasn't all on his side. Not since first meeting Archie in the park that day, long ago, had she felt such agitation. Yet, dour and stately, Paulo could not have been more different from her husband.

Now, glowering at him, fiddling with her wedding band, Mary Beth vowed not to let these feelings interfere with her investigation. As much as Bill and Sarah Hall, Abigail Pitt, or Lorenzo, Paolo Varonne was a suspect.

Their conversation ended abruptly as the camp's portly cook came trundling out of the mess hall. Behind him paraded four POWs with poles on their shoulders and bearing litter-like a steaming iron pot.

"Tempo di pasta!" the fat man hollered. "Mangiamo!"

The celebrations instantly stopped. The scuffling, too, as the eighty-eight remaining prisoners eagerly lined up.

"More than our politics, more than women and perhaps even money, we Italians love our spaghetti." Paolo was smiling at her now. "And that's another reason I love *them*."

"Don't let me interrupt," Mary Beth huffed.

"Happy hunting, Captain Swann," Paolo saluted her. "I hope you find your man." And brushing past her—intentionally, perhaps—he left to join the others on line.

*   *   *

Driving again, continuing north, she paused to survey the emplacement. The flag was flying as usual, and she assumed the big cannon was manned, but otherwise the base looked empty.

Coming toward her was an aubergine Master DeLuxe, the last of the limos Detroit turned out before retooling for Sherman tanks. It sped past her without so much tapping the brakes and gassed in the direction of town, but not before she caught a glimpse of the passengers. Inside were a pair of middle-aged aristocrats, the man in a gray, double-breasted suit and his wife in a silken curvette. They scarcely glanced at Mary Beth, as they no doubt ignored all the locals they passed speeding to and from the ferry. The Mercury coupe idled a second or two before turning onto the unpaved access road.

She pulled up just as Sergeant Perl emerged from one of the bunkers. He was beaming as usual, delighted to be alive on this early June Sunday, thrilled to receive the bounty often brought by Lieutenant Colburn's parents.

"Sausages, pies, real Java coffee. And this caviar—can you believe it?" His eyes were smiling, too. "I don't know whether to eat the stuff or fish with it."

"Your commander must be grateful."

"His men, yeah. The officer, not so." His smile went from bright to rueful. "The lieutenant is happier with SOS."

The thought of anybody preferring creamed chipped beef on toast—Shit on a Shingle—to caviar mystified her.

Perl's smile stiffened as a new voice broke in.

"SOS, hash, C-rations, that is what a soldier eats, not foie gras." Colburn marched up to her, a paragon of spit and polish, a pillar of discontent. "Imagine how I feel knowing what millions of others are enduring right now overseas. Imagine the disgust."

Mary Beth closed one eye, trying to discern his meaning. She smelled his Pepsodent, his Brilliantine and Barbasol and something else, bitter. And through his aviator sunglasses, she could still feel his eyes.

"Dismissed," the lieutenant barked at Perl, and then instructed Mary Beth to follow.

Instructed, not asked, and she was half inclined to ignore his order and return right then to her coupe. But the thought that he had something special to impart to her, a clue, perhaps, made her walk behind Colburn on the track to the bunker's face. There, beneath the long black barrel of the six-inch gun, he stopped and peered seaward.

"This war will be over soon, the greatest event in modern history," he stated, "and I will have missed it. Classmates of mine from boarding school and college, people of my milieu, will be coming home as heroes. They will have flown fighter planes and led brave men through jungles. And what have I done?"

It was not a question, at least not for Mary Beth. She had no idea why he was telling her this and had never even heard the word *milieu*.

Colburn, meanwhile, went on. "Guarded a coast that needed no guarding, that's what I did. Never fired a rifle, never faced danger of any stripe except from overeating. My friends will come back and write novels about their experiences. They will run for office and perhaps become presidents. They can raise their families with pride. And I will go into my father's business, sail yachts and drink martinis and play at being a man."

The lieutenant looked down at the surf exploding below. The rocks abutting this second cliff were especially jagged, close-packed like obstacles to invasion. Breakers burst on them like shellfire. Mary Beth shook her head.

"You men and your need to prove yourselves, I'll never understand it," she admitted. "But I might understand the need to satisfy it by, say, killing some enemy soldiers." She took out her notebook. "Even those already captured."

Colburn removed his sunglasses, yet the eyes behind them were grim. *I know I'm low*, they seemed to say, *but not that low*. "I may be a pencil-pusher, Captain Swann," he said finally. "But I'm no coward. And killing prisoners is cowardice."

"Then who would?"

The lieutenant shrugged. "A person with a chip on his shoulder. With something to hide or fear. Or someone just plain nuts."

"Or maybe all of that together."

Mary Beth ceased writing. She understood now why Colburn wanted to talk to her. To cleanse himself of any suspicion and share his thoughts on who the perpetrator might be. Most of all, though, he just wanted to talk. Now it was her turn to peer at him, a handsome man, yes, but also pathetic. The attraction she felt for the far less stunning Paolo Varrone was replaced in this case by pity.

"Just know that I will help you in any way that I can, Captain Swann. I will be at your service."

"And I'll be at yours, Lieutenant."

With that, he led her back to the bivouac bunker with its sign WATCH YOUR GI HEAD, the whitewashed stones, and the snapping American flag. There, she shook his hand and wished him a good day, at a loss for further words. It was a relief to climb into her coupe, a relief even to head into town with its gossip and secrets and whispers.

Driving up the access road, though, she had to swerve suddenly to avoid the oncoming jeep. Inside were two other soldiers, apparently returning from an afternoon jaunt. One, in the passenger's seat, she recognized as Dabrowski—that's what Perl had called him—diminutive and pale. The other was Falcone. His bulk barely squeezed behind the steering wheel; he waved a bottle with one hand while honking wildly with the other. His half-closed eye winked at her as she passed.

Neither of these men seemed at the least displeased by being left out of the carnage in the world, Mary Beth thought. Neither was itching for a fight, not even that burly Falcone. For them, Fourth Cliff was the next best thing to paradise.

*   *   *

Mary Beth always wanted to be a cop. While other little girls idolized Shirley Temple, she revered Charlie Chan and Bulldog Drummond. Other girls played with dolls and she with her mother's rolling pin, which doubled as a baton, and an assortment of tongs, basters, and wooden spoons that substituted for sidearms. And while normal girls hopscotched on their neighborhood streets, that tomboy Swann patrolled them.

People generally indulged her. The obsession, they knew, came from her father. A man whose wife, dying of diphtheria, left him with an eight-year-old who craved, but rarely received, attention. A coarse man, Phineas Boyle, a hard-ass of multiple hatreds though none perhaps as virulent as the one he felt for himself—ungainly, unloved, never rising above the rank of corporal. And who resented having to care for a child who reminded him of her mother, that same stubborn streak, that refusal to seek help even when she was ill. Who kept even the most passionate feelings to herself, bottled up and festering. That was the man who Mary Beth had to please, and what better way than to emulate the one thing he was proud of.

But rather than gaining his affection, Mary Beth's ambition only brought her contempt. Her father laughed at her, often in public, and openly derided the few women serving on the force. Charged with keeping hussies and children off the streets, they weren't the real police anyway, he snorted, just jazzed-up truant officers. His daughter, especially, was not cut out for the job. Better she find a man and mind his kitchen and use those wide hips of hers for childbearing. Neither from him or her teachers or Father Devlin did she receive any support, even after she underwent some training and swore to uphold the law.

Then came Archie. The only man who took her seriously, who never once questioned her decision or doubted her ability to enforce. Not that there was much crime to find, much less fight, on Fourth Cliff, but he nevertheless made her a partner in every assignment—ejecting unruly tourists, staking out a reported fish thief on the docks—and referred to her on the two-way, formally, as Officer Swann.

Archie never let her down and yet she felt she was now disappointing him. Unable to sift through the motives, to find a murder weapon or cull the possible suspects. Feeling sorry for Colburn and something else entirely for Paolo, hardly professional, and too easily persuaded by the Hall couple and Abigail Pitt. Some detective, her father would scoff. Older now, overweight and scarred, he'd still find the bile to pour on her and douse her delusions of policework. If only he knew.

Fortunately, he didn't, not yet. But with not one but two killings on this tranquil fishing and vacationing island, two POWs entrusted to her safekeeping now dead, the story would soon make the mainland press. Reporters would show up, and who knew what officials, all demanding answers. All accusing her of failure. Go stand at the intersection, they'd say, directing imaginary traffic. Go get a job picking cranberries.

Gunning the coupe, her knuckles white on the steering wheel, Mary Beth scarcely saw the sun setting over the coast. She needed to sleep, she knew, and to eat something other than crackers. She needed a drink as well, but remembered her promise to Archie. Most of all, she needed a friend, someone to confide in and give her solace. That someone was waiting just behind the unadorned doors and the blinking Schlitz sign at the entrance to the Flotsam Bar.

*   *   *

Something was wrong. The tables inside weren't just wobbly, they were awry, and one was even overturned. The bullseye of the dartboard looked up from the floor. Through the feeble light, she could see the glint of broken glass. Minnie Beaudet in a magenta turban, her back to the bar, realigned some bottles. Her voice, though Dietrich deep, was shaky. "Your usual?" she asked, followed by the fizzle of Moxie.

"What happened here?"

"What happened?" Her shoulders shrugged as she poured. "What always happens. Here or in Vermont or the Cape. Everywhere. It's always the same."

She turned finally as Mary Beth took a stool and showed her what even the shadows couldn't hide. Along with the hefty jaw and flattened nose, she bore a swollen mouth and a look of weary indignance.

"Who did this?"

Minnie placed the Moxie on the beer-splattered counter. "Want some pretzels with that? Ham sandwich?"

"Tell me."

She shook her head. "What good would it do? You'll go after them, and they'll deny it, and the entire island will take their side." She poured herself a shot of gin and chugged it. "They'll call you Black Bass again, and me..." She refilled her glass. "I'll be off to some other town, some other bar, waiting for the whole damn thing to repeat itself."

If Minnie were the crying type, Mary Beth figured she'd be sobbing. But her tears were exhausted long ago. All that remained was bitterness and a residue of love she kept hidden somewhere, like a fifth of ten-year-old Scotch.

Now it was Mary Beth's hand that gripped Minnie's wrist and squeezed. On another occasion, the bar owner might have taken this for an invitation, but tonight she merely smiled and gently pulled away.

"But there is something you can do for me, Swann. For us." She leaned forward onto the shards. "Catch that bastard. Catch him and arrest him and make sure he gets the chair."

Mary Beth nodded and grimly bit her lip. "Here," she said, pushing her glass toward Minnie, "want to tip off my tonic?"

This earned her a smile of a different sort—wry, defiant—and an infusion of gin in her Moxie.

"And I'll take one of those, too."

"Atta girl."

Into her fattened lips, Minnie inserted two Viceroys, lit them with her Zippo, and transferred one to Mary Beth. Eyes closed in what looked like ecstasy, she inhaled, blew out, and bolted half her drink. "He's playing with me, Minnie. The killer. Don't ask me how I know it, I just do. Just like they play with you."

She rose from her stool, somewhat unsteady, but dogged nevertheless. "But we're not going to let them anymore. *I* won't." She hitched up her duty belt and tugged down the brim of her cap. "From this moment on, we're in control."

*   *   *

Driving home slower than usual, aware of the fuzziness in her head, Mary Beth tried to remember the course of her day. It began with Antonio De Luca floating face down in cranberry swamp and proceeded to upsetting conversations with Paolo Varrone and Aldrich Colburn. A drag, a drink, and a promise followed before she finally flopped into her coupe. And now the road was wobbling from side to side—either that, or her car.

Unhindered, though, she managed to reach the station. No sign of Hogan anywhere, no ominous *brring* of his bicycle. No messages left, no more notes with floral writing and hearts. Only the map of Fourth Cliff and the whaler on the wall, the mounted cusk and spindle wheel. The Motorola scratched and the Philco hummed with the president's voice.

"The Italian people are a peace-loving nation," he said, recalling Galileo and Marconi, Michelangelo and Dante, and "that fearless discoverer who typifies the courage of Italy—Christopher Columbus." He praised the millions of Italians who immigrated to the United States—"They are not Italian-Americans. They are Americans of Italian descent"—and their vast contributions to industry, science, and the arts. "We want and expect the help of the future Italy toward lasting peace."

A fireplace crackled, a dog named Falla barked, and Mary Beth switched off the radio. She left the station and returned to the coupe. Usually, she'd go back to the lodge where she and Archie once lived, but increasingly she found herself ascending the stone spiral of the lighthouse. It felt like she was rising through time, above worry, to a place where memory reigned.

Here was the old Red Sox schedule and the twin photographs—the one she adored of Archie in policeman's blue and the other of him in Marine fatigues, which she resented. The gramophone and the records they danced to, the mattress on which they spent entire Sundays entwined. The old brass telescope that she no longer used for whale-spotting but for following the passage of warships out to sea, hoping that one of them would be sailing the other way, bearing her husband home. Here, on the wide sandstone plinth, once turned the Fresnel lens that guided all helmsmen through the shoals. But the great glass was gone, its gears long rusted. In their place sat a simple kerosene lamp that illuminated the map of the South Pacific with its constellation of pins. It enabled her, as the stars rose over the ocean, to read his latest letter.

June 15, 1944

Mary gasped. The letter had taken a full three weeks to reach her.

My Darling Maple Buns,

Then she smirked. "Maple Buns? He's got to be kidding," she said out loud and read on.

Finally, we are moving out. I'd tell you where but they'd only censor it, but somewhere away from this hell. After all these weeks of rain, rain, rain, the jiggers and jungle rot, I'll almost be happy to see a Jap. I'm telling you this because I don't know when you'll hear from me again, maybe in a month or two, and I don't want you to get worried. I'm fine. My men are the best. Our navy and planes are the best. And, besides, you know me, Mr. Lucky. How else could I have met you?

My greatest comfort is knowing that you're okay. Keeping the peace and preventing the old salts from running amok. Fortunately, nothing ever happens on Fourth Cliff, as your letters always show. But summer is approaching and with it those brats from Cambridge. Just because a kid's got an H on his shirt doesn't mean he can't be fined for drunkenness or chucked on the first ferry to Falmouth. Just remember who's captain around here, who wears the pants and the badge. Wherever I'm off to, I go confidently knowing our island is in the surest of hands.

And you should know always how much I love you, Mary Beth, how I live for you and for the day we can be together again on our beach or up in our lighthouse, shining.

From somewhere far away but close to you, I remain,
Your adoring husband,
Archie
PS: Sorry for pestering you, but please remember to oil the Harley. You could also dust the carburetor for sand. It's that round thing on the right side behind the distributor, just like I taught you. And make sure the key is still in the can.

"Screw your Harley," Mary Beth said out loud. "Screw your rain and screw your war. And screw…"

Her breath cut short. Silence filled the room, broken only by the pounding surf below. Mary Beth folded the letter carefully and placed it inside her jacket. But the pocket wasn't empty. Inside were two pieces of paper. The first was the handwritten note telling her that Francesco Albertini had been sleeping with Abigail Pitt. The second was the rubbings of the tire tread and half footprint she'd found on the road. She pinned them all to the corkboard alongside the map, her very first link chart.

But there was something else, something at once soft and prickly. She extracted it and held it up to the dwindling light. A sprig. Evergreen leaves and dark pink petals peeled back to reveal their stamens. Mary Beth studied it, stymied at first, but then recalled how Paolo had brushed past her in the camp. Stealthily, he'd stuck it in her pocket, but for what purpose—a token of affection or a subtle clue? She tacked it to the board together with the other evidence. Garland-like it hung over the islands where Archie would once again be fighting, the sweetly piercing flower of cranberry.

PART THREE

6.

Approaching through the dunes, a person might think a massacre was underway. The screams, the howls, the anguished cries for help. The sun pummelling mercilessly. But emerging onto the strand, seeing the children shrieking in water too cold even for their toes, their mothers scolding them for going near the waves, that person would be relieved to discover that, rather than an atrocity, this was merely summer on Fourth Cliff.

But the summers in recent years were different. Instead of mayhem, the shore was strangely silent. Always a poor cousin to Cape Code, the Vineyard, and Nantucket, the island was never overcrowded, even at high season. But with the war, its beaches were nearly deserted. Few vacationers came, not even the day trippers on the fifty-minute ferry ride from Falmouth, and most of the summer homes stood empty. It was as if rollicking in the surf and barbecuing under the stars were distasteful suddenly, with fathers, brothers, and sons shivering in foxholes somewhere or getting blasted out of the sky. As though the island had returned to its Puritan roots, when fun was considered unseemly.

Mary Beth didn't mind. A quiet summer meant fewer drunkards and city kids to deal with. It meant exchanging her leather jacket for a simple service blouse, the captain's bars migrating from her epaulets to her collar. There was more time now to listen to the Philco and the reports of Allied advances in France.

That's all the radio talked about, ever since the Normandy invasion—this port taken, that town. Next to nothing was said about another battle raging on the other side of the planet, yet another hellhole that nobody ever heard of, a Japanese stronghold called Saipan. A sideshow in which—it would later be shown—more than 50,000 people died. And though she hadn't received any letters since the battle started, instinctively she knew Archie was there. Leading his men, charging the enemy, being his usual brave dumbass self. When not praying with all her might for his survival, she fantasized about slapping him silly.

When not fretting and fuming over Archie, Mary Beth focused on the murders. The trails of both cases—Francesco Albertini's and Antonio De Luca's—were cold. Though the killer did not strike again, neither did he leave any clues. Perhaps he'd fled, departing for the coast, or decided to lay low. Either way, no more bodies showed up, nor did anyone so much as badmouth the Italians. Still, it unnerved her, not finding the culprit and knowing how her failure secretly pleased many of the islanders. She was letting Archie down just when he needed her most, failing to keep her promise to Minnie.

For one thing, alone, she was thankful—that the incidents had not been reported by the press. A single article in the Saturday Evening Post or an off-the-cuff remark by Walter Winchell would have sufficed to flood the island with detectives, both amateur and pro. Fourth Cliff would have become a circus and her life a bitter joke.

But instead of reporters, other visitors, scarcely less disruptive, arrived. Their landing was once again heralded by Patrolman Hogan's bell. Its *brrring brring* caught her that day leaning on the hot hood of the Mercury coupe and sipping a Moxie while watching the ferry unload. More interested in who was leaving the island rather than entering it, on the lookout for suspicious individuals who might be making an escape, she missed the black Dodge rolling down the plank and proceeding slowly into town. Of the two men in the front seat, she never got a glimpse.

Not until Hogan showed up. Not out of breath this time but clearly agitated, sweating straight through his tie.

"Captain Swann. Captain Swann," he stammered, and would have blubbered on if Mary Beth hadn't cut in, "I know my own name, Lemuel."

"Down on the dock, Captain," he drooled. "Come."

She glanced up at the cartoonish face, the Bugs Bunny teeth and eyes befitting Elmer Fudd. "Can't you see I'm busy," she said. But Hogan for once didn't budge.

"No kidding, Captain," he insisted. "You got to."

Mary Beth scowled. The last of the passengers, fish merchants mostly, had boarded already, and her Moxie had gone flat. "The dock, you say, Lemuel. It'd better not be a tuna."

*   *   *

Almost any catch would have been preferable to what Mary Beth did see, starting with the Dodge. It was parked as near to the waterfront as possible, just outside the diner, and its passengers had already questioned Pascal, the three-fingered cook, and were busy grilling the waitress, Trudy. That's when Mary Beth burst in.

"What's going on here?" she demanded. She looped her thumbs on her duty belt and drew herself high, displaying both bars and badge.

But the men barely glanced at her. They were of the same indeterminate age, north of thirty-five but far from fifty, and wearing identically shiny suits. Their fedoras were both tipped down at the

brim, Bogart-style, and their ties were similarly dull. Their bland faces seemed cut from a mold that all but removed unusual features—
an overlong nose, for example, or a droop in one eye. Only height
and diameter distinguished the two, the one tall and slender and the
other thickset and short. Together, they handed the menu back to
Trudy and in unison ordered chowder.

"I asked what's going on, and I expect an answer."

"Chowder's probably pretty good here, I reckon," the taller one
said, but not to Mary Beth.

"Reckon is right," his stocky companion agreed. "'Cause it's
pretty much all they serve."

"Figures."

"Figures."

"Enough!" She stomped forward and planted a fist on the table
between them. "Tell me right now or else."

Neither man looked up, only exchanged shrugs and chortled.
"Else what?"

"Else I'll haul you in for making a public nuisance."

The lanky man lamented, again not to her, "And they told us
these maritime folk were friendly."

"Friendly, yeah, like crabs."

With this, simultaneously, the pair opened their jackets to reveal
shoulder-holstered .38s and a golden eagle perched on a shield. DE-
PARTMENT OF JUSTICE, the inscription read, and FEDERAL BUREAU OF
INVESTIGATION.

Special Agent Dobbs and Special Agent Sitwell, they introduced
themselves, adding, "And we know who you are, Policewoman
Swann."

"*Captain* Swann."

Another set of shrugs. "Call yourself what you like," Dobbs, the
fireplug said, "though we prefer ineffective."

"In-ef-fec-tive," his partner agreed, drumming each syllable with his spoon. "So ineffective, in fact, that our director's decided to step in. Can't have a murderer running around killing our prisoners of war."

"Especially if they're Italian."

"*Only* if they're Italian."

Mary Beth was nonplussed. "But how? It wasn't in the news."

The shrugs became smirks. "And why do you think it wasn't in the news, Policewoman Swann? Who made sure it wasn't?"

She could have guessed, but they told her anyway. Tens of thousands of Italians were now fighting on the Allied side, even former prisoners. Germany and Japan had to be conquered unconditionally, but not Italy, which would soon join the free world in its struggle against the Reds.

"The Italians had a bad day," Sitwell added caustically. "Otherwise, they're just like us."

"*Just* like us," said Dobbs.

"And wouldn't it be a shame, what with our boys still dying over there, to spoil it all with a few miserable murders back home. That kind of thing gets out, you know, it could change a whole lot of hearts and minds."

"Hearts and minds," Dobbs repeated, "What with the Nazis telling the Eyeties, 'Surrender and those crazy Americans won't just work you to death, they'll strangle you.'"

"Or stab you."

"Or worse."

Even before Sitwell said it, the situation was sinking in. Mary Beth twisted her ring.

"Which is why your Mr. Gainor over at the shipyard contacted us. It's why we came lickety-split."

"Why we're taking over this investigation."

Sitwell smiled at her. "You go back to catching dogs or jaywalkers or whatever."

"While we go and nab this creep."

They paused as Trudy, her arthritic back bent, laid steaming bowls on the table.

"I reckon this chowder's pretty good," Sitwell predicted as he once again took up his spoon.

"Reckon is right," Dobbs said with a snap of saltine. "The best."

*　　*　　*

Mary Beth Swann was steaming. Archie would have sent them both packing, she was sure, Feds or not. But Archie was gone and the country at war and who was she, a policewoman who'd never arrested anyone more dangerous than a hobo, to chase down a two-time murderer who threatened national security? What was her pride compared to the destiny of millions?

And yet still she seethed as she watched them snoop around the docks, buttonholing fishermen as if each were a likely suspect. Things weren't done that way in Fourth Cliff, anyone could have told them, and people, even the lowliest deck swabber, received deference. But these agents were unlikely to listen. Fourth Cliff was candy compared to the waterfronts and slums they'd worked. And in contrast to the gangsters who gunned down their enemies in the street, the quiet killer of two defenseless prisoners was two-bit.

So Mary Beth stood apart and said nothing, not even when Doc Cunningham emerged from his office even paler than usual, his limb blonde hair plastered by sweat to his forehead. "They knew about everything," he muttered. "They knew about Newport."

She remembered the incident with one of his patients, the scandal, the shame. And yet she said, "So?"

"So they threatened to make it public—again—unless I told them things." His tone was almost soprano.

"Things?"

"Like who might have had a beef with Italians. Like who might have come in for a stitch or two, the kind of cut you get from piano wire or a butcher's knife, especially if their target is resisting."

"And you told them, I expect."

Cunningham nodded—or trembled, Mary Beth couldn't tell which—and struggled to light a Chesterfield. "And more."

"Like?"

"Like whether I'd administered sulphanilamide to anyone in the past year. That's for the treatment of gonorrhea."

The crease crinkled. "I know what it's for."

"Or this new-fangled drug, penicillin."

"And you told them that as well."

"What choice did I have?" A frayed cuff dragged across his brow. "What choice do any of us have?"

Not much, Mary Beth gathered as Sitwell and Dobbs made their way through town and uphill toward the intersection. They lingered for some time at the First Congregational Church, no doubt extracting intimate information from Reverend Miller. Though these Protestants didn't have confession, she knew, an understanding nevertheless existed that secrets uttered within the church remained there. Perhaps the agents also questioned the minister's wife. Viola Miller would disclose any confidence willingly, without the slightest coercion.

From there, the pair of agents turned south toward Mrs. McQueen's boarding house, entering not by the front door but a side entrance, traipsing through the victory garden tenderly planted by Abigail Pitt. There they remained for an hour or more, clearly unstirred by her feather duster. A far harder nut than Viola Miller, she was unlikely to divulge anything, and not only for fear of her husband, Orson. Most Fourth Cliffers were like her, tight-lipped seafarers who could have easily coined the verb "clam up."

Dobbs and Sitwell emerged flustered-looking, fedoras jammed over the foreheads, trampling the garden. They sauntered back into town to retrieve their Dodge and drive it northward. Mary Beth was prepared to follow, climbing into her coupe, when a gentle voice called to her from behind.

"You mustn't let them bother you," it said.

The captain snapped, "Nobody bothers *me*, buddy," before looking over her shoulder at Paolo Varrone and gasping, "Sorry."

He stood slightly downhill from her in his usual prisoner's uniform and Italy patch, but also with a fatigue cap that made his pointy ears stick out. Armed with a push broom, a dustpan, and a garbage barrel on wheels, he was charged with cleaning Fourth Cliff's streets of the occasional gum and fish wrapper. Mary Beth felt embarrassed for him. This aristocratic man, an officer and architect, reduced to street sweeping.

But if Paolo's expression showed any discomfort, it was ironically only for her. "War inflicts indignities on all of us," he said, "Public sanitation is the least of them."

"It's not fair." She blurted and immediately blushed. She was not a woman to share feelings lightly, especially not with a stranger. Certainly not with a suspect. Archie would have been stunned.

"No, it's not," Paolo continued. "None of it is. But I suppose those FBI men have a job to do and ours is to let them do it. From the look of them, though, they haven't got—how do you Americans say?—a ghost of chance."

He punctuated this with a smile as wide as a watermelon slice. Mary Beth was once again taken aback by the contradictions of this man—the ludicrous cap and trash can alongside the clarified skin and the pencil moustache right out of Robin Hood. The hardened war veteran who'd secreted a cranberry sprig deep in her jacket pocket.

This prisoner who made her feel captive. Unconsciously, she played with her ring.

"Thank you, Mr. Varrone."

"Paolo."

"Paolo…"

"But I do suggest you keep an eye on them," he added with a noble flourish of broom. "I'd hate to have to clean up their mess."

*   *   *

She tried her best to follow them, tailing them at a distance as they stopped at the general store and held a lengthy conversation with its owner, Tom Bruton. Better perhaps than anyone else on the island, he saw the comings and goings—what people ate and, more revealingly, drank, and the amount of bicarbonate they guzzled. The store doubled as a pharmacy and an ironmonger's, nursery and newspaper stand, filling station and post office. His thirteen-year-old son saw things as well, delivering groceries and hurling the Barnstable Patriot from his bicycle. It was Jimmy who presented the War Department telegram to Bill and Sarah Hall, Christopher's parents, the one that began, "We regret to inform you…"

The older Brutons told her how the agents had ordered everyone out of the store and kept its front door locked. How they'd taken each one, father and son, separately, into the storage room and questioned them for a full hour. Had any new customers come in recently, any unusual purchases? Strange letters, suspicious parcels? And did they sell bundling wire or hunting knives, the kind with two-edged blades?

"There'nt much to tell," shrugged Tom Bruton. "That Mr. Haggerty bought a pellet gun—he's got rabbits in his rhubarb—and Mrs. McNeice an extra pound of bran to get rid of something else."

He was a tense man, as tightly bound up as his packages, with dusty hair that stood straight up and features that looked fashioned from twine. His eyes reminded her of the pennies minted the previous year, with steel instead of copper.

"But did they ask you about the Italians?" Mary Beth pressed him. "About Francesco Albertini or Antonio De Luca? About other prisoners?"

"All that and who'll win this week's series with the Yanks."

She chewed on what little lip she had. "That's it?"

"I had a shipment of socks come in, this new nylon stuff, but they weren't interested." He pulled out his suspenders and let them snap, as if to say, *And that's that.*

Jimmy was a little more forthcoming, as he was about everything. A jumble of big teeth, gibbous eyes, and freckles, in blue jeans and a Jughead cap riding his chestnut crop, he didn't wait for Mary Beth's inquiries. Bouncing on his bicycle seat, he told her everything.

"They showed me their badges and they showed me their guns. Holy cow! And I asked them if they'd been there when Dillinger was shot and the Barrow gang." He paused for breath and sighed. "They weren't." But then, just as quickly, revived. "But they're going to put the kibosh on this guinea killer, they said, and how. Fill him full of lead!" Over his handlebars, an imaginary Thompson rattled.

"That's great, Jimmy," Mary Beth pressed, "swell. But did they mention any clues they might have found? Some leads?"

Jimmy shook his head. She could see he was anxious to get on with his errands, conveying a consignment of canned milk and powdered eggs to the Whitmans.

"Did they say anything about…me?"

The smile Jimmy gave her sent his freckles splaying. One eye burgeoned and the other one winked. "They said, Captain Swann, you shouldn't get your unmentionables in a twist," he chuckled, and peddled away on his Schwinn.

*   *   *

The agents' trail was easy enough to follow and even simpler to anticipate. From the general store, they proceeded past Old Man Gainor's shipyard and straight to the Flotsam Bar. That was their last stop—for the day, at least—as the hour was late and the last ferry would soon be departing for the coast. Pulling the coupe behind one of the skiff wrecks alongside the road, Mary Beth watched as Sitwell and Dobbs entered the establishment and remained for more than the standard hour. They left looking not flustered, but irked. As if they, and not their witness, had been interrogated.

"Let me guess, they knew all about Nantucket."

Exhaling a defiant stream of smoke, Minnie simpered. "The Cape and Montpelier, too."

"And what did you tell them?"

"Nada of what they wanted, I'll promise you." Without waiting, she poured out two tumblers of whiskey, stuck a cigarette in Mary Beth's lips, and flipped opened her lighter. "Told 'em that everything that happens in this joint stays in this joint, and if they didn't like it, they could go and jump in the chowder."

Mary Beth dragged and gulped. "They must've loved that."

"Love it, lump it, all's the same to me. There's only one badge on this island, far as I'm concerned, and you, my sister, are wearing it."

They laughed together, whether from nervousness or relief or both.

"Truth was, they seemed more interested in threatening me than questioning me," Minnie went on. "Like they knew they weren't going to get much out of me anyway."

"But what do I do now?"

"You wait. You watch, eyes and ears open and your knickers on."

The remark met with befuddlement.

"Don't play dumb with me, Cap'n Swann, I know you too well. And saw you in town the other day, speaking with that jailbird."

"You mean the prisoner of war? What's wrong with speaking?"

"Bird, prisoner, whatever. And nothing's wrong with speaking with him, only how you were speaking. Like his every word was honey or worse. A drug."

Mary Beth blushed, so deeply not even the sparse lighting could hide it. She was used to Minnie being jealous of her relationship with Archie, even being angry, but never disappointed. "Jeepers, aren't there any secrets around here?"

Minnie flattened her hands squarely on the bar. "Only one, Captain, and you've got to solve it. I know what it's like to be lonely, but there's a murderer out there somewhere. Forget the dreamboat, forget the G-men." She pressed her hard sweet face right into Mary Beth's. "Go and do your job."

*   *   *

Feeling guilty, frustrated, and just a little drunk, Mary Beth drove home. Guilty because she hadn't suppressed her feelings for Paolo and focused solely on him as a suspect. Frustrated because she hadn't the nerve to stand up to those jokers, Sitwell and Dobbs, to chuck them out as Archie would've done and fling their fedoras into the sea. And drunk because she'd bolted not one but three shots of rye and tomorrow would likely have a hangover. Just in time for the agents' return.

They would be back, she was sure of it. With their fancy badges and guns stashed in their armpits, disturbing the peace and turning up nothing. Of that Mary Beth was certain, and not only because slickers like them could never really understand these islanders—polite but backbiting, pious yet cynical, hardworking though rarely ambitious. The Puritan stock salted by generations of suffering, by inbreeding and brine, and clinging barnacle-like to their ways. Hell, she hardly knew them, either, even after half a decade of trying.

But not only was their foreignness working against the Feds, but also their methods. The assumption that their prey was cowering somewhere and had to be ferreted out. That he, like most criminals, was a coward who struck from behind and didn't have the guts to confront them. But that was not the man Mary Beth was beginning to suspect she hunted. Call it a hunch, but the murderer was hiding in plain sight. And playing Dobbs and Sitwell much as he was toying with her.

Reaching the promontory, she killed the coupe and dallied. Fireflies sparkled, crickets trilled. The lighthouse beckoned to her, but she felt too tipsy to climb it. Instead, she teetered past the tin-roofed shed with its storm supplies and tarp in the shape of a motorcycle and entered the keeper's lodge.

This was what she once called home. More whitewashed walls, more nautical knickknacks and shells. A Frigidaire, a stove, a four-poster bed, and an armoire where they hung their Sunday clothes and uniforms. A mantle over a fireplace they lit only in winter, but which Mary Beth kept decorated year-round with flowers. The earthenware vase that always stood empty and would remain so until Archie's return.

Yet it wasn't. Spilling over the brim was a bouquet of hydrangeas—fuchsia, white, and periwinkle. Fourth Cliff was famous for them, especially in summers, and not just among tourists. The natives, too, cherished them, seeing in the hearty blossoms a symbol of their own fortitude. A reminder of forbidden trysts and of passions too potent to contain.

7.

MARY BETH HAD NEVER OWNED A PISTOL, MUCH LESS FIRED ONE, until she reached Fourth Cliff. The Boston police wouldn't give sidearms to women cops, who were expected to deal with nothing more threatening than street walkers and urchins for whom a basic baton would do. But there it was beside her on the bed, waiting for her gift-wrapped when she wakened. A present for her twenty-fifth birthday, an event she'd once expected to celebrate totally alone, a spinster. But then came Archie. Then came the Colt.

Stainless steel with a walnut handle, a barrel nearly six inches long—"no pea-shooter for *my* birthday girl," Archie said—and .45 caliber bullets, capable, he claimed, of stopping an elephant. Though the chances of aiming it at anything more murderous than a milk bottle were negligible, he wanted her to have, if not the first, assuredly the last shot, and he taught her where to place it. In the chest, preferably, anywhere beneath the neck.

Her first attempts hit everywhere but. She moaned and even cursed, but Archie merely chuckled and embraced her once more from behind. Laid his arms over hers and raised them toward the silhouette. "Line it up with the sights and slowly, slowly squeeze." She did, cringing before each blast and then, firing, feeling the weapon jerk upward as if in sudden realization or disgust, and seeing the slugs zip through the dunes. "Breathe out before shooting," he counseled. "Imagine it's a water pistol. Imagine that silhouette is your father." Her next round punctured the heart.

The badge she had earned and the gun he'd given to her, but the bars she'd claimed for herself. Two days after he shipped out to Camp Lejeune, leaving her lonely and scared and clueless how to perform her job, she found herself pacing the lodge. Opening the armoire, she stared at his black leather jacket with its silver insignia. She smoothed the salt-cracked sleeves and savored its resinous smell. Then she tried it on. A neat fit, with her height and shoulder width.

In the wardrobe's full-length mirror, she was not at all laughable.

"Yes," Mary Beth said out loud. "Goddanged it, yes."

Archie learned of her decision matter-of-factly, in a letter that explained how, in his absence, somebody had to uphold the law. Though they might not at first salute the woman, Mary Beth wrote, people would instinctively respect the rank. "Talk about self-promotion," she quipped.

His reply was equally pithy. "Wear it proudly, Captain Swann," he replied to the photograph she sent him somewhere in the Solomons. "And guard our island home."

If only it'd been that easy. The badge and the gun were hers to keep, she learned, but the bars she would have to earn. The people of Fourth Cliff would have to believe that Mary Beth was capable not just of escorting drunken men home or old ladies across the intersection, but of actually catching a killer.

But instead of arresting him, she was merely spinning aimlessly in the coupe, tracking down leads that led nowhere and flirting with a prisoner of war. And now he'd sent her hydrangeas. *How laughable I look in the mirror*, Mary Beth thought. The shield and weapon were real enough, but the rank was still malarkey.

* * *

"Malarkey," she muttered while leaving the lodge that morning. Down the pot-holed path she drove, through the thickets and onto the main road, for a change heading south. Her patrol had just begun, the sun peeking over the Atlantic, when she suddenly slammed on the brakes. The car swerved left then right, into a patch of goldenrod, narrowly missing—once again—Alva Fitch.

"Can't you ever look around you, Alva?" Mary Beth snarled through her open window.

The madwoman bared her driftwood teeth; her ember eyes flared. "And can't you," Alva replied, "ever see?"

Most mornings she'd take an interest in what Alva was saying. But this particular morning, feeling on the verge of madness herself, Mary Beth hadn't the patience.

"I see you've done well for yourself," she said brusquely, and motioned with her chin toward the tin pails that Alva held. Both were brimming with clams.

"Pascal, over at the diner, pays me twenty cents each."

"Don't let anybody say he's stingy."

"He's a gremlin is what he is. An imp." Then she said, in a conspiratorial tone that let Mary Beth know she was serious, "I've seen the ghost of his missing fingers. Each of 'em's got claws."

Mary Beth's palm struck the red Roman god in the cap of the Mercury's steering wheel. "Well, I'll be darned."

"And damned you will be if you don't start using those peepers." Alva gave her a look at once concerned and critical, like the one she probably shot her husband and sons the day they took to their fishing boat and ignored the hurricane warnings.

"My vision's not what it used to be, admitted," Mary Beth humored her. "I'm thinking I might need specs."

But Alva just went on. "I told you—watch out for that fourth cliff. But you just keep puttering round in that jalopy of yours, blind as any of these steamers." She raised the pails, one after the other, and put her face, shriveled as old onion skin, through Mary Beth's window. It smelled of sand, clams, and insanity. "Why, you don't know what goes on right under your own nose, do you?"

Mary Beth stared at her warily. Perhaps she, too, had witnessed her speaking with Paolo—maybe everybody did. Alva might even know about the flowers. *You don't have to lose a family to go cockeyed,* she thought.

"What?" the captain snapped. "What goes on in this town that I don't see? You tell me, what's happening in broad daylight?"

Alva cackled. She shook her head violently, whipping it with her hawser-like hair, then tossed it skyward. "Them!" she shouted at the climbing sun. "They're back!"

∗   ∗   ∗

Who "they" were didn't require much guessing. Sitwell and Dobbs, of course they'd returned. The only question was: where? Not in town from the looks of it, no sign of the black Dodge down by the docks, nor had any of the fishermen seen it. Most of the merchants were just then opening and, at the diner, Pascal was stirring up his first pot of chowder. Not until she drove up the bluff toward the church did Mary Beth learn of their direction, and from what was becoming her trustiest source.

"Thataway," said Hogan. Though his eyes indicated opposing directions, his finger left little doubt.

The cranberry bog? Mary Beth thought. *The emplacement?* No, she realized. She knew exactly where the agents were heading and had a stomach-churning inkling why.

"Good work, Lemuel," she praised him, reaching through the

window and straightening his tie with a tug. "Keep this up, and I'll have to promote you to corporal."

The patrolman smiled with a profusion of teeth and went ram-rod stiff on his seat. Turning southward and speeding away, she could still hear the excited *brring* of his bicycle.

She hoped she could get there before them, but when she pulled into the camp, the Dodge was already parked in front of the mess hall. The agents must have arrived on the very first ferry, shortly after dawn, to catch the prisoners before they left for work. Most of them had in fact been netted and were loitering outside their bunks, smoking and looking bitter.

"Where are they?" was all she said to Lorenzo as he approached the coupe practically crying. The squat, ill-shapen man seemed short-er and more contorted, and his once-bright expression was downcast.

"Inside…" He wasn't singing anymore, but practically choked. "They take everything."

Everything, she soon saw, included radios, pin-ups, even the wooden crosses. "Against regulations," Sitwell explained. He was beaming even as he sweat and shoved a box of personal possessions alongside the others crammed into the Dodge's backseat.

Dobbs followed with an even bigger crate, straining but no less cheery. "We'll show these guidos," he exulted.

"But what about what the director said?" Mary Beth hounded them. "What happened to hearts and minds?"

"The director ordered it," Dobbs informed her. Though both equally bland, she was beginning to tell them apart, and not only by height. Dobbs had a mole in the middle of one cheek, and Sitwell a scar over his left eye. Sitwell's mouth was as thin as a shoelace while Dobb's was more like a strop. Sitwell cleaned his teeth with toothpicks. Dobbs needed to.

Sitwell said, "Grab 'em by the contraband, and their hearts and minds will follow." Removing his fedora, he drew a wrist across his forehead. "There's a big difference between confiscating wirelesses and murdering people, you'll agree, Policewoman Swann?"

Dobbs bounced on his gum-soles. His eyes were leaden, Mary Beth noticed, and Sitwell's were moldy. "Nothing wrong with putting on a little heat."

"You can't do this," she tried to step in. "It's against…"

Sitwell smiled at her. "Regulations? We *are* the regulations." He glanced critically at the deserted guard towers, the wire that wasn't even fastened for show. "And the only ones, from the looks of this place."

The "heat," as Dobbs called it, was applied—fittingly—in the kitchen, on a stool drawn up under a lamp. There, one by one, the agents questioned the inmates, asking them where they were from and if they were ever active fascists. Where they fought and where they were captured and what they thought of the United States.

"We think it's a Mussolini lover who's doing this," Sitwell explained to her. "That or a plot. Kill a few paisanos here and get your buddies back home to keep fighting." His eyes, unlike his partner's, were squinty. "All quite simple, really."

The drilling went on all morning and well into late afternoon, until the agents broke for lunch. They left the kitchen, but not before appropriating its spices. Little bags of them spilled from Dobbs's arms as he exited, trailing scents of *origano*. The portly cook lumbered after him, protesting.

"Ever ask yourself why he's the only porker around here?" Dobbs, passing by Mary Beth, taunted. "Ever ask him whether he's a smuggler or not or look into what he did in the war, massacring the natives in Libya?" He turned and snarled at the fat man, who froze in his steps and went speechless. "Cook, hell, this guy's a crook."

Outside, with their suits shining in the sunlight, the FBI men took in their handywork: a car packed with appropriated items and a yard filled with hassled men. Lorenzo approached them, hands pressed prayer-like in front of his chest. "Ti prego," he began, but the agents merely ignored him.

Instead, "Preliminary investigations," Sitwell informed Mary Beth, adding, "But I think we're onto something."

"We'll nail 'em, just watch," winked Dobbs.

And then, in twin fists of dust, they drove off. The air cleared leaving Mary Beth alone and coughing and so violently wrenching her wedding band that it almost broke her skin. Seconds passed before she realized she was surrounded. The prisoners gaped at her, some beseechingly, others enraged. But one of them stood apart, in his street sweeper's hat and pencil moustache. He leered at her crossly, pityingly, and—most unsettling to her—dispassionately. This was not the Paolo who listened to her fears and bolstered her confidence. Not the Paolo who snuck a sprig into her jacket pocket and who, she was almost certain, stuffed her vase with hydrangeas.

*   *   *

Her plan was to follow the Feds back into town and make sure they caught the ferry on time. Beyond that, she hadn't the foggiest. She imagined returning to the police station and phoning a switchboard on the coast. "Saipan," she'd ask the operator, "a Major Archibald Swann." She pictured him pausing in the thick of battle, filthy and black-eyed, but nevertheless taking her call.

"Okay, big guy, what's my next move?" she'd ask him, and Archie would laugh that laugh of his straight out of high school "Don't worry yourself, Maypole," he'd assure her. "Just follow your gut."

Her reverie crashed on the concrete blocks of the army emplacement. There seemed to be some kind of picnic going on, the soldiers seated around a makeshift table outside. They weren't alone, though.

Between the flagpole and the bunkers, close by the jeep, sat the black Dodge. Mary Beth turned in the coupe.

The table, she saw, was made of two-by-fours laid across empty ammunition crates. Or at least she assumed they were empty, as several of the soldiers were smoking, strictly forbidden inside the bunkers and especially the one with the thick metal door and the high explosive shells stored behind it. The table was anything but empty. Salamis, hams, thick cheese wedges, and condiments of all kinds crowded it. "Courtesy of Mr. and Mrs. Colburn," Sergeant Perl smiled. "The best of Beacon Hill."

"Ah, war-time," Sitwell sighed and heaped his plate with rice pudding.

They were all feasting, laughing, and telling jokes. The special agents with their fedoras pushed to the back of their heads and the GIs with their garrison caps worn crooked. Only the lieutenant looked stiff. He did not laugh or even eat. Through his sunglasses, he stared at the bounty as if it were rancid or a poison gradually killing him.

"Why the long face?" Dobbs egged him. "We all play our part." He popped a fistful of almonds. "Take Mrs. Swann over here, valiantly protecting the home front."

Like Colburn, Mary Beth didn't eat. She didn't sit, either, but remained standing and watching them.

"He won't touch the stuff," Perl whispered to her out of the corner of his smile. "Nothing but C-rations."

Sitwell helped himself to a second slice of pie. "And soon our boys will be in Paris," he said. "Just ask Ernie Pyle. Paris—wine, women—you can't feel guilty about a little sub."

"Or a hero," Dobbs added.

"Around here, they're called grinders," Perl informed them and was then, himself, corrected.

"You mean spukies, sergeant."

Mary Beth glanced at the far end of the table, at a bear of a soldier who seemed to be bursting from his uniform. "Where I come from, in the North End, we call it a spukie," he declared and brandished a taper-tipped roll bulging with lunch meat and cheese.

"Don't listen to that *doozy bots*," Perl assured her. "Did I at least get that right, Falcone?"

Falcone seemed to wink at him, with an eye that was already half-closed. "Bingo, sarge," he said, and pointed his sandwich like a spear. "And you, you're a *strunz*."

"This is what we're fighting for," Sitwell exulted to Mary Beth. "Wops, Hebes, Micks, all of us. America."

With this, abruptly, Lieutenant Colburn stood. Behind his sunglasses, she could tell, his eyes were hollow, his handsome cheeks even more so. He stood at attention and his men did likewise, leaving only Dobbs and Sitwell seated. "What did we say?" they wondered, but nobody answered them, least of all Colburn.

He about-faced, rather, and strode back into the bunker, almost forgetting to duck under the warning WATCH YOUR GI HEAD. Then he was gone, away from the world of grinders and spukies and back to a war in which there were no longer subs for him to sink, and no heroes.

*   *   *

She hated them. The way in the following weeks they continued to roam the island as if they owned it, interviewing every resident, sometimes twice, as well as the very few tourists. Threatening Doc Cunningham and Minnie Beaudet with exposing their secret pasts. But the agents' favorite target remained the POWs, grilling them repeatedly and making them sweat. Many went back to their bunks with lips split and eyes blackened with visions of a federal firing squad.

Of all the prisoners, Paolo Varrone received special attention. Hours of it. Perhaps because of his aristocratic air, his refusal to suck up to them, his face was slapped red and his fingers bent back to the point of breaking. Yet each interrogation only tempered him. His expression hardened, and not only toward Dobbs and Sitwell but also to Mary Beth, who anxiously waited for him outside. No longer cool but visibly contemptuous, his manner seemed to excoriate her for being so helpless, for not being the formidable woman he'd thought.

Paolo's scorn only added to her misery, already compounded by the feds. "Pistol packin' mama," they called her, after the popular Bing Crosby song, or "the seafood mama," after the Andrew Sisters'. And they did it publicly, loudly enough for everybody to hear. All of Fourth Cliff was witness to how, in pathetically short measure, she was reduced to an underling and exposed as a fraud. At this rate, by autumn, she might as well turn in her badge. The captain's bars would have long been torn off.

Though now she could tell them apart, Sitwell and Dobbs had become in her mind a single cancerous mass, black and spreading. The mere sight of it made her queasy. And that Labor Day, it nearly made her sick. Not even a federal holiday could keep them from tormenting Fourth Cliff. She hated them and hated to admit that she hated them even more than she did the killer.

So blinding was that enmity that she scarcely noticed the other car parked by the docks. Not far from the Dodge yet totally humbling it, a dove-gray Cadillac sedan. *No doubt some other government bigwig*, Mary Beth thought, *or a buyer from Chicken of the Sea*. She didn't get a chance to glimpse inside, though, for a ruckus suddenly escaped from the diner. Broken dishes and what sounded like smashing chairs, followed by a series of grunts and curses. Moments later, the door burst open and Dobbs and Sitwell came stumbling out.

They staggered, each with a hand stretched out before him while the other tried to wipe clean his eyes. Both were slathered in a creamy white liquid that coursed off their chins and dappled the front of their suits. They lurched right past her without even acknowledging her presence, fleeing for the Dodge. The liquid, she noticed, was studded with what looked like bits of onion and celery. And clams.

Emerging behind them from the diner were a pair of giants, six-footers at least, bollard-shaped and jetty-jawed. Half-shaded by their fedoras, their expressions were empty of anything but threat. Their cheap suits bulged conspicuously at the breast. They stood on the street right next to Mary Beth, but with their eyes fixed on the feds as they dove into the Dodge and gunned it out of town. Still, both goons remained frozen while yet another man exited the diner.

Far slighter and more elegantly dressed with a silken tie and pocket square, a camel-colored jacket and hat. His shoes were two-tone wingtips. Mid-thirties, maybe, unmarried or simply allergic to rings. He, too, watched the Dodge depart while sipping soup from his mug.

"Tasty," he said to Mary Beth. "But not my mother's minestrone." His hat jerked almost imperceptibly, but it sufficed to send his two henchmen hustling into the Caddy. "I hope our agent friends didn't cause you much trouble."

"Oh, none at all," she lied, and the man, from his simper, seemed to know it.

"Glad to hear it, Missus…"

"Captain. Swann."

"Captain, of course, my apologies."

"And the Bureau, its director, they don't worry you?"

His laugh had a contemptuous edge. "The Bureau, Captain Swann, deals with bootleggers and bank robbers, and Mr. Hoover knows better than to tangle with us," he assured her. "Besides, the government kind of likes us now."

"Likes? You?"

He curled his fingers into the palm of his free hand and examined their tips. "Sicily, Captain Swann. Ever wonder how the American troops marched in almost unopposed? Why they were cheered in Palermo? Ever wonder why there hasn't been a single dock strike in New York, not once, since the war began?" He blew hard on his nails. "Let's just say we have influence."

"In Sicily, maybe, and in Washington." Mary Beth's fists found her waist. "Not here, in Fourth Cliff."

"Sorry to disappoint you, but yes, in Fourth Cliff, too." He aimed his hat brim in the direction out of town, northward. "The old man at the shipyard, Gainor, he took some persuading but, in the end, he agreed as well." His chowder mug rose in a toast. "Be grateful, those FBI fatheads are finally out of your hair."

"And you, I suppose, are now in it."

Not a question but a statement that she regretted even as she made it. The man had a kindly face, his cheeks smooth, eyes limpid, and in any other setting she would have taken him for a schoolteacher or even a priest, but in this place and moment there was no mistaking his profession.

"Easy, Captain. We are on the same side here."

"And what side is that?"

"Peace. Quiet. The safety of your Italian guests."

She closed one incredulous eye. "You mean the prisoners."

"Maybe to you prisoners, but to us, associates. Antonio De Luca, for one, a key link in our efforts to ship certain items to the coast."

"And Francesco Albertini, he was a smuggler, too?"

He sipped once again before answering.

"Family. Many of them, some quite close. And in my world, anybody who harms the family brings greater harm to himself and *his* family." The man's milky moustache smiled. "Massive harm."

He said this as if he were reading a weather report or even recit-ing a prayer. Mary Beth, taken aback, replied, "You're not at all what I'd have pictured, Mister…"

"Corvelli. Louis. And what exactly were you picturing? Bloody baseball bats? Violin cases with tommy guns? I'm afraid you've been watching too many Cagney films, Captain."

"And you, Mr. Corvelli, have been watching too much Betty Boop. Make no mistake about it, I'm the law on this island. Me and only me. And if you or any of your associates think otherwise, I'll boot you right off."

Maybe it was the weeks of aggravation with the feds, the thrash-ing nights, and loneliness, but these words simply spilled out of her. Mary Beth stood tall, thumbs on her duty belt, collars thrown back with their bars. But Corvelli merely seemed entertained.

"Yes, ma'am." He smirked. "Or is it aye-aye? In any case, you and I have a common purpose. We're both looking for the same mur-derer."

"Meaning?"

"An alliance. A joining of forces…" He cleared his throat. "Of force."

Her response was a nervous laugh and an instinctive twist of wedding band. "Not a snowball's chance in hell."

He laid the empty mug on the sidewalk and extended a delicate hand. "Welcome, then, to hell."

8.

From the top of the lighthouse she could see, roaring overhead and into the twilight, a formation of P-51s. Albacore-fleet and shiny, the fighter planes practiced diving and strafing, rolling and precision bombing. In each of them sat a young man with his dreams of glory, his delusions of what real war was like. Poor boys, Mary Beth thought, they'd be there soon enough. Impossibly distant from their loved ones and home, killing people they'd never met while being shot at by total strangers. Insane. And yet the mere sight of the aircraft brought a warmth to her heart, a sense of security and of something else, hard to define. Transcendence.

It was the feeling she'd have in church sometimes, as a child, of being in the presence of something greater than herself—larger, in fact, than the world. But it had been some years since she'd gone to Mass, and longer still to confession. Her father, on the rare occasion they spoke, never let her forget it. But this evening, watching the airmen soar, she found herself wanting a priest. Just someone she could spill her guts out to candidly. The insecurities, the desires, the frustrations, the fears. The misery of exchanging Sitwell and Dobbs for Louis Corvelli—two devils for one Satan—and of failing both

Archie and Paolo. A priest would listen and bless her nevertheless. A few Hail Marys and, presto, all would be absolved.

But instead of atonement, all she got was more guilt. It flowed from the wrinkled photograph of Francesco's family, the woman in black and the two braided girls, still leering at her in what looked like judgment. Perhaps this, too, was a clue? Unsettling as it was, her conversation with Corvelli had suggested another motive for the crimes, not hatred or even passion, but an inter-family feud. What did they call it on the North Shore? A vendetta. For all she knew, a spat that began in the hills of Sicily ended with murder on Fourth Cliff. Corvelli himself could have carried out the murders—he or his henchmen.

Sighing, Mary Beth added the photo to her link chart, together with the note about Abigail Pitt, the rubbings, and the sprig. Next to the 1942 Red Sox schedule and the nailed-up pocket mirror. Alongside the map of the South Pacific.

The latest pushpin marked the island of Saipan, vaguely horse-shaped and neighboring on nothing. Press reports about what transpired there were dim and further obscured by the astounding victories in Europe, but somehow she knew it was hellish. Archie's last letter had told her as much, at least between the lines. *My Darling Mary Beth*, it began, using her real name. A sure sign of trauma.

I cannot tell you what I have seen and done in the last few weeks. I would never burden you so even if the censor let me. Suffice it to say that I never imagined what human beings could do to one another or that my eyes could witness it and not melt. I never imagined what I, myself, was capable of, and how I'd pray to erase that knowledge.

What we've done here, I know, will shorten the war by many months, maybe years. From here our bombers can at last reach Japan and flatten it, if necessary. Anything to make them surrender. And then I can come home to you, my beloved. I can come home but will you still have me?

More than my fear of what the enemy can do to me, I fear what he's already done. Changed me. Hardened me. Brought out sides of me that should always have remained buried. My greatest fear is that I'm no longer the person you married or would want to spend your life with.

One thing that hasn't changed and never will is my love for you. It's eternal. They can strip away everything from me, hack it off, and that love will remain, I promise.

You take care of yourself now. Don't let the Labor Day tourists irk you. Say hello to Hogan for me and please check the oil in my Harley. Better yet, take it for a spin—for me—just the way I taught you.

Your adoring husband (still),

Archie

The letter came with a snapshot, the first she'd had of him in more than a year, but scarcely recognizable. It showed a man slightly Archie-like but much thinner, almost skeletal, and with dark round circles for his eyes. His jungle fatigues looked too burdensome for his shoulders. He leaned on his rifle as if it were a crutch and attempted to smile but managed only a frown.

That photo, too, she'd tacked to the wall. It joined the earlier images of Archie in his policeman's uniform and Archie before sailing overseas. In the dwindling light, she stood back and stared at them. Tried mightily to convince herself that they were all of the same man.

Another squadron of planes zoomed over, this one very low. Crossing the mattress on the floor, Mary Beth reached the old brass telescope and trained it on a pilot. She could see him in the cockpit with his leather helmet and goggles, a scarf tied rakishly around his neck. A hotshot, no doubt, a future hero. Still, Mary Beth said a prayer for him, hoping he, like all those countless sons and husbands, would come home safely. That God would preserve him from this endless war and its infinite ways to die. She prayed and she watched, gasping, as the silvery Mustang banked suddenly and spun, spiralling before plunging sideways into the sea.

PART FOUR

9.

Five was the best time for trawling and October the most propitious month. Yes, the winter storms were already brewing, whipping off the white caps as easy as heads of beer. But the ocean floor was calm enough for an oakwood pot to sit placidly, inviting any visitor with four pairs of legs and two claws to come right in and feast. To enter the "parlor" and then the "kitchen," as the fishermen called it, set with juicy skewered mackerel and sealed with a wire-mesh trap from which there was no escape.

Their entrapment meant freedom for Calvin Trott. Unlike so many of the islanders who eked out their living from the sea, often one slim season away from poverty, his income was invariably handsome. Even in wartime, there were always rich Bostonians willing to pay top dollar for a Cold Water, more for a Canadian or Maine, while the military had zero use for his catch. Soldiers could fight on corned beef or Spam but never would they ask, "Hey, where's our C-ration of lobster?"

Calvin Trott indeed was free, so much so that he hardly had to work at all, especially now with his two boys off serving somewhere in the Aleutians, with more to fear from frozen limbs than from any remaining Japanese. Yet he enjoyed the roll of his boat, said it becalmed his arthritis, and a mug of spiked cider in his mitts. The pre-dawn hour was the most beautiful, he held, almost seductive, with stars still shimmering over a lavender veil of night. And then there was the thrill of hauling his pots aboard and welcoming their spiny guests. It was a sensation he experienced every morning but Sunday, going on forty years, without rest. War or no war, shorthanded or not, he was not about to forfeit it.

The Italians helped as well. The only two prisoners who didn't mind getting picked up in the middle of the night and freezing their butts off scanning for his buoys and hauling up the Quonset-shaped pots. Nice young men, Emanuele and Giuseppe, or was it the other way around, for Calvin could never tell them apart. Bird-boned and tremulous, they rarely said anything in their own language, much less English, and were only too happy to take a soft-shell or two back to their camp as a succulent present for their cook.

That was surely the source of their excitement as they hoisted up the last of the pots and began shouting. Emerging from his cabin, Calvin was expecting to find a two-pounder at least, but the pot, he saw, contained only a single lobster, and that one was visibly under-weight. And yet the quiet men still babbled. Only when he pushed between them and peered through the wooden slats did he see what the wire-mesh snared.

"They'll eat anything, or try to," he later explained to Mary Beth. "Heck, I've caught 'em with tire irons in their claws and beer cans. Once even a lady's girdle." With his hard, red complexion and bulg-ing eyes, Calvin himself looked lobster-like, she thought. "With kid-neys where their brains ought to be, what more can you expect?"

Not much, Mary Beth admitted, but not this. Even with the ocean occasionally giving back the bodies of the many sailors and pilots it stole, what this lobster clasped was beyond explanation. Be-yond horrific. So much so that even the POWs, both of whom had seen what shells and bullets could do to flesh, were terrified. It wasn't merely the human hand that set them screaming, but the iron ring it wore.

*   *   *

"Two, three days at most," was Doc Cunningham's estimate for how long it'd been in the water. "Just after it was chopped off."

"Chopped?"

"Like with a hatchet." Retrieving his scalpel, he scraped the surfaces of two exposed bones. "You see how clean these are, as if the radius and ulna were simply detached. As if the hand belonged to a mannequin."

Through the smoky lamplight, she squinted at the doctor's examining table. The hand was displayed there, palm up, as if to check for rain. Her initial disgust at seeing it, wrapping it in oilskin, and transporting it to the office above the diner was surpassed only by the knowledge that other parts were no doubt still floating out there and liable to be snagged, that she might have to reassemble them puzzle-like. This single segment would do just fine for now. Already, it told her a lot.

"No manual laborer, this one," the doctor concluded. "No calluses. And not much of a fighter, either. No bruises on the knuckles, that is if he led with his left. No skin beneath the nails."

Yet key deduction came not from the hand but from the ring the doctor removed from it. Leaning over the table, Mary Beth saw that there were eagles embossed on each of its sides, and on its face, a bundle of what looked like sticks.

"Fasces," Cunningham said.

"Excuse me?"

"Fasces. The ancient Roman symbol for strength. One rod is easy to break but try it with a bunch of them tied together—impossible." He lit one cigarette with the smoldering end of another. "It's where they get the word fascism."

"An Italian ring…"

"Not necessarily. We use it, too. Just look on the back of a dime."

Mary Beth fished into the pocket of the black leather jacket she had just started wearing again, for the fall, and found an old Mercury head. Holding it up to the light and turning it around, she gasped. "Jiminy Cricket." Smack in the center of the tails side, right next to E Pluribus Unum, was the same laureled bundle of sticks.

"But, yes, Italian." With a yellowed finger, the doctor pointed at the inscription inside. "Oro Alla Patria."

"Meaning?"

"Gold for the Homeland. That is, if I recall what I learned at Boston Latin. Whoever owned this iron ring got it in return for donating his wedding band."

Mary Beth was stumped. "But why? To whom?"

"For the war effort, of course." Cunningham clicked his heels comically and raised on one frayed cuff toward the ceiling. "To Il Duce."

*   *   *

Gold for the homeland, not Fourth Cliff, certainly. Another prisoner had been killed, savagely, another resident at least nominally under her care and who she'd failed, once more, to protect. And as harrowing as the first two murders were, this one was worse. This one had no name and no clean means of identification. The first two, if not saints, were at least peace-loving. This one, it appeared, was a fascist.

Alone in the station, Mary Beth measured her next move. Should she show the ring around the prison camp and ask if anybody recognized it? But even if someone did, why would they tell her? Why, if this person had died in the way that Louis Corvelli suggested, a victim of a family feud, would they want to involve an outsider, a foreigner and a woman to boot? What if Lorenzo, the ex-stonecutter, were the guilty one, or the fat cook, good with knives and known to be a killer in Libya? Who was to say that Corvelli hadn't wielded the hacksaw himself or—God forbid—Paolo? Better to keep her inquiries lowkey for now, she reasoned. Better to be discreet.

Discretion, though, was in shorter supply than sugar on the island. There was really only one man who might tell her something and one man she might trust. But did she dare approach him again, in the wake of all that gossip? In the shadow of that disdainful look he'd shot her the last time she'd seen him in the camp, and of the image of Archie half-starved and hollow-eyed on Saipan? Turning the iron ring over and over in her fingers, toying with the golden one on hers, Mary Beth realized she had no other choice. She rose from her black ash desk, retrieved her cap and jacket, and headed into town.

She found him not down by the docks, as usual, but high up near the intersection, under the shadow of the First Congregational Church. With his fox-face and bat ears, his icy eyes and pencil moustache, he still looked like a cross between Bela Lugosi and Errol Flynn. Yet no Hollywood actor would be caught dead diligently sweeping the street as he was, gathering tiny molehills of dust.

Engaging the brake, lowering her window, "You still think this is noble?" Mary Beth asked.

Paolo Varrone looked up and smiled. "Exalted."

"You make it sound holy almost. A sacrament."

"Un sacramento, sì," he laughed. "Christ was a carpenter, so who am I not to sweep?"

"Then don't let me keep you," she apologized with a blush, already regretting her decision to speak with him. Strive though she might, Mary Beth simply could not regard him as a suspect. She reluctantly released the brake.

Before she could roll on, though, Paolo added, "I understand your problem with those two *idioti* has vanished."

Mary Beth parked the car and got out. "They're gone," she said, "but another's taken their place. And I wouldn't call him an idiot."

Paolo scowled. "I know his kind. We have many of them where I come from. Racketeers, extortionists, assassins. They helped ruin my country and they'll ruin yours as well if you don't stop them."

"Stop them." She kicked some imaginary trash. "Yeah, right."

He jabbed the broom up and down angrily spear-like. "Just like Albertini, that Lothario, and De Luca, a smuggler right out of Carmen, those gangsters destroy my people's good name."

Whoever Lothario and Carmen were, Mary Beth hadn't a clue, but could produce one of her own. The ring. Paolo peered at it and froze.

"Where did you get this?"

"Let's just say from a man who didn't need it anymore." She chuckled at her own private joke. "He handed it to me."

"It's nothing to laugh about. I know this ring. It belonged to a very dangerous person. A lover of Mussolini."

"Well, he won't be endangering anyone anymore. Or loving."

Paolo glared at her and Mary Beth fixed him back. "Name?"

"Flavio Filippani. A Blackshirt, an officer in the Italian SS. The Butcher of Benghazi, they called him."

Paolo, disgusted, kicked his trash barrel, but Mary Beth went on with her questioning. "I call him victim number three and I need to know why. Who would've wanted him dead?"

"Many people," Paolo lamented. "Most. Those who want the Allies to win. But that doesn't mean they'd murder him."

"Jealousy? Revenge? Any motive other than just politics?"

"I assure you, Captain Swann, fascism is no mere politics. It is the enemy I am sworn to fight."

She blushed again, deeper. Who was this man, she wondered, who fought valiantly for his country even as he hated its leaders?

Who despised some of his fellow prisoners yet seemed eager to find their killers? Who planted a cranberry sprig in her jacket pocket and stuffed her vase with hydrangeas?

"I have to find the man responsible for Filippani's murder. For Francesco's and Antonio's too. I need your help, Paolo."

She said this with a tone that revealed her desperation—too much, she realized. Yet rather than comfort her, Paolo straightened suddenly, as stiff as the steeple behind him. "At your service, Captain Swann," he stated and presented his broom like a lance. "Who better to find dirt than a street sweeper?"

*   *   *

The cold black water churned. Salt and sleet diced the air. Up from the depths emerged first a foot and then a shoulder, a knee-cap and a thigh. The flesh was bloodless, pimpled, and pale, and the pieces kept surfacing. Only the face was missing. A snarly face, a hole where the nose should've been and pits in place of eyes, yet still recognizable. Flavio Filippani? No, she didn't even have his picture. Archie? Hardly, the hair and the teeth were all wrong. But the dignified chin looked familiar, and the pointy ears. From somewhere offshore a foghorn blasted and became, all of a sudden, a scream.

The scream was Mary Beth's, and it reverberated around the lighthouse where she'd fallen asleep that night. The drinks at the Flotsam did it, the whiskey that Minnie kept plying her with, getting her to ease up and stop fretting about what other people thought but focus on the detective task at hand. She tried, but the more she guzzled the farther Mary Beth wandered, burbling on about lobsters and mobsters and how Archie was the only man she'd ever slept with and how could she even think of another.

Finally, with a shot of straight Moxie, Minnie sent her home. An October squall misted her windshield and slickened the road. A miracle that somebody didn't find her dead in a ditch instead of lolling with a massive headache on the mattress she'd curled onto, still in her cap and jacket.

Mary Beth lay there before daybreak, temples throbbing, and stared up at the lighthouse wall. Alongside the Red Sox schedule, the photos of Archie, and the map was the link chart with its seemingly unrelated clues. What really did she know? That the killer was a man, and not only because Alva Fitch had told her so. None of the women on Fourth Cliff, herself included, was strong or vicious enough to strangle, stab, and dismember fully grown men and leave their bodies to rot. And a man who liked using a wire, a knife, and a hacksaw—anything but his bare hands—and drove a car with strange tires. That the man was either a vengeful American or an Italian upholding his family honor, a democrat or defender of fascism. Or one other possibility. That the perpetrator was a maniac, a person who butchered just for the joy of it and because, cloaked in wartime fog, he could.

She studied the evidence and the latest entry. Tacked to the corkboard and attracting the sun's first grimy rays was Filippani's iron ring. She thought about its owner, angry and animated by hate, and imagined how much angrier and more hateful he'd be knowing his innards were chum. She pictured the other victims, Francesco and Antonio, by comparison almost immaculate, their faces water-withered. And then she remembered the dream. The aristocratic chin, the pointy ears, and the pencil moustache. Mary Beth gasped. Floating on her mind's murky surface was the face of Paolo Varrone.

*   *   *

Unlike her old neighborhood, where autumn storms cleaned up the streets, the summer's gum wrappers and racecards surging into sewers, October's storms usually left Fourth Cliff littered. The docks were kelp-covered and the beaches strewn with jetsam—milk bottles and cigarette packs, socks and sailors' caps, even a Mae West life-jacket from the USS *Parrott*. Fortunately, no more parts of Flavio Filippani washed up. No left arm with an SS blood type tattoo. No torso that once boasted an Iron Cross.

The town, too, had been rattled. Though the winds weren't especially strong, the first blows always unhinged their share of shingles, splintered hulls moored too close to piers, took down a power line or two. The latter, alone, concerned Mary Beth as she surveyed the damage from her car. With Louis Corvelli sniffing about, on top of three unsolved murders, the last thing she needed was some well-meaning Italian picking up a wire and frying himself.

But apart from the autumn leaves that covered the street like ticker tape, she encountered no serious debris. The island was stirring as it always did after dawn, the fishermen chattering on the docks, storefronts opening. Driving north, she saw that the POWs had already cleaned up the camp and were heading off to work. They waved at her as they passed, young men mostly, veterans though scarcely hardened, singing what sounded like love rather than war songs, hands massaging the air. Vainly, she searched for Paolo, for no other reason than to verify that he was still alive and not bobbing piecemeal on the waves. But there was no sign of him anywhere. Most likely he was already out on the street and pumping his broom, head down but eyes open for any hint helpful to Mary Beth.

Farther on, she noticed some activity outside the base. All four soldiers were filing out of their bunker, ducking their GI heads under the concrete door. But rather than line up for inspection, they gathered around the flagpole clutching tools.

"Top of the morning to you, Captain," Perl greeted her, smiling, as she exited the coupe. "Ain't that how you say it around here?"

Mary Beth smirked. "We're in Fourth Cliff, Sergeant, not Ireland. Everything all right here?"

"A-okay. Just a little patch-up for Old Glory."

The topmost pulley had blown clean off, leaving the flag to flap erratically while its lanyard snapped. Two of the privates gawked at a third who'd shimmied halfway up the pole and was hammering a new block into place.

"How's it goin', *doozy bots*?" Perl called out to him.

The soldier, agile in spite of his size, grunted and laughed. "Great, you big *strunz*."

Perl laughed as well, briefly, then turned to Mary Beth. "Crazy lug," he said quietly.

"Seems like a nice enough sort. Harmless."

"Yeah, that's what they said about Himmler, too." He went back to smiling. "At least he can fix things."

Mary Beth eyed him keenly. "And your lieutenant, does he fix things, too?"

"Not really. He...searches." His squirrely nose twitched in the direction of some dunes.

Mary Beth squinted, following the jeep tracks to where a lone figure stood between the beach grass and the elder, gazing seaward.

"Searches for what?"

"What do you think? U-boats."

"But there aren't any. Not anymore."

The smile returned, but rueful. "Don't tell *him* that."

Through the unravelling mist, Lieutenant Colburn scanned. With binoculars in place of his sunglasses, he swept from horizon to shore. His patrician head lowered; his strapping shoulders heaved. Watching him, Mary Beth wondered if the two of them were not alike. Looking desperately for the slightest sign, the merest inkling, of the one thing that would give them peace. A precious little periscope of hope.

10.

THE STORM HAD PASSED, BUT NOT THE TEMPEST. MARY BETH KNEW that the instant she saw the scarf around Office Hogan's neck. It was not the type of garment, cream-colored and silky, found anywhere on Fourth Cliff, much less on a man who never left it. And he wanted nothing more than to show it off. Summoned from the station by the *brrring* of his bike, she found him sitting proudly in its seat, chin raised, eyes aimed crosswise to the sky.

"What do you think, Captain?"

"I think you'd better tell me where you got it."

The eyes descended and his jaw dropped, exposing a phalanx of teeth. "You don't like it?"

"Policemen shouldn't wear scarves, Lemuel, not on duty. But who gave it to you?"

"It was a gift. From Mr. Louis."

Mary Beth sighed. "He was here? On Fourth Cliff? Today?"

"Yesterday, too," Hogan reported. "And he'll be here tomorrow, he told me."

"And what exactly did you tell him?"

The private raised a shoulder to his ear. "Nothing much. Just the people you've been talking to even since, you know, what happened."

"People?"

"The Halls, for instance, and the Brutons. Abigail Pitt and Wallace McKee. And Minnie."

"Oh, Lemuel…"

Hogan seemed near to tears. "Did I do something wrong?"

She didn't pause to answer him but ran back inside for her cap and jacket, her duty belt and keys. She would have to speed, as fast as possible on the still-slick road. Before he could cause the island any further damage, or any person harm, she had to find Louis Corvelli.

*   *   *

She didn't understand how, on an island of less than thirty square miles with only one main road, she managed to miss him. Or how, gunning the coupe, she couldn't catch up with a dove-gray Cadillac no doubt proceeding leisurely. And yet wherever she went that morning, whoever she met, Mary Beth learned that she was only a minute or two behind. Louis Corvelli had been there already, been polite or intimidating or both.

Wallace McKee the cranberry farmer was positively charmed, or so it seemed from the farmer's responses, which rarely exceeded one word.

"He questioned you?"

"Ayuh."

"About Antonio?"

"Ayuh."

"And you said?"

"Enough."

"Enough?"

"Ayuh."

With his half-toothless smile, Wallace sent him away, Mary Beth heard, and a bushel of freshly harvested cranberries. "For his missus to make for the holiday." With that, he ducked his hump into the Model T's cabin and puttered away, leaving her to wonder who Corvelli would next inveigle.

"He admired my establishment," Tom Bruton said. "That's what he called it, my establishment. Checked out the shelves and even bought Jawbreakers for his pals."

"Pals?"

"Big fellas. Two of them. Didn't say anything, just stood behind him. They sure liked that candy, though."

Tom was acting nonchalantly, but Mary Beth could tell he was scared. His features not only taut but knotted, his dusky hair literally on end. After all, it wasn't every day that a general store owner accustomed to serving housewives and pensioners had a conversation with a real-life gangster. "At least they didn't tear up the place like those FBI gumps," Tom Bruton hastened to add. The steel pennies of his eyes widened into nickels. "At least he paid for the gas."

His son Jimmy was not less agitated, but for entirely different reasons. "I asked him if he'd ever shot anybody. I asked him if he'd ever been shot." Jimmy's teeth were in full display and his freckles burst like fireworks. He could barely sit still on his Schwinn.

"And he said?"

"Do your chores and be good at school." The chestnut hair and jughead hat atop it drooped in disappointment. "Make my father proud."

"Good advice, considering."

But the head and the hat shot up again, his face reignited. "Do that, he said, and someday I could visit him in Chicago!"

With other islanders, though, Corvelli was less indulgent. At Mrs. McQueen's boarding house, his henchmen pummeled the counter bell and nearly busted the counter itself before Abigail Pitt appeared. She was her usual delicate self, with a face that one would find gracing a Dresden miniature, as lustrous as it was frail. Though permed and kerchiefed, her hair had escaped in random strands, and her eyes looked just wiped of tears.

"Did he hurt you?" Mary Beth asked.

"I've had worse," Abigail admitted, and then quickly lit a cigarette. Her hands, Mary Beth noted, were quivering.

"What did he want to know?"

"Names and faces. Regulars and guests." She dragged and shrugged. "People like him, I guess."

"And you told him?"

"Not much. You know me, Mary Beth. Nobody gets anything out of me unless I want to."

"I *do* know you, Abigail." No more Missus Pitt, it was Abigail now, as Mary Beth felt a jolt of sympathy for the woman. Though there was no comparing Archie, who treated her like a queen, and Orson Pitt the wife-beater, she and Abigail were both alone and fending for themselves. Defending themselves in a world of perilous men. "I know you, which is exactly why I'm concerned."

"No need," Abigail replied. "There's nothing your Mr. Corvelli can do to me that hasn't been done already." She waved her feather duster dismissively but so violently that one of its plumes flew off. "Compared to my husband, Captain Swann, he's candy."

But what was done to Abigail could never have been imagined by the Halls. Braking sharply in front of the house, Mary Beth ran across the uncut lawn, ignoring the old Newfoundland lying there, and bounded onto the slump of the porch. The gold star pennant that once hung proudly in the window's center now dangled near the sill.

She knocked, one hand on the holster, which this time she didn't leave in her trunk. Sarah Hall took her time answering. Mary Beth could see why. Her hair was more disheveled than usual, her skin more desiccated. The depression around her mouth looked deeper somehow, perhaps because the lower lip was cracked.

"Oh, no."

Sarah threw back her head defiantly. "Don't you 'oh, no' me, Mrs. Swann. This is all your fault."

"My fault? How?"

"Running about playing detective. With your gun and your cap, dragging innocent people into your game."

Her eyes were rivets; Mary Beth felt nailed by them. But she didn't dare avert her own. Do that and the last of her authority would vanish. So, too, would her chance to check on Bill.

"Let me in, Sarah, please. I won't ask again."

The sharp-witted little girl who still lingered in her look reasserted herself. Akimbo, Sarah stood in the doorway. "No," she said.

"Move away from the door, Sarah Hall, and that's an order."

Mary Beth didn't know if such an order was even legal, but she was pretty sure Sarah didn't know either. Still, she was surprised when, after a few moments of staring at the duty belt and bars, Sarah stepped aside.

The scene inside was more shocking that any she'd prepared herself for. Overturned rag rugs, upended embroideries, and a china cabinet in which all was smashed but the pewter. The only furniture left undisturbed was the Franklin stove, too heavy to flip, and the rocking chair that remained stationary while Bill Hall sat.

Unlike his wife, he looked physically unharmed. Though seemingly melted in his chair, his entire body slouched, he was not bruised or bloodied like Sarah was, perhaps because of his still-muscular build.

"What did he want from you?" Mary Beth asked.

A flinch, a wince, both barely perceptible. "Information about that Albertini boy. And the other one."

"And you told him?"

"Told him to shove it in his porthole. Told him that I didn't care which of the prisoners were killed and by who. They can all kill each other, I said."

"Not the smartest, Bill. He could've really beat you or worse."

He laughed curtly, painfully, and motioned to the opposite wall. The photograph of Corporal Christopher Hall had been knocked off its hinges, its frame splintered and glass cracked. Not because of his muscles had Bill been spared but because, more than mere fists and even bullets, this unbearably hurt.

"Happy?" Sarah snorted.

Not happy, furious, Mary Beth wanted to snap back at her. Instead, hitching up her belt and tugging her cap brim, she stormed toward the door. Like Corvelli, she had also lost her patience. Ready, finally, to fight back.

*   *   *

But where could she find him? So far Corvelli had gone to those she'd already questioned. Vulnerable people—senior citizens, a single woman, a kid. Perhaps he'd think twice about taking on the fishermen, generally a curmudgeonly bunch, or even the merchants. For all the fear his henchmen could instill, there was only so much information one could squeeze from Fourth Cliffers. Like trying to crack lobsters with your teeth.

"He didn't get nothing from me," Minnie assured her. "Nada."

Unlike with the Halls and Abigail Pitt, Corvelli seemed to have treated her gently, almost gallantly. "He even left a tip."

He was a smart man, clearly, an insightful reader of people. He knew who to humor and butter, and he knew who to squeeze. Minnie Beaudet was clearly not one to be pressed.

"I suppose he could've worked me over real good, for all it would have done him," Minnie went on. She threw back her turban triumphantly, her already-flat nose stretched with the width of her smile.

But her expression turned somber. "You, Swann, have to be careful. Men like Corvelli can change on a dime—I know, I've dealt with them—and go from sweet to vicious just like that," she snapped. "From kind to killer."

Mary Beth nodded as if she understood, but her mind was already churning. Where could Corvelli go next? Who on this pocket-sized island remained to be interviewed, cajoled, or threatened? And then it struck her. How had she not thought of it first?

Back in the coupe she raced, shrieking around the intersection and down the bluff toward town, where she pulled up in front of the diner. She scurried up to the story above it, where the scent of Pascal's fresh-brewed bisque succumbed to the tang of a doctor's office. She entered and sighed. Once again, she was late.

Doc Cunningham didn't get up from his chair. He didn't look at her when she entered, but only at the tip of his Chesterfield. He wasn't browbeaten like Abigail and the Burtons, or physically harassed like the Halls. Yet his very composure told her what had happened.

"Filippani. The hand," she said. "The ring."

The doctor nodded. "I don't do well with beatings," he explained.

Mary Beth fell back against the examining table. "So Corvelli knows. It'll make him even more dangerous. It'll drive him insane."

Cunningham turned his face up to the light. He, himself, looked cadaverous, his skin almost translucent, his eyes the faintest blue. His voice, usually strident, was sotto. "Might I suggest, Captain, that you take a cue from our FBI friends and take a step back. This apparently is an affair between Italians—*in famiglia*—a matter for the Goombahs to settle. Besides, it might not be the best for your health."

She stood, glowering. "No," Mary Beth said. "No more," and strode out of the office. Behind her, rising from his chair and lifting one tattered cuff to his forehead, Horace Cunningham saluted.

*   *   *

There was no doubt about his next destination, only the amount of mayhem he would cause before she got there. Once inside the prisoner of war camp, Corvelli would go wild, siccing his goons on every inmate he could, tearing their bunks and their kitchen apart until someone divulged who was behind the vendetta. The fact that they were all Italians wouldn't matter. People like him were always targeting their own, Mary Beth remembered from the news, shooting them in barber chairs or beating their brains out with bats. She could only imagine what the poor POW would look like once he was forced to confess.

Hurling uphill, past the trash barrel and push broom abandoned on the curb, she screeched through the intersection and tore north. The speedometer was pushing ninety when suddenly her foot shifted from gas to brake and the cab filled with the stench of burnt rubber. Parked along the side of the road, in front of one of the skeletal skiffs foundered there by some forgotten storm, sat the dove-gray Cadillac. Corvelli and his henchmen were there, hatless and sweating as they hunkered over Paolo, cornered with his back to the hull.

"Stop it! Stop!" Mary Beth, bursting from the coupe, shouted.

Corvelli scarcely glanced at her. "I see you finally caught up to me, Mrs. Swann," was all he said, and turned his attention back to Paolo.

"What's going on here?"

"Just having a little chat with your friend." His voice was as silken as his tie.

Mary Beth winced. "He's not my friend, but he is my responsibility. You let him go right now."

The henchmen lurched forward, ready to strike, but Corvelli motioned them back. He looked at her now, unsmiling. "This man has blood on his hands. Our blood."

"The only thing he has on his hands is Fourth Cliff trash. And if there's anything more, that's my business, not yours."

"I beg to correct you, Mrs. Swann. It is entirely my business."

"That's Captain Swann, and you scram, all of you, before..."

Her hand shifted to her holster, and the henchmen's delved into their coats. Corvelli's hand rose again, halting them.

"Are you sure you want to go there, lady?"

"Yeah, I'm sure. Try me."

Her fingers were now curling around the Colt's walnut handle, releasing its safety. Her eyes were fixed on Corvelli, for an instant picturing him as one of Archie's targets, aiming for the heart or anywhere beneath the neck. But even if she hit him, she knew, the others would get off their rounds. She'd be dead in seconds, Paolo too. Yet still she tightened her grip.

"Please, Mary Beth, no."

It took her a moment to realize the words were Paolo's. Though his hair was disheveled and face reddened and wet, his expression remained calm, almost tranquil. He'd been through worse than a few slaps and punches, she reckoned. His only worry, it seemed, was for her. He'd even uttered her name.

"You might want to listen to him," Corvelli suggested, his mien no longer priestly but murderous.

"Beat it," Mary Beth said.

Statue-still they stood—Mary Beth with a finger on the trigger now and Corvelli's men reaching for the bulge on their breasts. The wind blew raw and briny, whistling through the ribs of the skiff.

"This one time," Louis Corvelli said finally, and signaled his flunkies to follow. They filed past Mary Beth on the way to the Caddy. Only the gangster paused. "There won't be a second," he whispered.

*   *   *

"You're shook up, I can understand," Mary Beth reassured Paolo while driving him back to town.

But the prisoner said nothing. He merely gazed at the windshield as if it were a mirror, scowling at his own reflection.

"I'm sorry you had to go through all that."

Still, silence.

"I can take you back to the camp if you'd like. Call it a day. A little rest…"

Finally Paolo spoke, though only to the window. "I survived Eritrea," he said, "Tobruk and El Alamein. Salerno and Monte Cassino."

"And fought bravely, I'm sure."

"I do not fear the likes of your Mr. Corvelli."

Mary Beth shot him a grin. "Hey, a bullet's a bullet," she began, only to be interrupted.

"I didn't need your help."

"Like hell you didn't."

"I didn't ask for it and I don't want it. Ever."

"Well, excuse *me*."

Through the intersection they rolled and turned wordlessly downhill. Entire minutes seemed to pass until they reached the abandoned broom and barrel. Paolo started to get out, but not before Mary Beth needled him. "Let me understand. Being saved by a woman is humiliating to you, but sweeping up garbage is honorable?"

He climbed out the coupe, brushed off his uniform, and flipped on his cap. A street sweeper again with a dustpan and a moustache—less a movie star than a character straight out of Looney Tunes. "Yes," he responded, raising the broom handle like a flag. "Christ was a carpenter," he reminded her. "But Mary never saved him from the cross."

The door slammed and Mary Beth drove off. "Men," she griped to herself, "utterly ridiculous." Professing love then running off to war. Expressing concern, even affection with one breath, then all of a sudden, insult.

White-knuckling the steering wheel, stomping the pedal, she sped. "Screw them all," she grumbled, this time out loud. Archie could stay in the South Pacific for all she cared, and Paolo could remain with his trash. *Keep your crosses, your hydrangeas and sprigs*, she thought. *I'll stick with a crown of thorns.*

11.

If, three hundred years earlier, there had been a first Thanksgiving, the history books didn't record it. Rather than welcoming pilgrims to their island, the Wampanoags who named it Hockomok after the evil supposedly lurking there probably warned them off. In any case, there were no wild turkeys around to be basted, and no cranberries to be boiled into sauce. The feast, if one indeed took place, probably consisted of fish and more fish, with fistfuls of crustaceans thrown in. Lobsters were considered unclean.

Even if the Indians had hosted them that fall, their guests were not especially grateful. A century later, all the natives were either dead or driven off, decimated by pox or sold into slavery by the settlers of Fort Wheelock, as they called it. A century later, after their descendants demilitarized the name to Fourth Cliff, the people took up Abe Lincoln's call and proclaimed a national holiday. Birds and stuffing, pumpkin pies and cobbler—all served with love and abundance, with thankfulness and myth.

Eighty years had passed and still the townies took that last November Thursday off, gathering around their stoves and fireplaces with whatever family members remained stateside. For there was much to be thankful for, what with the armed forces within striking distance of both Japan and Germany, with a bumper haddock catch, and the Sox at least breaking even, seventy-seven losses and wins. And there was peace, which was a far cry from much of the world. The fact that an Italian or two had met an unconventional end did not change that fact, at least not for most of the citizens. The killer was long gone, they assumed, chased off not by that upstart Boston girl but by agents of the FBI or that scofflaw, Louis Corvelli.

Mary Beth sat alone at her desk. Set on the blotter was a plate of seafood poutine that Pascal had fried for her and Hogan was good enough to cycle over. But she barely touched it. Instead, she huddled in her leather jacket and stared at the wheel and the whaler and the mounted fish on the wall, at the map of Fourth Cliff and the Philco radio that reminded her of a mausoleum. The two-way Motorola crackled.

She sat and tried to remember what Thanksgivings had been like with Archie, each of them an only child with no close family around, declining invitations from Reverend Miller and other good Samaritans, delighted to dine alone. She couldn't remember what they'd eaten exactly, whether turkey or leftover stew, only how they'd rushed through the meal. How they clambered kissing up the spiral steps to the top of the lighthouse and the mattress spread on its floor.

She tried to remember but the images were steadily fading. Of their five years of marriage, Archie had been absent for two. No more companionship, no more lovemaking under a goose feather comforter with the ocean thrashing below, no more tearing across the dunes on his Harley. She fingered the poutine and wondered what Archie was doing right then. Would the Marines give him a break for the holiday? Serve gravy along with his Spam?

She tried to focus on Archie but invariably came back to her father. Since moving to Fourth Cliff, she'd had almost no contact with him, couldn't bear the constant complaints about her life. And yet on

Christmas and Easter, sometimes on his birthday as well, she called him, held the receiver far from her ear and endured. But Thanksgiving was a separate case. This was the anniversary of her father's undoing, the day that the tyrant who raised her, who blamed her for the death of his wife, was cowed. Humbled and shocked and all but silenced, all that remained of the father she'd known was his undiminished criticism of her. Reluctantly, she reached for the phone.

Lucinda at the switchboard took her time answering, but eventually she was put through. Though he'd only acquired a telephone recently, she suspected it remained unused. And when it rang, she imagined, the clang could be heard throughout Southie, resounding like a five-alarm bell.

"Who is this?" he nearly shouted.

"Who is it supposed to be, Pop, Eleanor Roosevelt?" she chided him. "And how about a little hello?" she asked and removed the receiver from her ear.

Just in time, as her father roared, "How about a happy Thanksgiving, for chrissakes? How about making it home?"

She sighed. "I *am* home, Pop. And I can't get away. Work is, well, heavy."

"Hermit crabs giving you a hard time, I bet. Seaweed's clogging the drains."

She considered telling him but only for an instant. Doing that, Mary Beth knew, would only invite invective, contemptuous snorts at her pretensions to police work, followed by worse—his insistence on coming to help.

"Crabs and seaweed, that's about it," she lied. In fact, she rarely told him anything of substance—certainly not that she'd promoted herself to captain and insisted on being addressed by the rank. Her father would choke himself laughing. Instead, she offered, "Without Archie around, I sure got my hands full."

Another snort, this one phlegmier. "Well, maybe he'd still be around if you'd been more a wife than a flatfoot. Stayed in the kitchen instead of the street."

So it began, always, her father's litany of complaints. They began with her childhood, so different than the other girls', the way she roughhoused and scuttled around playing cop. Such a tomboy would never be interested in men, he groused, at least until Archie came around. And then it became her marriage to "that heretic," her desertion of the church, and lack of children. The list was prodigious. The grievance deep.

Worse, perhaps, was the way she resembled her mother. Not only in her cookies-and-cream coloring and severe good looks, but in the complexity of her character—insular and passionate, independent and needy, a safe with no known combination. Mary Beth could almost empathize with him for being stuck with a daughter so very much like his late wife, but who he could no longer love in the same way, only torment.

Torment came easy to the Boyles. The son and grandson of South Boston cops, horse-faced, ungraceful men who grew fatter and redder and more acerbic with age, who might have taken to drink if not so addicted to rancor. An angry man indeed, Phineas Boyle never reached the rank of sergeant—for that, too, Mary Beth was blamed—or got the citations he thought he deserved. A God-fearing man nevertheless who, two years earlier, got a front-row glimpse into hell.

"Taking your pills, Pop?" she asked, changing the subject. "The blood pressure ones, and those little greenies for, you know, your nerves."

"Green ones, blue ones, they're all the same shite. Put me to sleep but don't do nothing about the dreams."

She knew which dreams he meant. Those that kept haunting him nightly, that still appeared to him after awakening.

They began at 11 p.m. on Thanksgiving, 1942, when he was peacefully walking his beat and the captain's car sped by. "Get over to Shawmut, fast," he managed to hear. "There's a fire."

He'd seen his share of them, sure, mostly single-dwelling affairs and even a tenement or two, seen humans charred and incinerated. But this fire fit nowhere in the policeman's experience. The flames furling fist-like toward heaven, smoke balls barreling down the street. And the screams. As if he were transported back to his childhood, picturing the scenes of Father Hurley's sermon, of the tortures awaiting the sinful. Yet, the horrors accosting him inside the Cocoanut Grove nightclub exceeded his grisliest visions.

Flesh melted off skeletons, innards still sizzling on the floor. The blackened husks clinging to the fake palm trees, the carbonized logs still lined up at the bar. Most hideous, though, was the couple—a woman in sequins and a man in his tux—seated at a table, unsinged and raising their flutes, asphyxiated in mid-toast.

"Pills don't do nothing to the sight of five hundred dead people," her father went on. "Pills don't do nothing for the smell."

Plying a corpse from a still-glowing girder burned the skin off the back of his hands, but that was the least of his injuries. As if someone had pulled the plug on his bitterness, he became so docile that no one feared him anymore, much less the toughs on his beat. Failure to break up one family scuffle—he cried even more than the wife—put him first at a desk job and then on indefinite leave. His only scorn remained for his daughter. With her, the old Phineas Boyle was still intractable, judgmental, and brusque. Knowing that was how he and his forebears expressed their affection did little to assuage the hurt. For Mary Beth, just once, a simple "I love you" would suffice.

"I'm sorry to hear that, Pop," she said. "Things will get better soon, I know."

"Things will get crummier. Things were and are and always will be shite."

Once again, she held away the receiver. How she wished she could tell him about her life, about the murders and the mobsters and the feds. How she wished she could confess to him her loneliness and fears of inadequacy. And how she longed to share with him the one trait she inherited from him and not her mother: a deep, indomitable rage.

But "Happy Thanksgiving, Pop" was all she ended up saying. To herself, as her father had already hung up.

*   *   *

Winter in Fourth Cliff. Scoters, eiders, and long-tailed ducks bobbled white on the slate-gray waves or scoured the docks for chum. Fishing vessels of various stripes—drifters and gillnetters, crabbers and lobster smacks—rocked at their mooring. The town looked virtually deserted, the storefronts as bare of goods as they were of patrons, the streets ice-flecked. Only Alva Fitch stayed outside and coatless, futilely scraping moss from the fishermen's memorial. Only the church, rising on the bluff above the intersection, remained unbowed. Through the mist, its spire ascended like the hand of a child who knows all the answers. Or the arm of a drowning man sinking fast.

It was to the church that Mary Beth headed that morning, parking the coupe near the spot where she used to chat with Paolo. The prisoner and former officer and architect was nowhere to be seen, and not only because the sidewalks were too slushy to sweep. He was avoiding her, she suspected, still nursing his pride. That didn't prevent her from stopping there on her patrol route, sometimes getting out to peek around. One of those times she found yet another note stuck to her windshield. This, too, was written in black, but in place of Francesco and Abigail's names was Paolo's and her own, separated by the same red heart.

When she returned home and climbed to the top of the lighthouse, she pinned the new note on her link chart, directly next to the old one. They had definitively been written by the same hand. Not only was the ink the same but, more tellingly, two of the letters. The o's were closed with a curlicue and the a's concluded with a tail. The hearts were identical.

Still, that was hardly astonishing. More so was the invitation she received in the mail. "Join us for Christmas Eve Eucharist," it read, signed Viola Miller. The *o* was corkscrewed, the *a* entailed. After Miller was a holly-red heart.

With the latest note and the Christmas invitation, Mary Beth returned to town and climbed the whitewashed steps to the church. The tall wooden doors were white as well and decorated with twin wreaths. She removed her cap and entered.

Inside was silence, though not the dark, mystical silence of her childhood church, no incense and echoes and shadows of fluttering nuns. On the contrary, even the meager light the morning meted out was gathered by the tall, mullioned windows and magnified by their scalloped glass. The pews were waxed and the altar free of statuary, only a simple gold cross. Though she had drifted from the church she grew up in, finding it too stifling, Mary Beth missed it increasingly these days, and now more than ever. Where could she make confession in this church? From where would she draw the passion?

But where else would she find a woman like Viola Miller, fastidiously tidying as she always did Advent week, preparing for the Christmas prayers? Her sweater and scarf—both handknit, both dun—made her look larger than she was. In fact, she was uncommonly slender, some might even say gaunt, regarding most foods as indulgences. Her head, though hatless, boasted a chainmail of kinks the exact same color as her yarn. Her face was stark with judgment.

"Mary Beth Swann," she said, looking up from her precisely stacked hymnals.

"Viola."

"So much to do here. So much to get ready, what with the reverend scribbling away."

Reverend Charles Miller, plump and introverted, was every bit his wife's opposite. Though kind-hearted, he kept that kindness mostly to himself, cloistered in the parsonage behind the church, drawing up sermons or to-do lists. Good for a funeral or a wedding, Charles—not Charlie, never Chuck—rarely interested himself in his parishioners' lives, which were far too hard for his constitution. And he certainly was no busybody. That distinction was Viola's.

"So much to do," Mary Beth nearly smiled, "and yet you find time for note-writing."

Viola went rigid. Though roughly Mary Beth's height, straight-backed she seemed taller, practically looming. "What on earth could you mean?" she said, speaking down.

From her jacket pocket, Mary Beth withdrew the notes. Viola's face went from sanctimonious to pale.

"You wrote them both. Same o's and a's. Same symbol of love— or is it spitefulness?"

Viola fixed her in her nail-head eyes. The beak of her nose descended. "You should talk. You and your Italian paramour. To think," she huffed. "a married woman."

Now it was Mary Beth's turn to stiffen. "A very married woman, I'll have you know, Viola, with a husband in the service. And Mr. Varrone is no more my paramour than Mr. Albertini was Abigail Pitt's. But that didn't stop you from gossiping."

"Not gossiping, Missus Swann, exposing." She picked a speck of nonexistent dust from a psalter. "What with most of our menfolk away and these papists let loose to rut, somebody has to. Reverend Miller is far too busy."

"That's Captain Swann to you," Mary Beth informed her, and proudly stated, "And *I* am a papist."

But Viola Miller merely smiled at her. Her teeth, as evenly aligned as her hymnals, looked serrated. "All the more reason for vigilance."

Such nastiness was only to be expected from Viola. She never liked Mary Beth, who she blamed for alienating Archie, always a churchgoer, from his faith. But accusing her of philandering, insulting her church, went too far. "Stuff your vigilance!" she barked.

Viola retracted into her scarf. "Your voice," she gulped. "This is a place of worship."

"That's what the people believe, and I'd like to believe it as well. But if I find you leaving any more of these notes, so help me..."

"So help me what?" As fast as she'd retreated, Viola was herself again, prim and self-righteous. It wasn't shyness that kept Reverend Miller in his parsonage, Mary Beth realized, but fear of his vengeful wife. The same fear that drove their five grown children far from Fourth Cliff. "What could you possibly do to me, Missus Swann?"

Between the bow, her smile and her malignly arched brows, Viola's face made the perfect target, the ideal place for a punch. But instead of striking, Mary Beth straightened her jacket and lowered her voice. "I will consider you a suspect, Mrs. Miller. In the murder of Francesco Albertini."

Viola's laughter reverberated through the pews as Mary Beth turned and exited. But it was an anxious laugh now, accompanied by the thud of some books on the floor. The captain didn't pause, though, and didn't alter her stride while passing through the doors.

"Merry Christmas," she announced, though acidly, to the frigid Fourth Cliff morning outside.

*   *   *

"Not rummy enough?" Minnie asked as Mary Beth cuddled her mug.

"No, it's fine. I shouldn't."

"Yes." Minnie pouted and poured. "You should."

She'd been sitting at the bar for an hour at least, spilling out her woes. About Viola Miller and her incessant backbiting, and Louis Corvelli, whose Cadillac was seen combing the island that very week, no doubt for more innocents to arm twist. Minnie listened and ladled more hot spiked cider into Mary Beth's mug, smoked, and dished out wisdom.

"Forget about that fat mouth Miller. I'm surprised she even knows *how* to write. And as for Corvelli, don't press your luck. The guy's no Gentleman Jim."

Mary Beth complained about her father and Doc Cunningham's failure to shut his trap, about the weather and the war, and all the while Minnie stood there, in a pink terrycloth robe that accentuated her roundness and a matching cloche that threw her roughhewn features into relief. She seemed genuinely concerned about Mary Beth, squeezed her wrist as she always did, and bucked up her sagging esteem. Only when she mentioned Paolo again did the bartender pull away.

"You know what I think about that," she scolded her. "And not only because of Archie. It's because, sister, you have a job to do and don't need any distractions. Especially not with that cold fish."

Mary Beth nodded into her mug. "Some job," she said. Three unsolved murders and not one serious suspect. First the FBI and then the underworld butting in, embarrassing her in front of the townspeople. Fishermen calling her Black Bass.

"Things are tough all around," Minnie reminded her. "So stop feeling sorry for yourself. Start putting yourself in the murderer's shoes. Start asking the whys and hows."

There might have been some peace for a while, just two old friends in a bar, the tables empty, and a Christmas tree flickering in the corner. They might have talked of something else for once—safaris in Africa someday, a Caribbean cruise—had a car engine not growled up outside. If the doors hadn't just then burst open.

*   *   *

"Ho! Ho! Ho!" someone shouted, and another bellowed, "Home alive in '45!"

Mary Beth swiveled on her stool to see two of the soldiers from the emplacement barge in, in field jackets and helmet liners, tottering and soused. One of them, short and wan, was Dabrowski, if she wasn't mistaken, and the other a bear of a man, with arms and thighs too thick for his uniform, narrow-browed and knobby featured. His name, she recalled, was Falcone.

"Whiskey for my friends and me!" he commanded and scooped up a handful of darts.

Mary Beth turned back to Minnie only to find a much-changed woman. In place of the glowing warmth was a coldness suddenly, and instead of soft wisdom, fear. The ash from her cigarette dropped. "Minnie?" Mary Beth whispered. "You all right?"

Falcone tossed a dart toward the board and hit the outermost ring. Still, Dabrowski applauded. No doubt who was the leader here.

"Whiskey, goddamn it!" Falcone barked.

From Minnie to the men, Mary Beth looked, and then back again, confirming what she already knew. This was not the Falcone she'd seen at the emplacement, the good-natured guy fixing a flagpole or waving a ham and provolone sandwich. This was another, menacing side, a man not with a chip but a veritable log on his shoulders, Mary Beth thought. And he'd been here before, she sensed, and had also acted boorishly, perhaps even violently. Was it he, Mary Beth wondered, who roughed up the bar a few months ago? Who'd fattened Minnie's lip?

"I think you've had enough, gentlemen," she said. "I think you should call it a night."

"Leave it, please," Minnie rasped, only to be ignored.

"You heard me, now. Go peacefully."

Falcone pivoted, dart in hand, and glowered at her. His droopy eyelid was nearly shut, and the white beneath it glinted. "Is that any way to treat the men who're defending our country? Who might have to give their lives?"

"Well, you're hardly out in the South Pacific," Mary Beth chuckled. "And I wouldn't call Fourth Cliff France."

He hurled the dart, this time striking nearer center. Drabowski cheered, "That's our doozy bots!"

Falcone ignored him and turned back to Mary Beth, steaming. "Are you saying, lady, that I'm not doing my part?"

Mary Beth chuckled again, if only to show her mettle. His eyes, she noticed, were close-set and vehement, the color and viscosity of oil. "Not at all. We appreciate all our men in uniform. Our women, too." Her voice lowered, no longer joking. "And it's captain to you, private, not lady."

"Or maybe you're suggesting that people like me, with names like mine, are not real Americans?"

"Not at all."

"One in every ten GIs is Italian. Did you know that?"

"And eighty-eight out of the eighty-eight of our prisoners. Those not murdered."

Falcone lurched forward and pointed a dart at her forehead. "Don't! Don't you dare!"

Mary Beth felt a tap on her shoulder. Minnie was holding out a bottle, whispering to her to let them have it and go. But Mary Beth merely shrugged and kept her eyes on Falcone. The big man would have lunged at her if Drabowski weren't holding him back. "I think you should leave now, private," Mary Beth said. "Unless you want me to report you to Sergeant Perl."

Falcone snorted. "Herb the Hebe, fat chance."

"Then Lieutenant Colburn."

The snort became a chortle. "That crackpot. Him and his subs."

"Leave," she stated, "or I'll have to arrest you."

Now he did lunge, and might have reached her if not for the grip of his friend. Cursing, Falcone wrenched himself free and cocked back his arm to throw. "A khaki wacky and a queer, some dive," he spat, and hurled the dart not at Mary Beth but at the target, smacking it bullseye.

"That's our doozy batz!" Grabowski announced as he slapped Falcone's shoulder and herded him out of the door. But then he turned back. "Don't be so hard on him," he said, practically whispering. "He's had it tough."

Mary Beth snorted. "Too much foie gras."

"No. His parents were arrested as enemy aliens, his brother, too."

"But, why?" Minnie asked. "They're American."

Dabrowski shrugged. Sweet-faced, barely eighteen from the looks of him, blue-eyed and sandy-haired, Mary Beth could imagine him wearing, instead of fatigues, an altar boy's robe. "They did that to a lot of Italians, even the guys born here. Put them in camps, just like the Japs. His mother died there."

"Jeepers."

"So I wouldn't be putting him in the same boat with those prisoners. He blames them for everything."

Dabrowski came to attention suddenly, a soldier again, saluted, and about-faced toward the door.

"Who'd guessed," Minnie commented after he'd exited.

"Who'd have guessed and how."

"And who'd have thought you'd be suicidal?"

Mary Beth gaped at her.

"First you take on that Corvelli hood and then this bonehead, Falcone." She refreshed her best friend's mug. "It's hard to solve a murder, sister, when you're dead."

Two refills later, Mary Beth stumbled outside. Snow was falling, thick wet clots of it mingling with the sand, coating the dunes like mountaintops. In the flickering Schlitz sign it shimmered blue and silently filled up the lot. It buried everything—the cracks, the dirt, the salt whisked and gathered from the sea. The outlines of GI combat boots and the tracks of a departing jeep.

*   *   *

December 26, 1944

My Beloved Archie,

This is the second Christmas I've spent without you—that we've spent without one another. I remember how we laid under our tree and laughed in the torn-up gift wrappers, how we danced to Jo Stafford and Duke Ellington on your gramophone. How in the lighthouse, with the ocean like some great green carpet spread below, we looked out and claimed to see clear around the world. All the way to tomorrow.

I remember, Archie, and I remember the feel of you and the smell of you—I hope this isn't too rich for the censors—but mostly I remember your presence. Strong, sturdy, rolling like a buoy when you had to, other times pylon-stiff. You were my lighthouse. Your beam guided me to port.

Forgive my sappiness! It must seem strange to you, even inappropriate, after all the hellholes you've fought in, with worse maybe ahead of you still. There's talk here and on the radio of another major invasion, another island close to the Japanese coast. The enemy will surely defend it even more fanatically than before, fighting to the death. I don't care if they die, only that you live. That you survive and come home to me, and that we lie in our wrappers again, dance, and welcome the dawn.

Nothing much is happening here. Fourth Cliff life as usual. Pascal's brewing up his best holiday bisque and Minnie's doling out the cider. The haddock catch is especially ample this year, the fishermen say. The alewife, too.

Christmas eve, I stopped at the First Congregational, not so much to pray as to show the flag and shake some hands neighbor-like. The mood was muted by the news from Europe, the Germans breaking through our lines in Belgium. Reverend Miller gave a sermon about faith and fortitude and the need to stand strong in the face of adversity. He looked frailer than usual, though, like a candle about to be snuffed. More than the war, I'm afraid, he's worn down by his busybody wife, Viola.

Still the church was beautiful, what with all the decorations and mistletoe. The parishioners seemed to glow—Abigail Pitt and Doc Cunningham, the Brutons and the Halls. Alva Fitch showed up as well, to everyone's surprise, brought out of the cold by our sweet, simple Lemuel Hogan, who gave her his coat. Together we sang Joy to the World though the world seems anything but joyous.

Later, I drove out north alone. Snow had fallen earlier in the week and flurries were twirling down still, but the coupe kept hugging the road. The cranberry bogs glistened but the emplacement was dark, all except for the cannon, which someone had garlanded with tinsel. The only lights came from the camp, where a young priest had come from the coast and was leading a midnight Mass. The prisoners were each holding a candle, huddled together and singing. Astro de Ciel, I think I heard, to the tune of Silent Night. I sang along, too, warmed by memories of childhood, of my mother baking biscuits for me and my father playing Santa. Still, I kept my distance. There was happiness enough knowing that our *former enemies could find some comfort at last and, like me, remember what Christmas was like before peaceful people became killers. When love was what this holiday was about suffering.*

From there, I thought about continuing on to second or third cliff (depends who you ask!) and our little strand of beach. I thought about standing barefoot on the shells and pebbles and staring out at the waves as they swallowed up the snow. I thought about it but in the end turned around and went home. Well, not to home, really, but to the lighthouse, and put on one of your Louis Armstrong records. I sat on the mattress and looked at your photos, the ones you took in your uniforms—blue, green, and muddy.

I don't care what you look like, Archie, when you come home, what the war has taken from you and can never give back, or what nightmares it planted, just as long as one day you walk up that spiral staircase and call out "Mairzy Doats!" or whatever dumb nickname you made up for me that day, your arms stretched out like lighthouse beams.

Merry Christmas, darling.

Your always-loving wife,

Mary Beth

PS: This morning, while heading to the general store to mail this letter, I stopped outside the shed. The snow had melted—no need for warning signs and salt—but there was the tarp and under it your Harley, and I thought: what better present? Consider your motorcycle oiled. And, yes, the key is still in the baking powder can, waiting for you.

*   *   *

No Yuletide rest for this trapper, not once in forty years. The morning after Christmas he was out again, in the dark and hauling up his pots. But Calvin never complained. On the contrary, this was his task in life, just as it was for generations of Trotts before him, and he performed it willingly. Lovingly even, grateful for the bounty his catches brought him. Thankful for the food that filled his table at a time when others' lay bare, and that enabled him to send brown paper packages to his two sons serving on the same cruiser in the Aleutians. He didn't mind the cold or the lack of sleep, just as long as he had his rum and his "kitchens" were filled with guests.

But this guest was too big for the "kitchen," its tail extending across the "parlor" and sticking clear out of the pot. No "snapper" this, too small to keep, but a "jumbo" the likes of which he'd never seen, a seven-pounder at least. And a pure white shell which he'd heard of but never really believed existed, an old lobstermen's tale. But not only the size and color astonished him, but what the claws still clutched.

No weakling, Calvin Trott required all his strength to ply the object loose. Well before he did, though, he could see what it was. Half-axe, half-hammer, with a notch for removing nails—he'd seen tools just like it in carpentry shops. But its blade was worn, and not by wood but by something much harder, by stone or metal or perhaps some hefty bones. He considered tossing it overboard and consigning it to the sea, but instead stuffed it inside his sou'wester. After all, it wasn't every day that one caught a seven-pound jumbo, and a white one at that, and not every day that one found the head of a plumb hatchet, still salvageable, and stamped with the initials U.S.

PART FIVE

12.

By the time Mary Beth got there, the man was already dead. Laid out not peacefully on his bunk but indecorously where he'd collapsed. Under the hurricane lamps, his skin looked mottled, nacreous white with greens and purples, mother-of-pearl. His mouth was a frozen rictus. Horace Cunningham examined him, pried open his eyelids and poked under his tongue, but there was nothing to be done. Even if they'd gotten there sooner, even if there'd been an ambulance and hospital nearby, the case was hopeless.

Of course, Paolo didn't know that when, just before sundown, he snatched one of the camp's few bicycles and peddled frantically into town. He found Mary Beth at the diner staring at a plate of Pascal's seafood hash. Her thoughts were lodged on another island far away from Fourth Cliff, another Pacific slaughterhouse whose name, Iwo Jima, was almost unpronounceable but where Archie was known to be fighting. She didn't eat, didn't even stir her food, and scarcely looked up when Paolo practically pounced on her.

"Come. Now," he gasped. "Bring the doctor. Quick."

They hurried Cunningham downstairs and into the coupe with his medical bag and floored the gas pedal northward. The prisoner of war camp was dark by the time they arrived. Only the Quonset huts seemed to glow, and the towers with their static searchlights. The mess hall was fully illuminated, though, when the three of them entered to find Lorenzo sobbing into a handkerchief and the cook lying tinged and distended on a table.

"What happened here?" Mary Beth asked him, but Lorenzo couldn't talk, only burble something in Italian, of which "tragedia" and "povero Fiorello" was all she could make out.

"Fiorello?"

"That was his name, Fiorello," Paolo reminder her. "Fiorello. Like the mayor of New York."

Mary Beth scowled. "I know who La Guardia is. What I don't know is how this man died."

Paolo's face looked wolfish suddenly, but he managed to contain himself. He asked Lorenzo some questions and received staccato answers which he then struggled to translate. Seemed the bony little man had snuck into the kitchen early, ostensibly to say ciao, but really to see for himself the dish he smelled simmering. A savory aroma he remembered from his childhood, rising from his mother's stove. He instead found Fiorello poised with a spoon in his hand but without his usual smile.

"I cannot feel my lips," he said. "My nose."

His many chins began to wiggle and his bug eyes to bulge as Lorenzo rushed to steady him, steering him out into the mess and onto one of its tables. Fiorello fell backward, his arms and legs outstretched, crying they were numb. Soon he lost consciousness or almost, still whispering, "Lorenzo, Lorenzo," but not to his friend.

"Lawrence," Paolo explained. "The patron saint of cooks."

The doctor, with his yellowed fingers and a cigarette stuck to his lip, proceeded to examine the victim. Or, more accurately, the corpse, for Fiorello long had no pulse.

"Natural causes?" Mary Beth asked, hopeful.

"Depends how you define natural." Cunningham stepped back from the cadaver, rolled down his frayed cuffs, and squinted into the lamp. "What's that I smell?"

"Cosa stava cucinando?" Paolo repeated for Lorenzo.

"Risotto."

"Risotto with what?" the doctor pressed him.

"Risotto con capesante."

"Capensante," Paolo repeated for Cunningham. "Scallops."

"Go and fetch it."

Lorenzo ducked into the kitchen and returned a second later with a cast-iron pot. It still emitted a sharp scent of parmesan, a whiff of *origano* and garlic so tempting that the prisoner dug up a spoonful and raised it toward his mouth.

"No!" the doctor barked.

"Madonna mia...." The spoon dropped to the floor, together with the pot, spilling its creamy contents.

"Don't touch it."

Mary Beth and Paolo gawped at him.

"Paralytic shellfish poisoning," Cunningham explained. "A thousand times deadlier than cyanide."

"The scallops?"

"That or real cyanide. Either way, the man didn't stand a chance."

"Tell that," Paolo said, "to them."

"Them" referred to the crowd now gathered outside the mess. The entire prison camp, it seemed, dozens of men in their khaki uniforms and ITALY patches, suddenly looking less than friendly. The last people on the island to show her respect were now furious at Mary Beth, fed up with her failure to protect them. They uttered curses as she exited, all concluded with a spit. She fought the urge to unlock her gun or even quicken her pace.

"You'd been better off if Paolo hadn't found you," Cunningham quipped when back in the coupe.

But Mary Beth just hunkered over the wheel. "I'd be better off if I'd gone and eaten that hash."

*   *   *

Along with whelk and mussels, the hash indeed contained scallops, though they later tested harmless. If mollusks had killed Fiorello, they weren't the ones Pascal cooked with, nor was it certain whether those were pulled toxic from the sea or somehow poisoned afterward. In the end it didn't matter.

The death would be seen as yet another murder, a fourth major crime unsolved. She felt guilty about having once suspected Fiorello, the poor man, and certain of the islanders' reaction. Once again, they would hold her accountable. Black Bass would be the least of her nicknames.

Still, she spent much of the next day tracking down the source of the scallops. The prisoners, she knew, grew their own vegetables, many of their own spices as well, but where did they get the fresh seafood? Who gave them the parmesan cheese? Perhaps they were smuggled in with the military rations ferried to the island each week. Perhaps they were carted from the wharf to the camp by the Ballard brothers, the Great War veterans who saw to its basic needs.

But "Cheese?" was all they said. "Scallops? Lady, we're lucky to get hardtack." The two men shrugged and simpered. Though not technically twins, in their doughboy duds they were difficult to tell apart. Gnomish, grotesque, their bodies stunted by years of stevedoring, their faces disfigured by pain. Their brains, too, were mangled by the horrors they'd seen in the trenches. "Lady," they repeated, and she didn't have the heart to correct them, "we're lucky to get sardines." Their laughter seemed to nip at her, all the way back to her car.

Next, she visited the dock favored by the scallop dredgers, an insular group that didn't mix with the other fishermen, as tightly sewn as their nets. Any strangers loitering around here lately, she asked them, any sign of tainted hauls? Their answers were curt. No, no strangers, and no, their catches were just fine, thank you, bought up each morning by the Boston mongers who returned each time wanting more. Fourth Cliff scallops were famous, they'd have her know, clear across New England.

"And we don't need you spreading bullshit, neither," one of them added, a middle-aged man with one milky eye, raw skin, and a nose that appeared to have been chewed on. "We don't need you at all."

He pointed at her badge with a shucking knife and flung a fistful of membrane onto the dock. The other dredgers followed suit, shucking and flinging. Their warnings seemed to be echoed by the seagulls, screaming as Mary Beth hustled away.

Enough, she said to herself when back in the coupe, then repeated it out loud, "Enough." She didn't need this crap, didn't need the job or to live up to anybody's expectations, whether Archie's or even her father's. She could hang up her cap and duty belt, unpin the bars from her jacket, and lock up the lighthouse forever. No need to say goodbye to anyone—well, to Minnie possibly—before hopping the next ferry and busing to Bedford, to Swampscott, Marblehead, or Revere—anywhere far from Fourth Cliff. "Enough," she cried, and smacked her palms on the wheel.

For a long time she sat staring at the red Roman god in its center, combing through the facts once more. While Fiorello was ruled out as the murderer, it could still be some other prisoner. What about Lorenzo? He'd been in the mess hall earlier that day, supposedly to steal a taste of the risotto. Couldn't he have just has easily poisoned it? Couldn't he, short but sturdy, have garrotted and stabbed and dismembered? And all the time he was posing as her friend....

Mary Beth was still there mulling when Officer Hogan found

her. He didn't ring his bicycle bell this time, afraid to startle her, but tapped lightly on her window. "What now?" she snapped at him, and seeing his bucktoothed mouth descend, his cockeyed gaze fall, felt awful. "I'm sorry, Lemuel. Bad day." She treated herself to a chuckle. "Couple of bad years, it seems."

Hogan did not respond. "Old Man Gainor," was all he said.

"What about him?"

"He wants to see you."

"Me?"

"Yes, ma'am."

Old Man Gainor never asked to see her, not unless it was something urgent. Something grim. "When?"

Lemuel screwed up his lips and creased his brow, struggling to remember. "Oh, yeah," he declared, and flourished triumphantly in his seat. "Now."

*   *   *

Mary Beth rarely saw him, but neither did anybody else. A loner, almost a recluse, driven into solitude it was said by some unknown family tragedy. Said to be in his eighties, at least, he was nevertheless known by his moniker for as long as anyone remembered, perhaps because of his hoary beard and vintage wisdom. And though Fourth Cliff had no official mayor, Old Man Gainor was the closest it came. On him the inhabitants relied to manage the public finances, oversee taxes, and maintain the north-south road. To him they looked to ensure their safety, or least employ the individual who could.

He also owned the shipyard. There, on his dry dock, boats were caulked, defouled, and painted, rudders righted, and the few remaining mastheads aligned. But most repairs were now made in coastal shops, leaving the old man with little to do but read the Patriot and smoke his meerschaum pipe. Behind the hulls cannibalized for their bulkheads and frames, their cofferdams and ballast holds, half hidden by rusted funnels and propellers, sat the mahogany bridge that served as his office. From here, rarely moving, he watched over the island's wellbeing. Here he waited while Mary Beth wound her way through the junk and stood at the entrance removing her cap. Trying, but not quite succeeding, to smile.

"You wanted to see me, sir?" The final word sounded strange in her mouth. She hadn't used it since Boston.

He put down his paper and smiled back, paternally. "It's been some time, hasn't it, Missus Swann?"

She wanted to correct him—*Captain Swann*—but thought better of it. Instead, she said, "I haven't seen you around, sir. Not even in church."

He laughed. "You know how it is with us old folks. God pays us house calls."

Swiveling in his captain's chair, he motioned her to sit. She did, gazing around the office in which everything, from the knot tables on the wall to the binnacle coat rack, was nautical, and across the navigation desk that separated her from Gainor. "What do you hear from the mister?" he asked.

"Not much," she replied, matter-of-factly at first, then mumbled, "I haven't had a letter in weeks."

"Ah, yes, the battle of Iwo Jima. A tough one, I heard, even after the Marines raised the flag."

She looked up at him, at his face which also seemed retrieved from the sea. The urchin eyes, the foamy beard, and gull nose. His brows rose like whitecaps and his cheeks, when he lit up his pipe, looked phosphorescent. "I know things have been difficult, Mary Beth," he began, soothing her with the use of her name. But then he added, "Still."

She peered at him. "Still what?"

"Three murders on our island—yes, I know all about them—and now this, a man who was poisoned to death. No matter what country they were from, we're responsible."

"It's not clear whether the cook was killed or…"

He held up a corrugated hand. "How he died is not important, only how people think he did. And how you've been unable to protect them."

"But none of the townspeople have been hurt."

"What begins with the Italians might well end with us, Missus Swann." He was back to that *missus* again. "And there are federal agents, gangland bosses, and lord knows what else. Fraternizing with one of the prisoners. I'm afraid I have no choice, Missus Swann. You can keep the car for a week or two, until we find a replacement, but starting right now…" The hand now extended across the desk, gnarly palm up. "I must have your badge."

For a moment, Mary Beth just sat there inhaling the acrid tobacco. She considered not just giving him the shield but throwing it at him and telling him to stick it where the easterlies didn't blow. She thought about venting all her resentment toward the people of Fourth Cliff—provincial, ungrateful—and their unkindness to a woman who, all alone, was only trying to do her job. She considered announcing her imminent return to the mainland, to civilization, and to sanity, leaving this whole wretched island, fishermen and killers alike, to sink to the sea bottom.

But "Very well" was all she said. There was no use fighting, at least not this battle. So what if she didn't get a pay check? And what good anyway was just a shiny piece of tin? And what had she done to earn it, really, since she'd failed to arrest the killer?

"You can have it," she said as she unpinned the badge from her jacket and laid it face up on the desk. "But you won't get my self-respect. And you won't stop me from finding the murderer." She rose stiffly from her chair, flipped on her cap, and yanked up her duty belt. "You and the rest of you tars, just stay out of my way."

"Then you're on your own, Missus Swann. I warn you."

"That's Captain Swann, badge or no badge, Mr. Gainor." She strode, back straight, into the yard. "Or do you prefer Old Man?"

*   *   *

Through puddles stained with rust and outboard oil, she stomped back to her coupe. Nothing would have stopped her, not even an apology, and certainly not the harsh grating sound emanating from one of the hulls. Only the young man who emerged suddenly to lower his bandana and gulp the air, who found himself directly in her path, caused her to pause. With a surly "Morning," she sidestepped him.

"Good morning to you, too, Captain."

Mary Beth turned. It wasn't the gentleness of his voice that halted her, but rather the reference to her rank.

"Do I know you?"

She didn't. Men of this age, early twenties, were unheard of in Fourth Cliff, unless they were somehow marred. But this one appeared to be hale, whole in body at least, well-built beneath his fisherman's sweater, and his face—slender, clean-shaven—was fresh. Not weather-beaten like the rest of the islanders', not grief-streaked, but tender, almost child-like. His eyes were chips of teal.

"I'm Grant, Captain. A relative of Mr. Gainor's." Sweeping off his woolen cap, he unleashed a golden cascade.

She looked him up and down, now suspicious of everybody. "And you do what here, exactly, Grant?"

"Scraping, mostly. Tubeworms are my specialty." He held up a hand rake. "Those fellas sure do cling."

"Yeah, well, some fellas will." She eyed him more closely now. There was something incongruous about him—the army boots and the corduroys, the tool belt and the aviator's jacket. His intense yet faraway expression. "You're not from around here, are you?"

"Me, heck no. I'm from the Minnesota branch of the family, by way of San Angelo and Bassingbourn."

"I'd keep it to yourself, then. People here don't always warm to strangers."

"But we aren't strangers, Captain. At least you're not to me."

Mary Beth sprung at him. "Explain yourself!"

Grant, kneading his cap and hugging his rake, retreated. "I mean that I've seen you around town a bit. I've seen how you are with everybody, so considerate and strong. Your husband must be very proud."

These words at another time would have angered her, made her feel mocked. But the way the young man uttered them, as earnestly as a psalm, disarmed her. She backed up, collected herself. "Well, don't let me keep you from your work…"

"Oh, no, Captain Swann, it's an honor to meet you finally."

"An honor," Mary Beth replied. "Can't remember the last time I heard that." Then, tipping her hat brim, she walked past him. "Pleasure meeting you, Grant," she added and splashed through the rust and the oil.

*   *   *

Minnie had never laid eyes on him. "Any drinking he does, he ain't doing it in my bar," she said. Neither had he frequented the diner, according to the cook Pascal and Trudy the waitress. Mary Beth continued to ask around town, but always with the same result. Nothing. Not until she climbed up to Doc Cunningham's second-story office did she hear repeated the name she'd been asking about all day.

"Grant? Of course, I know him. Poor, sweet boy."

By the dusty light of the examining table, with the medicine cabinets the only witness, he told of a promising young man from Duluth. Football player, first in his class, dreamed of becoming a doctor, "like me." He paused to glance around the office. "Well, maybe not like me."

"And San Angelo? Bassingbourn?"

"Where they sent him for B-17 training. Where the bombers took off from in England, flying over France."

Forty-six missions he flew, Cunningham explained, four short of the maximum. Forty-six times that he was essentially wrapped in a cigar tube and placed in front of a firing squad at twenty thousand feet. Most of his friends were blown out of the sky, shredded and burnt then splattered on impact. Yet somehow he never got a scratch. "At least not externally. Inside, he was mush."

His family sent him to Fourth Cliff. Let him do the simple things, scouring off barnacles and working for his great-uncle. Give him time to heal.

"But can he?"

"That's where I come in," Cunningham said with a flourish of washed-out hair. "With Metrazol, the latest in the treatment of shock. Perfect for battle fatigue." Two injections per week were enough to offset the trauma, the doctor claimed, the convulsions they caused smothering the patient's psychosis. "Like fighting fire with fire."

"And if the patient goes up in flames?"

Lighting up a Chesterfield, Doc Cunningham frowned. His eyes went from powder to indigo, so it seemed to her, and his skin looked ochrous. "Progress has its price," he said sharply, and suddenly Mary Beth understood. The scandal at Newport, his sudden need to relocate to a place where no one knew him or even asked questions. Her initial repugnance of him resurged.

"I've got it under control," the doctor insisted.

"It's not *your* control I'm worrying about." She picked up her cap and zipped up her jacket. "The last thing I need around here is another crackpot."

*   *   *

And she certainly had no need for Alva Fitch, yet there she was when Mary Beth returned to the street. Bent over the coupe as if it were another memorial and scrubbing hard with a rag even filthier than her dress, Alva didn't look at her or even say hello. She was too busy chanting to herself, over and over, something about St. James and the scallops, murder and martyrdom. Mary Beth didn't care. She only wanted Alva to get away from her car and leave her in peace. As if peace were anywhere obtainable on Fourth Cliff.

"Cut it out, Alva, please," she practically begged. "I'm really not in the mood."

But the madwoman kept rubbing and humming, pausing only to spit on her rag. The wind whipped her hair like shredded sails. "Scallops and murder," she sang.

"Darn it, Alva. You're going to take off the paint."

She interrupted her song long enough to say, "Got to make it shiny for him."

"Him who? The killer?"

Alva showed her driftwood teeth, the fiery coal of her eyes. "Not him. *Him*. Who's waiting for you now at the station."

Mary Beth knew better than to ask. Instead, she jumped into the driver's seat and threw the car into gear. Alva shrank in the rearview mirror, waving at the coupe with her rag.

Tearing up the bluff, veering south at the intersection, the car rumbled onto the unpaved path. Pedalling toward her, Mary Beth saw, was Lemuel Hogan, signaling frantically to stop. She didn't. With a wave of her hand, she sped on while her mind raced through the possibilities. Lieutenant Colburn? Reverend Miller? Old Man Gainor ordering her off the island at once? Or could it be worse: her father? Could it be, sweet Lord in heaven, Archie returning home from the war?

She had half prepared herself for any of those scenarios, but not for the one that greeted her. Parked outside the station, empty, was the dove-gray Cadillac sedan. Slowly emerging from the coupe, she strode into the station, one hand reaching for her holster.

"No need for that," Louis Corvelli said as she entered. With softly gloved fingers, he traced the outline of the spindled ship wheel on the wall and the fin of the mounted cusk. He tipped up his hat and winced at the whaler's portrait. "What is it with you maritime people?" he asked. "It's like you were born in the sea."

She glanced around the room for a sign of the henchmen and saw that Corvelli was alone. Still, she tightened her grip on the Colt. "What do you want?"

"In Chicago we don't decorate our homes with fire hydrants. There aren't any alley cats on our walls."

"I thought I told you to scram."

"Scram." He frowned. "Now who's been watching too many movies?" His tone benevolent again, his manner priestly. "I want a deal."

"A deal?"

"A partnership. Like I offered you when we first met. An alliance."

"A partnership? An alliance?"

"Provided," he smiled, "you stop repeating every word I say."

The gun handle was still in her palm. "Go on."

"You see, Captain, though I don't wear any bars, I too have a rank. I also have to report to my superiors. And my superiors are not at all happy."

Mary Beth shrugged. What was he talking about, she wondered. Where was this treacherous man going?

"Like you, I made some mistakes. Worse ones, perhaps. And this—finding the murderers—is...how should I say this?" Not just a priest again, but also a confessor. "My last chance."

He studied the map of Fourth Cliff, tilted his head, first to one side then the next, as if to get perspective. As if to determine where on that hook-shaped slip of rock he was standing.

"The South Side of my city makes yours, in Boston, look like a country club. Compared to my Outfit, even your husband's, in the Marines, is kid stuff."

He turned to her finally. The look on his face was unlike any she'd seen so far. Angelic, pathetic, his eyes less limpid than sad. "And unlike you, Mary Beth—may I call you that?—unlike you, I won't only lose my job."

"And why on earth would I help you?"

Removing his hat, Corvelli crossed the office and took a seat at her desk. He switched on the Philco—Billie Holliday was playing—and turned it off, then ran his hand over the blotter. "Nice piece of furniture you got here," he commented, and then, almost as an afterthought, added, "Because you don't want Dobbs and Sitwell back here, do you, and there's a killer on the loose that we both need to find. One way or another, our lives depend on it."

Mary Beth collapsed in the chair opposite the desk. Exhaustion all at once overwhelmed her, a sense that further resistance was pointless. Still, there was no discounting the fact that Louis Corvelli remained a suspect, a man who, priestly or not, could easily strangle, stab, and dismember any number of enemies, and whose words were likely worth less than his deerskin gloves.

"Oh, I almost forgot." He reached into his camel coat, and Mary Beth reflexively flinched. All he produced, though, was a shiny piece of tin, which he proceeded to lay on her desk. Mary Beth stared at it. Her badge.

"How did you?"

"Your Old Man Gainor required some persuading. In the end, he had to agree."

She lifted the shield and gripped it so tightly it nearly cut into her palm. "You win," she said finally. "But we do things my way, you hear? No arm twisting, no threats of concrete shoes."

"You got it. No arms, no shoes."

"And no heat. The only one packing here is me."

Corvelli slapped the empty breast pocket. "Plum forgot it at home."

He said this so earnestly, she could almost believe him. But what choice did she really have? The townspeople would think even less of her working with Corvelli, but he could be the only chance she had of finding the killer. "Good," Mary Beth sat up, a captain again. "So where do we begin?"

"With everything you've discovered so far, up to the death of the cook, who just happened to be my boss's cousin. And we find out who gave him those scallops."

13.

MARY BETH SHOWED HIM HER RUBBINGS OF THE TIRE TREAD AND the half footprint. She showed him the iron ring with the fasces and Ora Alla Patria inscription. He ogled the first and scowled at the second. "No murder weapons?" Corvelli pressed her. "No motives?" Mary Beth nodded. She could only describe the state of the bodies—Francesco Albertini's garroted and Antonio De Luca's stabbed, and Flavio Filippani's hand chopped off clean at the wrist. And, yes, Fiorello the cook had been poisoned, most likely intentionally. "There we are." Mary Beth smiled painfully. "Nowhere."

They retraced their steps first to the docks and the shops around town, the diner and the general store. They stopped in at McQueen's boarding house, where Abigail Pitt was her usual vulnerable but impenetrable self. As anticipated, several locals grumbled at the sight of her accompanied by Corvelli, called her Black Bass and worse. Mary Beth was willing to put up with it all provided her new partnership led to a breakthrough. Her notebook, though, remained empty.

From town they drove northward, the Cadillac trailing the coupe, and parked at the Flotsam Bar. Minnie Beaudet put on a show of hospitality and Mary Beth played along, asking her questions about who'd been drinking there recently and when and receiving one and two-word answers. If nothing else, their friendship would remain a secret. Only when Corvelli excused himself for the loo did the proprietor lean over the bar and whisper, "Are you out of your freaking mind?"

"Gainor was canning me." Mary Beth shrugged. "What else could I do?"

"So you get into cahoots with Little Caesar?"

"I don't care if he's the Wicked Witch of East, just as long as he helps me out."

"You're playing with fire."

"Maybe. But I might also be getting warm."

Later, they swung by the cranberry bogs. Farmer McKee was there, with his rising hump and missing teeth, and though both Mary Beth and Corvelli questioned him again, all they received was the usual ayuhs.

"What do these people have against language?"

"It's a concession," Mary Beth explained. "A sign of weakness."

Corvelli frowned. "Fourth Cliff, hell. This place is tougher than Alcatraz."

Next stop, the prisoner of war camp. Mary Beth braked before entering, exited the coupe, and stuck her head through the Caddy's front window. "Remember what I said, no arm twisting," she warned. "Not even a hint of it. I have a fine relationship with these fellows. I won't have you spoiling it."

Corvelli held up two deer-skinned fingers. "Scouts' honor," he pledged.

Yet, to her discomfort, many of the inmates recoiled just at the sight of him. Cheerful greetings of *Buongiorno, come stai* and packs of Raleigh Golds did little to mitigate the fear. Reluctantly, Lorenzo led the way through the mess hall and into the kitchen, where he and Corvelli chatted—amicably enough, it seemed—in Italian. Shifting through pots, Mary Beth awkwardly looked on. Apart from words like "cuoco" and "capesante," she made out nothing, no more than she could of the process which brought her from a safe South Boston girlhood to this vexing island and this impossible job, collaborating with a mobster and interrogating a prisoner of war in the hope of capturing a killer.

Lorenzo flicked his chin and crossed his fingers then pulled down a bottom eyelid—more hand gestures, she reckoned, than Fourth Cliffers used in a lifetime. Corvelli took that hand and shook it. "Molto bene, grazie."

He waited for Lorenzo to leave before refiguring his smile into a grimace. "Here's the lowdown," he reported. "The scallops arrived around dawn, before the delivery of provisions. Your doughboy friends knew nothing of them and neither did the rest of the camp. Everybody was sleeping still, except for the cook, who had already finished the dish when Lorenzo snuck in for a taste."

"You mean, whoever brought the scallops knew exactly who to give them to. Knew that they had to be served up immediately and sampled."

"Precisely."

"Which meant that the supplier was known to the cook and had come by with delicacies before. Like parmesan."

"Like parmesan and ricotta, according to our friend Lorenzo. Prosciutto and olive oil."

"But why didn't Lorenzo tell me this before? Why only to you?"

Corvelli pointed to his temple, meaning, she guessed, use your head. "You're a cop, Mary Beth, a foreigner, and a woman. And my grandfather knew Lorenzo in Marsala. The important thing," he went on, "is that we now know that the cook had no reason to suspect the scallops and every reason to fry them right up."

Mary Beth glanced up at the single bulb that lit the kitchen.

"Fiorello was murdered, no question about it," she said. "Most likely by the same man who killed the other three."

Corvelli added, "A man who has access to wires and blades and a storehouse of hard-to-get foods."

"A man who was friendly at first."

"But a man who clearly enjoys killing people." Corvelli allowed his smile to return, but gravely. "And really dislikes Italians."

*   *   *

Though she fervently hoped not to, leaving the mess hall, they almost collided with Paolo. Mary watched as his body at first cringed and then stiffened and finally went catlike, shoulders lowered, ready to pounce. His, face, too, transformed. Surprise, outrage, and fury. She swiftly inserted herself between them.

"Paolo, I can explain," she began, even though she couldn't. How would he ever understand that the man who had worked him over and threatened him with worse was now her partner? She had difficulty enough explaining it to herself.

Corvelli spoke to him softly in Italian, repeating the word "scuse," and held out his hand. But Paolo just sneered at it as if it were something that had to be broomed. He cast a final look at Mary Beth—eyes gelid, moustached snarled—and stormed away to his Quonset hut.

"I wouldn't take it too personally," Corvelli assured her. "We're an emotional people, and our emotions sometimes get the best of us."

Mary Beth stared at the hut. "The best of us, yes," she sighed.

They returned to their cars and continued north, concluding their sweep of the island. Only the emplacement remained, ghostly in the mist. Its bunkers looked out over the sea, its cannon scanning the waves. The horizon, mud-colored in the dwindling afternoon, was empty.

But this didn't keep Lieutenant Colburn from searching. That's what Sergeant Perl told them as Mary Beth and Corvelli drove up—how his commander had placed his men on the highest alert, convinced that now was the time when the enemy would strike. With the war in Europe only months or even weeks from concluding, the U-boats would assault Massachusetts.

"Hence, the getup," the sergeant said, smiling, and turned to show off his gear—his Sam Browne belt with canteens and cartridge pouches, his .45 revolver and bayonet. Jokingly he tipped his helmet. "Kind of suits me, right?"

He and two other soldiers, Dabrowski and Falcone, were far from the bunker, laying a communications cable. "He wants to be able to report it directly to Washington," Perl explained. "The minute he spots a conning tower."

"And they call *me* doozy bots."

This was Falcone, a bulky presence even bent over the cable. With a wrench and pincers in his hands, an M-1 over his back and helmet sliding down his forehead, he looked even more predatory than usual, his knobby brow Neanderthal.

"Hey, no knocking the lieutenant," Perl upbraided him. "He only wants what's best for us. For the country."

Falcone glanced up from the cable, with a drooping eye that hid far more than it revealed. "And you, Sarge, are a strunz."

"I hate to interrupt these pleasantries," Mary Beth said. "This is Louis Corvelli, our guest on the island. He's helping me investigate the murders."

"Murders?" Perl's smile disappeared. "I thought there was only one."

"Three, probably four. And the killer's still out there."

With his altar-boy face paler than usual, Dabrowski glanced up.

Falcone, though, kept cutting. "Which is why," Corvelli added, "we'd like to ask you some questions."

He made the usual inquiries about suspicious movements and individuals, reports of people with grudges against POWs and rumors of tainted scallops, but Perl just shook his head. "Sorry, Mr. Carvotti."

"Corvelli."

"Whatever. But Lieutenant Colburn has us hustling around the clock." He tipped his helmet in the direction of the dunes, where the officer could be seen in full battle dress, glued to his binoculars. His jeep had carved figure eights in the sand. "He's going to get his sub in the end, even if he has to invent one."

"Merda!" Falcone cursed and sucked on the joint of his thumb. "Fa Nabola!"

"Since when do you cut a cable with a trench knife?" Perl excoriated him. "Doozy bots."

"Strunz."

Mary Beth exchanged glances with Corvelli. This conversation was getting nowhere, and time was running out. Less than an hour remained before the last ferry left for the coast. Stymied, they went back to their cars and sped in the direction of town.

*   *   *

"No suspects, no motive, and except for the scallops, no weapons." Parting with Corvelli at the wharf, Mary Beth looked downcast. "Looks like we all but struck out."

Behind his steering wheel, Corvelli pulled down his gloves and tipped the brim of his hat. His face wore its clerical deportment again, his voice satin. "Don't trouble yourself, Mary Beth. Something's bound to turn up. Or else."

"Or else what?"

"My two associates will return. You remember them, I'm sure. The very large gentlemen with the bulges in their coats?"

"I thought they work for you."

He barely suppressed a chuckle. "Until they're told not to. Then they work *on* me."

She nodded as if she understood but didn't. There were many things she found incomprehensible. Why did the murders have to happen on her watch, just when Archie was away, and why was Old Man Gainor trying to fire her? Who among her remaining suspects—Lorenzo, Paolo, Abigail Pitt and the Hills, and now this Grant fellow—could she fully rule out? The answer was nobody, not even the GIs, not the obsessive Lieutenant Colburn or even Sergeant Perl, whose constant smile might be hiding something darker. And how far could she really trust Corvelli? What was it about her that enabled the murderer to hide in plain sight and to play with her as if she were a child?

"I don't have much time," Mary Beth confessed to him.

"I may have less. My superiors aren't big on patience, you see. On second chances, either."

He no longer looked at Mary Beth but through the Caddy's windshield, along the ferry's gangplank and beyond. She turned away, heading back to the coupe, but then halted.

"By the way, forgive me for asking, but what is a strunz?" she asked.

Only now Corvelli laughed. "A stupid person. A fool."

"And a doozy bath?"

"Doozy bots." The laughter ceased as he pressed on the gas. "A lunatic."

14.

In the otherwise flat stretch of island between the town and the northern tip was a slightly depressed, somewhat moister swath known as the moors. Nondescript, scrubby, the area was best known for its saline soil, inhospitable to all but the most tenacious plants. Among them, though, was the broom crowberry, a thorny shrub with little to commend it most of the year. Only in late March did it make its presence known if not celebrated. With reddish-orange petals, many too tiny for a distant eye to see, the crowberry heralded the spring.

Stopping the coupe on the roadside, Mary Beth got out and admired them. Though scarcely flamboyant, these first flowers made her feel wistful. It brought her back to the early springs of her childhood, with black snow still clogging the gutters and the branches bare but the icicles dripping silver and the colors of old hopscotch courts resurrecting on the street. Such memories reminded her of her mother urging her to go out and play. "Winter's over!" she announced with the fullness of her strength. "Live!"

But life, for her, was ebbing. Already feverish, with a swollen neck and a bark-like cough, Colleen Boyle was exhibiting the disease that would swiftly kill her. Until her last breath, though, she remained indomitable, and in Mary Beth's mind, a saint. While often strict with her eight-year-old daughter, she also adored her, sewed and baked gingerbread for her, pampered her whenever her husband wasn't looking. Her mother smelled of cinnamon, applesauce, and bleach. Her hands were soft and unyielding.

They had a lot in common, the Boyle girls: severe beauty, hardy hips and shoulders, the same stubborn streak, and a refusal to complain even in the face of anguish. Her eyes, like her daughter's, were emerald. And while her father scoffed at her desire to become a policewoman, her mother encouraged it. "I can see you now, *mo stoirín*,"—my little darling—"with your badge and your cap. The bad guys will pick up and run!"

Mary Beth loved her mother, but for a long while hated her. Resented her for dying so young and leaving her to be raised by an intolerant man, embittered and cold. Angry that she made her go out and play when the temperature was still freezing and snow clung to the gutters, for wrapping her up in her coat, hat, and mittens instead of embracing her and promising that she'd always be there when she returned.

"Bluebells, cockle shells," Mary Beth recited out loud. "Eevie, ivy, over." Her shoes lifted up and down on the pavement. "Mother went to market to buy some meat. Baby's in the cradle, fast asleep."

Yes, it would be warmer soon and all the flowers would blossom, but her world would remain wintry. By the wind-lashed moors, Mary Beth zipped up her jacket and clutched its lapels to her throat. The crowberry could bloom and spring might come, but Archie had abandoned her, just like her mother. She was alone again, this time with a murderer on the loose and an island that wanted her gone. Through icy squares, it felt, she was once more hopping, and trying her best not to slip.

*   *   *

Pascal had whipped up a batch of his beloved scallop stew, but Mary Beth couldn't touch it. Instead, with her spoon in mid-dip, she stared at the chunks of white flesh rising ghostly from the cream and thought of unavenged victims.

"Something wrong, Captain Swann? Too hot for you, maybe?"

Short, round, bearded, and bald, Pascal often looked impish. Only when customers complained or left his dishes uneaten did he take on a disgruntled air. This rarely happened, thanks less to Pascal's talents than to his ever-shrinking menu. Gone were the fricots, tourtiéres, poutine râpées that were the chefs d'oeuvres of any Acadian kitchen. In their place came the chowders, bisques, and stews that these bland New Englanders preferred. What couldn't be soaked in cream was fried or fried and then soaked in cream. Salt and pepper were their herbs.

And yet here was one of his favorite customers once again playing with her food.

"The scallops are fresh, right off the boat, I swear," he pledged with a raised right hand. Though the gap of his two missing fingers—the result, rumor had it, of a knife fight in Nova Scotia—she could see his apron. Its stains were incongruously red.

"Pomme de pré," Pascal explained. "Cranberries. Would you like a slice?"

But Mary Beth just shook her head. Not even Trudy could get her to eat. The arthritic widow was a uniquely homely woman who, unexposed to the elements which eroded most Fourth Cliff faces to a hardened sameness, retained her bloated nose and pitted cheeks, her shrinking lips and eyes. And yet Pascal found her attractive enough, it seemed, as the two were purportedly lovers.

A familiar *brring* of a bicycle bell resounded outside the diner. And if Mary Beth's appetite was low before, it was lost when Patrolman Hogan stuck his head in the door.

"Captain," was all he said, breathless, unleashing a string of drool. "Quick."

The stew sloshed over the bowl as Mary Beth shot up from the table, grabbed her cap and jacket, and ran. Already she could hear the ruckus echoing across the street, but its source was yet unknown. Hogan had to tug her sleeve and point before, squinting through the drizzle, she could discern two figures trading blows. Or rather one figure punching and the other deflecting, all the while standing his ground.

It took her a ten-yard sprint to recognize Paolo Varrone. In his khaki cleaner's clothes and hat, with his broom in present-arms position, he did his best protecting his face. Jabbing at him, again and again, was John Devereux, the fisherman's son, the first person to speak to her on that day—could it be, ten months ago?—when Francesco Albertini was found.

"Hold on, there, John," she said, calmly enough, inserting herself in front of him.

"Out of the way, Captain Swann," the young man spat. "Let me at him."

This was not the John Devereux she knew, the quietly handsome gillnetter hand anxious to receive his draft notice, as fearful of missing the war as he was of entering it. In his place was a furious youth perfectly willing to kill. His reddish hair flamed. His eyes, a searing blue, seemed molten.

"I'll do no such thing," Mary Beth insisted, and it nearly cost her a chin. She ducked a fist meant for Paolo and locked her hands around the slender Devereux, pushing him backward.

"But you didn't see what he was doing." From the point of explosion, he now looked on the brink of tears. "It was...horrible."

"What? What was he doing?"

"That."

He pointed down at the fisherman's memorial, little more than a marble slab incised with the image of a boat and beneath it, two rows of names. Among them were the Fitches, Alva's husband and sons, a Dudley or two, and a Devereux.

"I'm sure he was just cleaning up," Mary Beth assured him. "It's his job." She glanced over her shoulder at Paolo who, behind his broom, was seething.

Devereux sobbed. "Then you tell him, Captain Swann. Tell him to keep his filthy mitts off my grandpa." He drew a sleeve under his oozing nose and and leered once more in Paolo's direction before bolting in the direction of the docks.

"Proud of yourself?" The question came from behind her, posed by a person whose expression was sheer contempt. "First it's a gangster and then this—how do you say—this punk. Who won't you befriend?"

"I wasn't befriending, Paolo. I was saving *him*."

"You mean, from murdering another Italian? I don't think anyone cares."

"I can't do anything right by you, can I?" She wasn't fiddling with her wedding band anymore, wasn't nervous around him, but enraged.

"I did not say that."

"Oh no? Then what did you say, then? Mary Beth, you're doing a great job? Mary Beth you're the cat's meow?" She stepped toward him, fixing him in furious eyes. "No. What I heard from you, I heard from all the puddin-heads on this sorry excuse for a rock. All I ever heard is crap!"

Paolo instinctively stepped back. His face looked more ferret-like than foxy, his moustache a twitching whisker. "I'm sorry…"

"Well, it's a little late for apologies. A little late for everything."

With a final sneer, she stormed off. She marched past Hogan, ignored Pascal and Trudy who were waiting outside the diner with her bowl of stew. Into the coupe she dove, released the brake, and jammed the gear before tearing out of town.

Beyond the shipyard she drove, past the bar and the moors, almost as far as the bogs. She fantasized about going farther, whizzing by the POW camp and the gun emplacement before vaulting off the cliff and crashing onto the strand where she and Archie last made love. From there, she would plunge into the surf.

That'll show 'em, she thought, as her foot flattened the pedal.

It was then, while hurling northward, that she passed another vehicle speeding south. A truck unlike any she'd seen before, mustard yellow, with a canvas roof and a pickup rear. Though she couldn't make out who the driver was, squinting into her rearview mirror, she noticed the blue out-of-state licence plate. The tires, too, were unusual. Wide and thickly treaded, they looked fit for any terrain.

∗   ∗   ∗

Other signs of spring appeared, other flowers—crocuses, forsythia, and even an audacious daffodil. Finches chirped and peepers peeped. The sky was pierced by Canadian geese, their black bills and white necks stretching toward the bogs where the wood frogs were already quacking.

In town, for the first time in a month, Mary Beth saw children playing. Around the docks and the memorial they scurried, still in caps and mittens, engaged in hide-and-go-seek. Watching them, she wondered what it'd be like if she had had children. Would she be strict and unforgiving as her father, or encouraging and adoring as her mom? Would she, too, bounce a baby on her lap and sing, "Ride a horse to Boston, ride a horse to Lynn," and then, spreading her knees suddenly, sing, "Careful little pumpkin that you don't fall *innnn*." And would her child scream with laughter, knowing that her mother would never let her drop?

She would have to try again, first thing after Archie got back. But when would that be? While American forces in Europe had pushed the Germans out of Belgium, crossed the Rhine and were heading for Berlin, in the Pacific, the Japanese showed no signs of surrender. Marines were still slogging it out on Iwo Jima, a name now synonymous with hell. Archie was there, Mary Beth was sure, exposed, endangered, but knowing Archie, resolved. That was her husband, easygoing even when the going was hard, caring for his men, his country. Whose love for her was genuine, of course, but no match for his sense of duty.

At least there were no more murders, but neither were there any leads. Corvelli twice visited the island that month, yet he and Mary Beth came up clueless. They learned nothing new about the case, only about one another.

"This was not exactly the career I dreamed of when I was young," he confided to her. Turns out, he really was a priest—or at least in his ten-year-old mind. "To serve God, serve my fellow man, that is what I wanted to do in life. Add some good to the world. Lord knows we need it."

They had stopped by the roadside with a thermos of coffee and two tin cups, their backs to the Caddy and their eyes on the clouds that seemed to be deliberating whether or not to part.

"I saw myself working in my old Chicago neighborhood, between Loomis and Racine, or else in some tough foreign mission." He stared into his cup. "I was a strong boy, but I wanted to use that strength for the right reasons."

"And the wrong ones?"

Corvelli shrugged. "You know how these things happen," he said. "You make your plans but somebody—God—has other ones."

"Don't I know it." Mary Beth had already told him about her

childhood, the loving, long-dead mother and the father for whom nothing was ever good enough, least of all her. She told him about meeting Archie in the Public Garden and their happy life on Fourth Cliff, and how the war came and snatched that life away. "One day you meet a guy and, bam, everything changes."

"And one day your cousin comes to you and asks you for a simple favor, and who are you to say no? It's family."

The favor was to deliver a package to a customer, the cousin said, a very deserving man. A simple package wrapped in brown butcher's paper and twine, "no bigger than an alms box."

The young Louis Corvelli, the future Father Corvelli, was predictably on time. No doubt the cousin knew that and knew as well that a parcel presented by the block's nicest kid just had to be a gift of some kind. It couldn't be that opening it would transform the customer into confetti.

"Goodbye, priesthood. Goodbye, life of service. Hello to doing things I never thought possible. Things you can't even confess." Corvelli toasted the sky with his cup. "I was already marked, damned, and had no choice but to enter the business. There, a smart, enterprising person can get ahead quickly. And I did," he drank and gulped, "until now."

"Why do they care so much?" Mary Beth asked. "Why would anybody in Chicago or anywhere give a fig about Fourth Cliff?"

Corvelli smiled at her. "Family." Or rather, families, each one with grudges against his. "It's too complicated to explain." But it came down to this: find the murderer or pay the price on a dozen other debts, all of them massive. "So you see, Mary Beth, when I tell you I haven't got much time, I mean it. Come Easter, you won't be seeing me anymore."

She laughed, but knew he was telling the truth. "Come Easter, we'll have closed this case once and for all and you can go back home a hero. They'll even give you a medal—or whatever it is they give in your world—or name a street after you. Just you wait and see," Mary Beth said and almost believed it herself. Almost believed that Louis Corvelli, like Archie Swann and Paolo Varrone, was a man she could trust to remain.

*   *   *

It was on her way back from seeing Corvelli off at the wharf that Mary Beth saw it for the second time. The mustard truck with the canvas roof cruised up the bluff and turned north at the intersection, out of town. Mary Beth tailed it but at a distance. She was curious where it was headed—to the Flotsam Bar perhaps. She needed to inspect it up close. More important to her, just yet, than the state on its license plate or even the identity of the driver was the tread of its tires. Broader and more rugged than any others on the island, they could have left the tracks she found by the bog where Antonio De Luca was murdered.

Short of the Flotsam, though, the pickup turned off the road. Mary Beth waited a full minute before following, but even then proceeded cautiously, easing the coup through the amethyst puddles of Old Man Gainor's shipyard. Parked at the far end, half hidden by a densely fouled hull, was the vehicle. Quietly, she stepped out of the coupe and advanced.

"Hey, you! Stop!"

She swerved to face a seven-inch knife descending toward her nose. Instinctively, she reached for her holster and shouted, "Freeze!" She lurched backward and at the same time drew her pistol, only to see the dagger fall.

"Oh, Jesus. Jesus Christ, I'm sorry."

Again and again, he apologized—"Forgive me, Captain Swann, I didn't recognize you." Mary Beth was amazed at how quickly Grant could change from murderous to gentle.

The knife, it turned out, was a filing rasp, which Mary Beth bent down to retrieve and then handed back. Grant accepted it and blushed.

"I don't know what gets into me, sometimes."

"What gets into all of us," she assured him.

"Doc Cunningham warned me this could happen once in a while, with the Metrazol. That I've got to be careful."

"Careful of what?"

"You know," he said, blushing deeper. "Blowing a fuse."

She eyed him as closely as she dared. This young man, scarcely more than a teenager, wholesome, unspoiled, with eyes bordering on turquoise. And yet a veteran whose war experiences made him inwardly ancient, worn down, and perhaps occasionally deranged. The rasp was used for removing barnacles, she understood, but it could also puncture skin.

"Too much time on Fourth Cliff is enough to drive anybody bonkers. You've got plenty of company, Grant."

He smiled at her, little more than a boy again, with golden strands escaping his cap. But there was also the bomber jacket and the combat boots and the utility belt holding any number of potentially lethal tools.

"Not you, Captain Swann, you'd never lose control. I've seen you—always calm, always in command of things. I just wish I could be more like you."

The smile was now hers, albeit saccharine. She didn't know whether to take him seriously or not, whether his innocence was native to Minnesota or a byproduct of the trauma he'd endured. A side effect of the drug he injected or a mask for some inner evil. For now, all she wanted to know was the make of his truck.

"Nice set of wheels you got there." She motioned with her head.

"We don't get many of those around here."

He shrugged. "You mean the Bantam? I drove it all the way here, through snow, ice, everything. Drives just like a jeep."

"A jeep? You don't say."

She started to move toward it only to find her path blocked by his muscular frame. The guilelessness had fled from him suddenly, replaced by some implacable threat. His hand still held the rasp.

"Well, it's been swell chatting with you, Grant. Come by the station some morning. I'll make you a cup of Postum."

"Thank you, Captain Swann." He was all honey again. "And you can come by here any time you'd like. I'll always be happy to see you."

She backed away toward her coupe with Grant trailing closely behind. He even opened the door for her. Mary Beth avoided his face now, fearful of which one—the angel or monster—she'd encounter, and kept her eyes on the ground.

That's where she saw it and froze. A crosshatched footprint.

*   *   *

What would Archie have done? The question plagued her back on the road. Finally, it seemed, a real suspect, a man who no doubt was suffering from severe mental distress, who had reason to hate the enemy and the physical strength to strangle, stab, and dissect. A man known to almost no one on Fourth Cliff, laying low in his uncle's shipyard. And a man whose military boots left the distinctive print she'd found near the bog, and whose truck probably made those tracks.

Archie would have wanted to get a closer look at that vehicle, if possible inspect its interior for bloodstains and other evidence. He'd try to trace Grant's whereabouts, who had seen him, where and when. Ultimately, he'd bring the young man in for questioning, present him with the facts, and pressure him into making a confession. Archie Swann would have done all that, Mary Beth was sure. But then again, she wasn't Archie.

Her husband wouldn't have thought twice about taking on Old Man Gainor, even if he did sign his checks, nor would he have hesitated to arrest a combat veteran recovering from the worst type of trauma. And if the entire island thought less of him, so what? Archie was the law and the law made no exceptions for anybody. Mary Beth, on the other hand, was already subjected to the island's antipathy, and had already been fired by Gainor. And forget about flying missions over France, Mary Beth had never been out of Massachusetts.

No, she would have to proceed differently, stealthily. She would ask Doc Cunningham about that Metrazol drug and whether the convulsions it caused could drive a man to murder. She'd have to inquire offhandedly about Grant, never letting on that he was targeted, and continue to trail him at a distance. She would have to steal back into the shipyard and get a closer look at that truck, maybe make a rubbing of its tires.

Most crucially, Mary Beth would have to be patient. She could not rush her investigation. One cut corner, a single slipshod move, could tip off Grant. Rather, she would act as if nothing unusual had happened, as if the spate of murders was over finally and their perpetrator had likely fled.

Only two people would know otherwise. Louis Corvelli, because she owed it to him, and Minnie, because she, alone among the islanders, could be trusted. People would continue to disrespect her, Mary Beth knew, but she would have to tune them out. *Focus on the case,* she told herself, *until you put Grant in handcuffs.* Make all of them—Old Man Gainor, Viola Miller, the fishermen who called her Black Bass—regret it.

15.

Twice a week, on Sundays and Thursdays, Mary Beth took a bath. The lodge came equipped with one, a chipped enamel tub with porcelain faucets, that was big enough for both Archie and her if they held their knees to their chests. Other than exchanging looks, though, romance was anatomically impossible. But now, alone, she could luxuriate. Light the kerosene water heater and set the dial to boiling. Step in gently and ease down, stretching her legs out as she descended. Then, in the steam and the sweat, Mary Beth slid until all but her face, knees, and toes were submerged.

Her body was not the one she would have chosen for herself. Not svelte like Lauren Bacall or busty like Lana Turner. Yet Archie never complained—on the contrary, he seemed perpetually grateful. As if merely looking at her was enough to make him question his own great fortune. No other man would ever see her that way, she was certain. No other man would behold her nakedness and think, *Can this really be mine?*

And it would only be his, of that she was certain. Lonely though she was, both yearning for and angry at Archie, she was not that kind of woman. But what did "that kind" mean anymore, since the men ran off to their war and left women with the thankless grind of keeping a house, a family, a nation until the heroes came marching home? The men who frequented cathouses from Paris to Cathay while their wives and girlfriends remained with their hearts and legs closed, waiting.

She allowed her head to sink so low that water nearly covered her eyes. Such thoughts were unfair, she knew. Archie would never even think of patronizing brothels. And when he came home, he wouldn't be marching, but more likely dragging himself. That is, if he came home at all.

The mere thought sent ripples through the suds. Life without Archie was too meaningless to contemplate. The only person in her life, since her mother died, who made her feel special, who worshipped and believed in her. Without him, she would never have come to Fourth Cliff, nor would ever have stayed once he left. Without him, she'd never have had the pluck to pin on his bars and commandeer his rank and to press on in the face of almost total opposition.

"Oh, no, Mitzi Bowls," she could almost hear his reply, "You've got it all wrong." She could imagine his boyish grin. "You're the strong one around here."

"Archibald Swann," she declared and heard it reverberate on the tiles. A name that was intensely close to her and yet impossibly far away; a name which, troublingly, evoked less and less desire. For though she yearned for him, the memory of their lovemaking was fading. And as much as she tried to cling to them, so, too, were his smell, his textures, and touch. Another year's absence, and who knew what would be left to remember other than those photographs pinned to her wall, of Archie gradually vanishing.

But the same could not be true of Paolo Varrone. She hated to admit it. The man was no matinee idol, unless the idol was Don Ameche. The tapered face and pointy ears, the eyes that alternately froze and heated her, and that ridiculous moustache—not exactly a heartthrob. And yet, the very thought of him, much less the sight, had her twisting her wedding band as if it were rubber. As if it were cutting off her veins.

Perhaps it was a matter of flattery. To think a man of such education and culture, a man of the world, would take even the slightest interest in her, a working-class Southie who'd rarely been over the Northern Avenue Bridge. Who could barely find Italy on a map, much less Milan. She felt intimidated and impressed by him, titillated and exposed. And though he exasperated her at times and even left her livid, she found herself wishing she could see him again. Anywhere. Here, in the frothy water beside her.

Of course, nothing would ever happen between them. However fallen church-wise, she remained at heart a good Catholic girl and an ever-loyal wife. Still, what harm was there in fantasizing? What danger lurked in merely gazing at her foam-capped knees and imagining him caressing them. Separating them.

Her hands, until now gripping the rim, plunged and swam toward her thighs. The surface swirled and broke. She didn't know what she felt—guilt, exhilaration, mystery—only a strange but irrepressible desire. It heightened, soared, and then instantly crashed when a sound came from outside the bathroom.

A clicking sound, followed by the softest thud. Not rabbit or mole, she was sure, but human. A footfall, a shift. Quietly as she could without splashing, Mary Beth rose from her bath. She reached for a towel and wrapped it around her and then tiptoed into her bedroom. There, from beneath the pillow, she retrieved her .45 Colt. With the gun in hand and the other on the doorknob, she counted one, two, three. Then she burst out.

She stood there, dripping and holding her breath as she moved the muzzle around the room. Across the walls with their maritime ornaments, she aimed, around the kitchen stove and Frigidaire, ending up at the armoire, but beaded on nothing. And yet something, she sensed, was different.

Slipping on her still-wet feet, pistol extended, Mary Beth approached the mantel. The earthenware vase was there, empty, the hydrangeas having long since dried up. But beside it was another flower, this one laid out in a fleur-de-lis pattern, and composed entirely of seashells. The fluted fans of scallops.

*   *   *

"Lily," Corvelli pronounced while viewing it. "Lovely. It's Italy's national flower, you know."

She didn't, but it wouldn't surprise her, not if, as Mary Beth suspected, Paolo had left it. Just like the cranberry sprig planted in her pocket, the hydrangeas in her vase, this flower fashioned out of scallop shells she took for a sign of affection. Who else but a swashbuckler like him would sneak into her lodge at night and scarcely make a sound? And who else but a gentleman would take care not to disturb her in the bath?

"Somebody who really likes you, it seems," Corvelli first needled her, and then stung: "Or somebody who really doesn't."

Mary Beth loured at him, puzzled.

"It could be a token," Corvelli explained. "Or could be a warning."

What if she were wrong, Mary Beth wondered. What if, instead of Paolo, another person had entered her lodge—some long-widowed fisherman, or Tom Bruton, whose wife ran off years ago with a Bumblebee buyer. Or, conversely, the many islanders who resented her and wanted to drive her off. Or just a crackpot like Alva Fitch? Or perhaps a mixture of each. A crazy person who both loved and despised her, who dreamed of caressing and harming her at once?

That's when she mentioned Grant. She told Corvelli about the rake and the rasp and the numerous other tools he possessed, any one of which could have inflicted the wounds found on Antonio De

Luca's body or been used to dismember Filippani's. She described the young man's brawn, which was more than sufficient to garrote Francesco Albertini, and the medicine he was taking, which could drive even a sane man wacky. She recounted the admiration he expressed for her as well as the aggression he displayed when they last met. She told him about the footprint and, finally, about the truck.

A strange transformation overcame Corvelli's face. From the priestly and pedagogic, it became once again stony, a gangster's mug. "We're going there."

"To the shipyard?"

"Of course to the shipyard. Where else?"

"But shouldn't we do this quietly, at night maybe, when nobody's there?"

"No time for that. Not for you, certainly not for me," was Corvelli's candid reply. "We've got to do this now," he said, flipping on his hat and tapping the face of his wristwatch. " Twenty-three skidoo."

He rushed past her, out of the lodge, and hurried toward his Caddy. Mary Beth barely had time to follow, flooring the coupe as it joggled over the potholes before reaching, in a sand-laced cloud, the road. Soon, the tip of the lighthouse was no longer visible above the dunes, and the spire of the First Congregational Church loomed ahead. At this speed, they'd enter the shipyard in a minute.

Just then the Cadillac screeched to a halt. Braking hard, Mary Beth managed not to rear-end it, but not without accidently beeping. It echoed in the soupy morning like a foghorn.

"What the..."

She burst out of the car, ready to remind Corvelli that this was Fourth Cliff and not Chicago and people here didn't drive like barnstormers. She had just rounded the grille when she saw them. Emerging from behind one of the skeletal hulls alongside the road were the two enormous henchmen.

They didn't acknowledge her, but just stood there facing the Caddy's dove-gray hood and staring into its windshield. In their oversized suits and fedoras, they seemed larger than Mary Beth remembered them, their expressions stonier, the bulges on their breasts more conspicuous. She'd never heard them utter a word, but with expressions like that—at once empty and threat-filled—they didn't have to.

Corvelli emerged from the car, slowly, and showed them his empty hands. Then, nodding at the two men as if to get their permission, he pivoted back to Mary Beth.

"Remember what I said about not having much time?" he asked. "Well, it seems mine has run out."

"But that can't be. I won't let them!"

Instinctively, she reached for her holster, but felt his soft-gloved fingertips on her hand. "I told you about my neighborhood, Mary Beth, my Outfit," Corvelli whispered. "It's useless."

The goons were already delving into their suit jackets, but Corvelli calmed them as well.

"Now, now, no need for that, boys. I'll come quiet."

He did, pausing to flash a final smile at Mary Beth and to assure her that she was onto something with this Grant fellow. "Just don't give up, Captain Swann. Ever," and removed his camel-colored hat. "It's been an honor."

She watched, wordlessly, as he climbed into the Caddy's backseat. One of the gunmen shoved in next to him while the other took the wheel. Mary Beth wrestled with emotions—anger, frustration, sadness. And helplessless, as the car disappeared down the road to the wharf. There, it would take the ferry to Falmouth, the Pilgrims' Highway to Boston, and Route 20 to Chicago. That was the place where Louis Corvelli had come from, she knew, and now would never leave.

*   *   *

Not even sunset yet and already her glass was refilled. "The one ally I had, and even that I screwed up," Mary Beth lamented and took an extra-long sip.

Minnie merely frowned. "I think the underworld had something to do with it."

"The underworld would've stayed under if only I'd come up with something."

"You did tell him about Grant."

"Too late."

"For him, maybe, but not for you."

Mary Beth drained the glass and smacked it hard on the bar. Minnie automatically poured, but at the same time admonished her. "Last round, sister. I won't have you wallowing in your cups and feeling sorry for yourself. You've still got a job to do."

"To do, yeah, but not doable. At least not by me."

"You bet your boots by you." The frown became a pout. "And you still have a friend in this world. You always have."

Looking up from her whiskey, Mary Beth confronted a pair of eyes that had gone from steely to wet and a prominent jaw that was quivering. Even the cigarette shook. "Oh, Jeez, Minnie, I didn't mean…"

Rising and stretching across the bar, Mary Beth hugged her, but a sudden shattering sound made her pull back. Minnie returned to her taps and Mary Beth to her stool, both gaping at the broken glass of whiskey between them.

"Sorry. I'm so sorry."

Minnie tried shushing her, but Mary Beth, flushed, kept apologizing. Finally, after a pause for breath, she gulped, "I think I need another."

"Sorry, Swann, time to take a powder."

Minnie's expression was now the deadpan she reserved for

drunks. If love still lurked there, it was hugging a bottom that Mary Beth could no longer plumb. Nodding, she swerved off her stool and faltered toward the exit. Halfway there, though, she halted.

"You are my friend, aren't you, Minnie?"

Framed in mugs and bottles, crowned with sputtering light, the big woman in the purple turban smiled at her. "Count on it," she said.

Outside, the sun had already gone down, leaving the island coated in a mist-thickened darkness. The coupe was the only car in the lot—Minnie lived in rooms behind the bar—and Mary Beth had no problem reaching it, although in a meandering way. She fumbled for her key and was fighting to insert it in the lock when a rustling rose behind her. She'd barely started to turn before someone looped an arm around her throat and hauled her backward, onto the gravel, where powerful hands flipped her onto her stomach and punishing knees pinned her legs to the ground.

The world went haywire. The fog outside was suddenly within her head and behind her eyes, blinding her. She felt the jacket being ripped off her shoulders, her shirt. Her hand reached for her duty belt only to be stopped by an elbow jabbed in her ribs. She called out for help, but her mouth felt filled with sand.

A liquory breath was on her neck, and on her back an impossibly heavy weight. Mary Beth gasped for air. She couldn't struggle anymore, couldn't resist. Her brain finally told her what her body sensed, that it was better to just lie there and not invite further blows, perhaps to feign unconsciousness. Whoever was on top of her was kissing her, alternating affection with violence. Stroking and hitting her, grinding her terror into numbness.

And then—*crack*—a tremendous breaking noise. Mary Beth feared for her leg bones, even her spine. But the sound was followed by others: shouting, curses, and a frantic shuffling of gravel. A second later, an engine, a growl of gears and whirr of tires. All was quiet after that, except for somebody's labored breaths.

"Mary Beth?"

The night, the fog, slowly came back into focus. So, too, did a face, creased with concern.

"Mary Beth, are you all right? Did he hurt you? Did he…"

Someone was buttoning her shirt for her, helping her on with her jacket and retrieving her cap from the dirt.

His features came into focus, the raven hair, the moustache.

"Paolo?"

"Sì," he said, though she could already see him clearly. Looking singularly unheroic in his streetsweeper's khakis and clutching a broken hickory broom. "I was on my way back from work."

"Well, you can go now, thank you. I'm fine," she insisted as she wiped something wet from her nape. "Fine," she repeated, and, glimpsing the blood smeared on her fingertips, promptly passed out in his arms.

*   *   *

He drove her in the coupe. Fortunately, there was no one outside in the town to see him, a POW, behind the wheel of a police car with Mary Beth slumped in the passenger's seat. Undetected, they passed through the intersection, southward and onto the promontory's trail.

Groggily, she asked, "You know where I live?"

"Should I not?" He turned in and deftly navigated the potholes. "There are very few mysteries on this island."

"Easy for you to say."

"Nothing is easy, I assure you."

He parked in front of the lodge and helped her inside. Turned on the lights and hung her hat on the wall peg, all while Mary Beth struggled with her duty belt. Paolo might have assisted with that, too, if she hadn't let out a gasp. Her hands were still spattered with blood.

"Not yours," Paolo assured her. "I hit him on the head with my broom."

"Did you get a look at him?"

"No, sadly. Too dark. Too foggy."

"Why didn't you kill him?"

"Who would believe a prisoner?" Paolo sighed. "I could find myself at the end of a military rope."

The floor started to churn. Mary Beth's head swam and her legs turned rubbery. She might have fainted if Paolo hadn't steadied her.

He edged her toward the bed and sat her on its hobnail cover, washed her hands with a dampened cloth and cleaned the back of her neck.

"Would you like me to call the doctor?"

"God, no."

"I will leave you, then."

"No."

A wave of what at first felt like gratitude swept over her and broke into a foamy desire. Yes, this was the man who'd filled her vase with hydrangeas and left her a scallop shell lily. Poalo, who's pointy ears and narrow nose vanished suddenly, taking the moustache with them. Only the eyes remained, no longer frosty but a fiery blue. "Stay," she whispered, and then did something she hadn't for a great many years, perhaps not since her mother died.

Mary Beth wept.

Paolo gripped her heaving shoulders and swept the wet bangs from her brow. "There, there," he tried to calm her. "Everything will be…"

She kissed him. Desperately, on the lips, yanking him toward her by his collar. Her mouth was open and trembling, but Paolo's remained still. He did not resist her, but neither did he give in.

"You have had a frightful experience and, I suspect, more than enough to drink. I suggest you lie down now and try to get some rest."

He said this softly but with force, once more the colonel. Mary Beth let go of his shirt and jerked backward. "What have I done?"

"Nothing," Paolo consoled her. "You've done nothing that a normal person would not do." Gently, he pushed her shoulders down onto the bed. "Now be normal and go to sleep."

He left her, on tiptoes, switching off the light before he exited and began the long hike back to camp. Mary Beth lay in the darkness with her heart pounding and tears drying prickly on her cheeks. Inside her, emotions collided: fury and panic, desire and embarrassment and guilt. She could still feel him on her lips and smell his scent—could it be, origano? But she also felt the crushing weight, the brutal hands tearing at her. Long into the night, Mary Beth remained awake, roiling.

16.

THE CHURCH BELLS SOUNDED THE DOG WATCH AND THE WORSHIPPERS paraded inside dressed in Fourth Cliff finery. Easter Sunday, a spanking day, salty and crisp. The air was ripe with the scent of rebirth—bloodroot, cowslip, hyacinth, and honeysuckle—and a whiff of approaching peace. In Europe, Allied forces were converging on Berlin, bringing victory within several weeks' reach, and in the Pacific, the conquest of that godforsaken island, Iwo Jima, was completed. But Mary Beth wasn't dwelling on the war, or even when Archie would return. Rather, she was watching as Reverend Miller greeted each of the congregants, eyeing the men, especially, for the moment when they'd remove their hats. One of them would be sporting one hell of a bruise, a bloody bump raised by a broom handle.

She suspected that someone was Grant. He would have had the strength to pin her down, as well as the fierce infatuation to both caress and molest her. Only the battle-fatigued Grant would have run once confronted by Paolo. Pity she hadn't the presence of mind to get a look at the vehicle her attacker fled in or the footprints he left behind.

But Grant didn't show up, and neither did Old Man Gainor. The first, she gathered, had lost his faith high over enemy targets, and the second never had it to lose. Or perhaps they were sticking close to home after the morning's incident. A phone call from someone—just who was unknown—claiming to see smoke from the shipyard. Fourth Cliff's only fireman, Bob Culliver, rushed to the scene.

A stubby, nondescript man married to a stubby, unobtrusive woman who gave him three plain and plump daughters, Culliver was content to spend the war at home and most every day reading the funny pages and smoking ten-cent cigars. Apart from the occasional overheated boiler or cat ensconced in some tree, he had little to do. But the call sent him dashing for his turnout coat and leatherhead and gunning his little red truck.

Hand siren cranking, Culliver arrived at the shipyard to find not a single flame, only the usual puddles and slicks and a flummoxed Old Man Gainor. Neither man could figure out why anyone would've sounded such an alarm. It was Grant who reminded them of the date, April 1, and suggested that someone was merely poking fun at them. The young man—according to Culliver—was the only one who laughed.

Grant and his uncle remained at home but not, it seemed, the rest of Fourth Cliff. The Brutons, the Halls, Abigail Pitt, and even Minnie Beaudet filed into the church, along with Lemuel Hogan and Wallace McKee. Pascal and Trudy, who were probably Catholics, came too, as did Alva Fitch, who no longer believed in any God but arrived in a borrowed muslin dress. Doc Cunningham in a worsted suit and his only presentable shirt, the Ballard brothers for once not in their doughboy uniforms. None of them showed signs of bruising.

The church doors closed and the organ inside started thundering. Mary Beth remained where she was, aware of the pain still radiating through her neck and lower back. Conscious of a tingling on her lips. She waited until strains of "Jesus Christ Has Risen Again" escaped the scalloped windows and floated up the spire. Only then did she abandon the memorial and climb into her coupe, drive up to the intersection, and turn north.

*　　*　　*

She thought about stopping by the shipyard, sneaking in and inspecting up close the Bantam truck and its tires. She thought about confronting Grant and whipping off the woolen cap he always wore to see if there was a wound underneath it. She saw herself arresting him for assaulting her in the Flotsam lot and on suspicion of perpetrating all four murders. Removing the Peerless handcuffs from her belt, she'd lock his wrists behind him and calmly pocket the key.

But as the shipyard passed outside her window, Mary Beth scarcely slowed down. Not only the thought of meeting Grant dissuaded her, but of running into his uncle. With no hard evidence other than a knock on his nephew's head, Old Man Gainor would once again demand her badge. A nasty altercation would follow, with words and perhaps even blows exchanged. Sure, she could always draw her pistol, but would she have the stomach to fire it? Could she press the trigger and shoot a .45-caliber slug, point-blank, into another person's chest?

The shipyard shrank in the rearview mirror, as did the Flotsam Bar and the bogs. In the windshield, the prisoner of war camp loomed. Mary Beth breathed hard. Could she stop in and risk seeing Paolo again? And how, after that kiss, could she face him? How could she not?

The camp was quiet as she passed. A priest had come over the coast, reportedly, and the men were no doubt at Mass. Driving on, she saw that the emplacement, too, was silent. The flag flapped, the cannon jutted seaward, but none of the soldiers were yet about. Lowering her foot on the gas, Mary Beth accelerated to where the road ended and the pavement gave way to sand. Through the scraggly dunes she steered and braked at the edge of a scarf. Below, bristling with shells and pebbles, lay the shingle where she and Archie had last loved.

That night seemed impossibly distant to her now, a figment from someone else's dream. The memory of Paolo's touch, though fleeting, was stronger than that of Archie's whole body pressed against her. Their marriage had been reduced to images: buying oysters down at the dock, decorating their tree, and in the lighthouse with the gramophone playing, dancing naked at sunset. All reduced to black and white and preserved in a dusty album. She would take it down and blow it clean, she told herself, and watch the pictures reanimate the day that Archie returned.

But would their relationship ever be the same, with all he'd been through? After all she'd endured since he left? Could they ever go back to the time when they parted or had the two of them permanently changed? If, lying on that beach that night, her love for him wrestled with anger, bitterness might now have the upper hand.

On a meandering path, Mary Beth made her way down to the beach. Mussels and cockles crunched beneath her shoes. Sea glass glimmered green and amber in the early April sun. She picked up a stone and tossed it into the verdigris water, the sound of its plop lost in the surf and the shriek of wheeling gulls. Beyond, the sea was empty—no more liberty ships and cruisers—and the sky was fighter free. Soon it would all be over, Mary Beth felt. Archie, and the world, would return.

And she would run to him. Who was she kidding? What anger could survive a second once he walked through the station door, or rather limped, and drew his denuded frame as straight as he could and gave her a discolored smile? She would practically fly over her desk to get to him, to wrap her arms around him and lift him too easily, and replenish his cheeks with tears. "Archie," she'd weep, and wouldn't care who in Fourth Cliff could hear her.

For there'd be no hissing Black Bass behind her back anymore, no more threats of dismissal from Old Man Gainor. And as for Grant, Archie would nab him in a week. The captain's bars would again be pinned on his collars, and Mary Beth demoted to her former rank. But she'd assure herself all that was as it should be, that she'd had her moment to take command and did her best given the circumstances. Being the nation's first woman police chief, and holding that title for nearly two years, was something to be proud of, she convinced herself, nearly.

No matter. Time would pass. Life on Fourth Cliff would resume its rhythm of winter storms and summer vacationers, the seasons of cod, hollock, and hake. They would have a baby, finally, Archie Junior, with his father's supple body and his mother's temperament, who'd run hellbent across the sand and smash the other children's castles. A family would follow, an entire flock of Swanns, who'd grow up and take wing, each in search of her or his own island. And their parents would watch them, follow their flight through the telescope for as long as they could until they vanished over the horizon.

Then they would be old, Mary Beth and Archie, handing over their shields to younger cops and retiring to the top of their lighthouse. The sun would set purple and Armstrong would play and the mattress, if it hadn't disintegrated yet, would be waiting for them, not to make love but rather just to lie there, together, holding hands, and remembering those sweet sore years of separation.

Forgotten would be the bodies of the prisoners, Agents Sitwell and Dobbs, and that star-crossed mobster, Corvelli. Forgotten would be Paolo Varrone, who would long have returned to his homeland and worked to restore its honor. Gone would be the case that Mary Beth couldn't solve because, as everyone knew, she wasn't up to it. Because a woman had no business even trying.

She picked up another stone, a bigger one, and hurled it into the swell. Its gunshot-like pop echoed off the cliff behind her. Hitching up her duty belt, tugging down on her cap, Mary Beth sucked in the sea air, exhaled in a huff, and pivoted. The mussels and cockles cracked as she marched up the path to the second or third cliff, depending on who one asked. Back to the coupe, to catch the Fourth Cliff murderer.

*   *   *

Her plan was to return to the station and make the unavoidable call to her father, to hear once again how she'd chosen the wrong career, married the wrong man, and generally disappointed him in life, and then have to explain why she wasn't spending Easter with a disabled father who was utterly alone in the world.

Returning to the road, Mary Beth drove slowly. So slowly that she once again got a look at the stately couple seated in the Master DeLuxe, the man in a polka-dotted bowtie and the woman's sere pill-box hat, as it exited the trail from the emplacement. The soldiers, she saw, were now gathered outside of the bunkers and signaling her to turn. And how could she ignore them, these young men who, though in no way endangered, were still far from home this holiday Sunday?

The table—two-by-fours laid across ammunition crates—was once again set, and with a bounty that made previous spreads look like pittance. Candied ham and pig knuckles, deviled eggs and asparagus, a rack of lamb and freshly shucked scallops.

"Not exactly kosher," Perl laughed, "but who am I to complain?"

None of the soldiers did. All three were busy digging in, too preoccupied to even notice Mary Beth. She sat but didn't touch a thing, her stomach souring and her attention diverted by the absence of two of the men.

"Private Falcone?" she asked.

Perl replied with the saddest of smiles. "In bed," he explained, and pointed toward the WATCH YOUR GI HEAD sign painted over the bivouac bunker's entrance. "Seems stupid doozy bots can't read."

"And Colburn?"

The squirrely nose wrinkled again, away from the bunkers this time and out toward the dunes. The lieutenant was once again pacing, in full battle gear and glued to his binoculars, scanning the ocean. Mary Beth excused herself, rose, and trudged through the sand and beach grass, working up a sweat before reaching him.

"Any sign of the enemy?" she puffed.

Colburn didn't answer, at least not at first. Waves shattered on the rocks below, thundering and sending up spray that no doubt fogged up his field glasses, and yet he kept on scanning. Moments passed before he turned to her with an offended child's expression and asked, "Are you making fun of me, Captain Swann?"

A few months earlier, she might have blushed and twisted her ring, but now, hardened by deaths and disappointments, she merely shrugged. "Not at all, Lieutenant. I know the frustration of every day looking for something and never finding it."

"He's out there somewhere," Colburn said, motioning beyond the surf. "I know it. I can feel him."

"So can I."

He continued scouring while Mary Beth leaned her back up against his jeep and just listened. "There's a wall at my college," he told her. "A memorial wall. Perhaps you've seen it?"

She hadn't, but refrained from explaining how girls from her Southie neighborhood weren't especially welcomed in Cambridge.

Colburn went on: "On it are engraved the names of all the alumni who fell in our nation's wars, beginning with the Revolution. The Civil War's list is the longest, followed by the Great War, and now this. Dozens of names, together with the classes they belonged to and the battles where they fell. A simple, glorious wall."

She shrugged again, though this time not to show her toughness but her lack of reverence. "A wall is a wall," Mary Beth remarked. "It holds things up."

"Yes, like tradition."

"And divides things. People like you, for instance, from me."

"Heroes from nobodies. Immortals from those who disappear."

Mary Beth snapped, "Those who survived from who didn't."

Lowering his binoculars, he squinted at her for a fleeting moment before veiling his eyes with sunglasses. He gazed out to sea again and whispered, "I'd rather be on that wall forever than live a life of shame."

She rose from the jeep and approached him. He no longer seemed so imposing, his movie-star looks tarnished by exhaustion. Less Laurence Olivier than Jimmy Stewart. The hair more charcoal than raisin, the rugged chin turnd fragile, and the eyes, once gemlike, now glassy. And in place of the fragrances he once gave off—the Pepsodent and Brilliantine—hovered a mustier whiff. Despair.

"One month from now, they say, it'll all be over," she comforted him. "You'll be back at your school with your debutantes and fancy parties, and you'll forget all about the war and that wall. You won't remember a thing about this place."

"*They'll* come back as well. Those who went overseas and fought. They'll write the books and get the girls and go on to lead the world." He raised binoculars again to his nose and used them to lift the sunglasses. "And I'll go to work in my father's real estate business. I'll be nobody."

Mary Beth stared at him. In his helmet and ammo belt, his carbine and grenades, he looked like a statue. The kind you'd find in Boston Common, ever vigilant and long dead.

"Today or in a month from now, it won't make a difference," he said to the sea. "I'll never leave Fourth Cliff."

Back on the road, with nothing but the scrappy landscape and the phone call with her father ahead of her, Mary Beth didn't rush. Which was fortunate, for speeding, there was no way she could have stopped in time to avoid a tragedy. Swerving to the side and screeching to a stop, she barely managed to miss him.

He stood clad in a yellow smock and matching hood with holes cut out for the eyes. He waved his arms up and down, pelican-like, and hopped from foot to foot, wailing. Mary Beth peeled her forehead from the wheel into which it had smashed and leaned angrily on the horn. But this just made the hooded man bellow even louder and whirl.

That was it. She opened the door and managed to stick one leg out when another two men, similarly dressed but in red, ran up and also started warbling. The three of them danced around the coupe, while inside, Mary Beth shut her eyes tightly, clamped her ears, and screamed.

The tensions that had built up since Archie left, especially in the last year, had finally burst their breakwater. The murders, the ridicule, not to speak of the loneliness and the fears, were suddenly overwhelming, unmooring her as easily as any nor'easter and dumping her hull by the roadside. *So this is what it feels like*, she thought, and realized how easy it'd be to become Alva Fitch. The three hooded demons danced and hooted and the screams that filled the coupe belonged to somebody else, a madwoman, anybody but Mary Beth Swann.

Through all the howling—theirs and hers—she heard someone shout, "Smettila adesso!" The voice, at first distant, grew near. "Smettila! Vatenne!"

The gamboling ceased. The man in yellow froze in mid-hop and removed his hood.

"I am so sorry, Capitana." Lorenzo, his bony head sweat-sheen-ed, bowed to her.

"Perdonaci. We did not mean to scare."

The other two figures also revealed themselves to be prisoners Mary Beth recognized, both of them contrite. "Scusi. Scusi," they repeated until another person pushed them away.

"Idioti!" he barked and then turned back to Mary Beth. "Did they frighten you?" Paolo bent down and put his face to the window. "Are you all right?"

Her hands slowly dropped from her ears and landed on the steering wheel. Blood rushed back into her face, transforming its pallor to flush. "I'm fine. Fine," she insisted and struggled to rein in her tears. She told herself to step on the gas, to get out of there and away from Paolo, but her foot felt frozen. Surrendering, Mary Beth rolled down the window.

"Ballo dei Diavoli," he said.

"Ball of what?"

"Ballo dei Diavoli. The dance of the devils. It's an Easter tradition we have from back home. It celebrates our victory over death."

"Victory," Mary Beth mumbled. "Death."

"And as far as I could see, you won."

She laughed, finally, the stresses sloughing off. The sight of that moustache spreading as he smiled hauled her back to reality, to sanity, only to replace it with another madness. "How is it you're always here when I need you?" she asked.

"I could say the same thing about you."

His face was in the window, his mouth only a slight lean away from hers, and Mary Beth leaned. The kiss was longer this time, wetter, and more intense. And too brief, as Paolo, at first passionate, again pulled away.

Hurt and furious, but above all confused, Mary Beth berated

him, "How could you do this to me?"

"Do what?"

"Lead me on. Tease me."

"Forgive me, it is not that I don't find you attractive. Beautiful, in fact, and lovely. But it is all so impossible."

His hand was on his heart, but still Mary Beth lunged. "The cranberry sprig you put in my pocket. The flowers you put in the vase on my mantle. The shells. If that's not teasing, what is?"

"The sprig, yes. In my country, it is a sign of good luck. But what flowers are you talking about? What shells?"

"The hydrangeas. Remember? And the scallop shells you shaped like a lily."

Paolo stood up straight and stepped back from the window. "I assure you, Captain Swann, I left you no such things."

Mary Beth gaped at him. She bit her lip and twisted her wedding band so violently it burnt. The images of the ruptured breakwater and the abandoned hull returned to her and she shook. *If Paolo didn't leave them, who did?*

*   *   *

Grant. The battle-crazed former pilot who attacked her in the parking lot and who could have done that and worse in her lodge, when she was naked in the bath, but chose instead to make a lily out of shells. Grant who was playing with her, humiliating her as handily as he was murdering Italians, just to show he could. Grant who didn't kill for revenge or for politics or even for pay, but merely because he enjoyed it.

The gas pedal met the floor as the coupe tore southward toward town. The moors flashed by her window, and then the Flotsam bar. Skidding into the shipyard, she'd plow through the puddles and the oil and bring her bumper right up to the Bantam's door. She'd check the treads and pick out the footprints, just for evidence, sketch them in her notepad. If Old Man Gainor came out and started threatening her, she'd threaten him back with charges of harboring a murderer. And if Grant appeared, she wouldn't bother whipping off his cap and inspecting his head for injuries. She wouldn't say a word except "Hands up," with her pistol aimed straight at his face.

But just short of the entrance, the patrol car slowed to a crawl. A paralyzing thought had just occurred to Mary Beth, a single word, and she muttered it out loud. "Paolo."

Far worse than that first kiss, when she was half-drunk and battered, this second one was given without prompting. Whatever she felt for him, whether genuine affection or mere lust, Mary Beth had succumbed to it. She now was the hussy that other women would gossip about, the unfaithful wife who betrayed a husband who was risking his life for her and their country. And who did she double-cross him for? A prisoner of war, a foreigner who, only a few months before, would have killed them both and a great many more in the name of victory.

Disgusted with herself, queasy, she drove past the shipyard and through the intersection, and, a short distance to the south, exited. The tires, bumping over the potholes, further churned her stomach, and she feared she'd have to heave into one of bayberry thickets. She made it to the lodge, though, and staggered inside. All was just as she'd left it—the whitewashed walls and knickknacks, the Frigidaire and four-poster. And the armoire with a mirror that showed a dishevelled policewoman with her cap and belt askew and an expression of addled shame.

She crossed to the mantle. The scallop-shell lily was still there, still taunting her. Paolo or Grant, what difference did it make who drew it? Either way, a man had made a simpleton out of her, a deluded, out-of-her-depth clod. Sweeping her jacket arm across the surface, Mary Beth sent the seashells flying.

Fleeing the lodge, she passed the tin-roofed shed which housed the tarped and oiled Harley-Davidson and trundled toward the lighthouse. Up the dizzying spiral she climbed until, panting, she reached the top. Here, at last, was comfort. The mattress and the telescope, the gramophone and the Sox's 1942 schedule. Even the map of the South Pacific with its pushpins put her at ease, and the link chart with its pathetic shards of evidence. The photographs of Archie in various uniforms, blue and green, in successive stages of vanishing.

She selected the last, the one of her husband looking wan and feeble after one of his many battles but still smiling at her, assuring her that she was the strong one and that everything would be okay. Pulling it off the corkboard, she brought it close to her face, her lips. How silly would it be to kiss it, Mary Beth thought. How useless. "Forgive me," she whispered.

Then, reaching her from below, came the *brring* of a bicycle bell. "Not now," she groaned, in no mood to deal with Officer Hogan and some small-town crisis—a beehive infesting a flowerbed or an unclaimed dog howling beside the memorial. "Go away," she commanded, though not loud enough for Hogan to hear.

Brrriing. The sound went right through her and yet reminded her that, whatever had happened, she was still Mary Beth Swann, the captain of the Fourth Cliff police.

Adjusting her cap in the pocket mirror, she made her way down the stairs. The sun outside was glaring and, for a moment, Mary Beth was blinded. She could only hear that relentless *brrring.*

"That'll do, Lemuel," she shouted. "I'm not deaf, you know."

"I know, Missus Swann, I'm sorry. I thought you might not be home."

She squinted into the light and could barely make out the outlines of the bicycle, much less its rider. But the voice, much younger and less halting, was not Hogan's. A second passed while the big teeth and bulging eyes, the freckles and Jughead cap came into view.

"Here, Missus Swann," croaked Jimmy Bruton. "This is for you."

He held something out to her, but no sooner had her fingers touched it when the Bruton boy pulled back. "I'm sorry," he repeated, and remounting his bike, hurriedly pedaled away. Mary Beth had to lean down to retrieve the delivery.

She didn't open it there, but instead moved closer to the rocks that separated the promontory from the sea. The afternoon was waning already, another lonely Easter ended, the sun cowering violet in the sky. With quaking fingers, Mary Beth opened the envelope and removed a single sepia-colored sheet. The bold logo on the top read Western Union, and beneath it, the date—April 1—followed by her name and address. And then, all in capitals, the message:

THE SECRETARY OF WAR DESIRES TO EXPRESS HIS DEEP REGRET THAT YOUR HUSBAND, MAJOR ARCHIBALD SWANN, HAS BEEN REPORTED MISSING IN ACTION SINCE TWENTY TWO MARCH IN THE PACIFIC. IF FURTHER DETAILS OR OTHER INFORMATION ARE RECEIVED YOU WILL BE PROMPTLY NOTIFIED.

PART SIX

17.

NEITHER OF THEM COULD REMEMBER THE LAST TIME, IF EVER, THEY'D seen Abigail Pitt in the Flotsam. Spying her walk through its doors, Minnie almost did a double take, and her sole customer, gazing into a glass, didn't register. Her only movement was to pinch another cigarette from the pack on the counter and reach for the butt-filled ashtray. Not until Abigail plopped onto the stool next to her and slapped a palm on the bar did Mary Beth at last look up.

"What is it, Abigail?" she slurred. "I'm busy."

"I need to know something, Mary Beth. Are you or are you not still our police captain?"

Mary Beth stared at her. What a mystery this woman was, with her chinaware skin and delicate features, her hair no longer in rollers and kerchief but flowing in auburn ringlets down her neck—pinup pretty, in spite of her overalls, and tough. Running Mrs. McQueen's all by herself, with no help, and nothing but strangers boarding. It was that Abigail who now confronted Mary Beth, who pushed the ashtray and highball away and demanded an immediate response.

"Well, are you?"

Minnie answered for her. "She's our captain and she'll stay our captain. Now what seems to be the problem, Abigail?"

"He's back."

For a moment both Minnie and Mary Beth stiffened, fearing another murder. It was almost a relief when Abigail added, "Orson."

"How?"

Abigail smirked. "Medical discharge. Seems he has piles."

"Well, that at least will keep him busy for a while," Minnie snorted. "Talk about a pain in the ass."

The two of them chuckled, but not Abigail. She helped herself to one of the Viceroys, lit it up and puffed, then unhinged a single strap of her overalls. Pulling down her undershirt, she revealed a blue and wine-stain bruise just below her collarbone.

"Ouch," Minnie said, and turned to Mary Beth. "Time you stepped in."

But Mary Beth merely shrugged, bolted down a third of her drink, and sulked. "Go find yourself another sucker."

"Don't listen to her," Minnie urged Abigail. "She's got a bad case of the blues."

Abigail slammed the bar again. "I don't care if she's got the willies. He's home and he's angry. And you know what happens when Orson Pitt gets angry."

"Maybe he's got a reason." Mary Beth said this to her drink, but it left both Minnie and Abigail gawking at her. "Maybe he's heard about some of the goings-on at McQueen's."

"Shame on you, Swann," Minnie scolded her, but Abigail just stood up.

"Well, I guess I got my answer." She made to leave the bar but paused beside the dartboard and turned. "Just remember, ladies, I came to you first."

Minnie waited for the door to close before lacing into her friend. "You crum. You chucklehead. Going into a decline like this just when you got to pull up your bootstraps."

Mary Beth could barely stand to look at her. The flattened nose and flinty eyes had never seemed so intimidating. "Leave me alone."

"Like hell I will. Not when you're downing my booze and filching my smokes. Not when there're thousands of gals like you who got the exact same telegram and worse and somehow find the strength to keep going."

"You're the only one who knows."

"Everyone will know once they see you like this. So buckle up, Captain Swann, and get back to work."

Stubbing out her butt and polishing off her cocktail, Mary Beth swiveled off the stool and meandered through the tables. "He's going to come back," she said, as much to the dartboard as to Minnie. "They're going to find Archie, just watch."

"Either way, you've got to do him proud."

*   *   *

Her first reaction was anger. What took the War Department ten whole days to inform her of Archie's disappearance? Then the disbelief. A man like Major Swann didn't just go missing, not even on Iwo Jima. There had to be an awful mistake. Or, more ruthlessly, a practical joke. After all, the date on the telegram was April 1.

Later still there was denial. It didn't happen—Jimmy Bruton, the telegram—except in a nightmare she'd awake from any second. And finally, she had hope. Not the misty-eyed, hands-over-her-heart variety, but a grim resolution, as if, by focusing hard enough, she could will her husband's return. They would locate him among the newly liberated prisoners or on a list of the more seriously wounded. He'd be lying in some military hospital, muttering, "Mary Beth, Mary Beth," over and over, his doctors convinced he was lost. But she'd find him and embrace him and prove them wrong. Just like Sara—Shirley Temple—in *A Little Princess*.

But at the end of all these emotions came self-pity. Now she was truly alone, a woman without any real family or many friends, possibly a widow and soon to be fired, who'd failed in every crucial role in life—as daughter, wife, and police captain. The obvious answers were cigarettes and Scotch, and she'd surely wallow in them if not for Minnie. If not for Abigail Pitt and her blunt request for help.

And she did need help. Orson Pitt was a frightful man, a crabber in civilian life and probably a troublemaker in the army, which was likely all too happy to be rid of him. Now he was back in Fourth Cliff, ornerier than ever and riled by the rumors of his wife's misbehavior, raging to take all of his disappointments in life out on her.

Minnie was right. Mary Beth couldn't let him. She was determined to stop him, by force, if necessary, though stopping a six-foot, two-hundred-pound behemoth might prove challenging. She'd have to confront him first and threaten him with detention. But where exactly would Orson be detained? Fourth Cliff had no jail.

These issues became more than academic the next morning, a sparkling early spring day, after the last of the fishing boats had departed and the dockhands retired to the diner for their Goo and Moo—pancakes, syrup, and milk. Cruising through town, Mary Beth spotted a burly figure seated on the dock, looking out to sea. Shirtless beneath his overalls, this could have been any islander, but there was no mistaking the massive shoulders and triceps, and the rolls of neck fat escaping his herringbone army cap.

"Good morning, Orson," Mary Beth began, neighborly enough. "Glad to see you back."

The shoulders rose and fell, followed by a grunt. "Yeah, like hell you are."

"All of us Fourth Cliffers are proud of our boys—our men—who served. Those who fought and those who didn't. Everyone did their part."

Orson scowled. "Lay off," was all he said, and lifted a flask to a mouth that was little more than a slit. His eyes were slot-like as well in a flat, square face, his nose long and menacing. His features reminded Mary Beth of the emplacement, gun and all, and left her with a sense of dread. Still, she needled him.

"You'll be glad to know that McQueen's never once closed its doors while you were gone. Abigail kept it in tiptop shape."

The scowl became a grimace. "I heard what kind of shape she kept it in, all right. Heard about it all the way in Colorado. And for who."

"Oh, I wouldn't go listening to rumors, Orson. Worse than old wives' tales are old fishermen's wives' tales."

She sat down beside him, gazing at the saw-toothed waves and the seagulls divebombing for chum. It was a mistake, she realized, but too late, as suddenly Orson was standing over her, wielding his flask like a weapon.

"You stay out of it, lady, you hear me? You keep your snout out of my business." He was shouting at her, and his breath smelled flammable. "You can dress up any way you want, carry a gun, but for me you're nothing but another dumb Jane, and no Jane stands in my way."

Mary Beth didn't flinch. To show any reticence at this point, she knew, was fatal—if not for her, then for Abigail.

"I'm sorry, Orson. Like it or not, I'm wearing the badge here, and this badge will not let you hurt your wife."

She stood and hooked her thumbs in her belt, legs planted, waiting for the blow. But none came. Instead, a change of expression washed over Orson's face, strangely drained of menace. "A guy cheats on his gal," he said, "people feel sorry for her." His voice softened, so low she could barely hear it. "Gal cheats on her husband, and people only laugh."

*   *   *

Orson's words stayed with her throughout the rest of the day, vying with thoughts of Archie. She fought back at any inclination to feel empathy for Orson. Whatever the excuse, there was no justification for hitting Abigail. And who knew what he was capable of? A man that muscular could literally break her in half. He could strangle to death one Italian prisoner, and stab and mangle two others. Morally bankrupt, mad at the world, he could also poison a fourth. On the face of it, Orson Pitt would be the perfect suspect. If only he hadn't an alibi.

But did he? His posting to Colorado, his assignment as a weapons instructor and absence for nearly two years, the only source for all that was Orson himself. For all anybody knew, he'd spent those years somewhere near the coast, an outboard dinghy's distance from Fourth Cliff, easily capable of sneaking onto the island at night and committing his crimes. Perhaps all four victims had been involved with Abigail. And she would be his ultimate target.

Mary Beth made a mental note to keep an eye out for Orson and stop by McQueen's whenever she could dream up an excuse. Next time, she'd contrive to make him remove his cap. Though several weeks had passed, the mark of Paolo's broom would still be there, a telltale bump or scab on his blubbery scalp. That, together with the military boots he still wore, would seal up the case for her. She had only to make the arrest.

But what about Grant? He, too, fit the murder's profile. He also had the physique and the footwear, the manic edge—violent one minute, harmless the next—and the maneuverability. And he had one thing Orson lacked: that truck. Heading out of town in her coupe, Mary Beth determined to return to the shipyard and finally get a look at those tires.

She did, but the Bantam wasn't there. Nobody was. The place seemed deserted, and Mary Beth wondered whether some emergency had occurred. That's when she heard the bells. A familiar enough sound but out of place on weekdays. And not so much ringing as tolling, in doleful segments of eight. Shifting into reverse, Mary Beth backed out to the road, turned, and hurried in the direction of town.

The bells of the First Congregational Church were knelling incessantly. Clearly, something terrible had happened, an event deemed tragic even by the locals' doleful standards. The dread in her doubled as, one by one, the townspeople emerged. Merchants abandoned their shops, fishermen dropped their tackle. Pascal and Trudy, Reverend Miller and Viola, even Abigail and Orson Pitt. A bedraggled Doc Cunningham descended from his office. They all came out and converged on the memorial, but then just stood there downcast.

Others arrived from elsewhere on the island—the Brutons and the Halls and John Devereux. Wallace McKee in his Model T truck and Lemuel Hogan on his bicycle. Most uncommonly, Old Man Gainor was present as well, accompanied by Grant. They joined in the throng surrounding the memorial, hung their heads, and shuddered.

Not one fisherman but an entire crew, Mary Beth fretted, another family like Alva Fitch's lost at sea. Which would only make that mad woman crazier. And yet among all those gathered there, she, alone, came shuffling over to the coupe. Displaying her driftwood teeth, eyes ablaze, she motioned to Mary Beth to lower her window. Alva stuck her head inside.

"You are welcome to stand with us, Captain Swann," she said.

"Stand for what?"

"Why, in mourning, of course."

Mary Beth peered through the windshield at the crowd in the center of town. "How many?" she asked. "How did they die?"

"Just one and naturally," Alva, of sound mind suddenly, informed her. "The president."

*   *   *

The grieving over President Roosevelt's death continued, on an off, for nearly two weeks. While joining in the overall sorrow, Mary Beth kept track of Orson. Down to the docks and then to the general store she trailed him, watched him as he uprooted Abigail's victory garden. She looked out for Grant as well, or at least for his truck, hoping to see it parked in town one day, unattended, its tires exposed for her to inspect. Each morning before or around sunrise, she went out on her usual patrol, beginning in town and ending at the top of the cliff—the second or third—overlooking the strand.

At the station, behind her black ash desk with its casket-like drawers, she sat with her hands folded on the blotter while the Philco hummed with *It's Maritime*. Nothing had changed. The walls still stood—tentatively, in the absence of any gales—with their spindled wheel and whaler's portrait and the cusk mounted in mid-flail. Behind its metal cage, the fan still scrutinized her. The yellowing map and sepulchral file cabinets, Captain Swann misleadingly stenciled on the door. She sat and listened to the Motorola crackle, all the while yearning to hear "Calling Mairzy Doats! Mairzy Doats come in!" suddenly come over the two-way.

Except for Minnie, she saw nobody, avoided conversations and took pains not to run into Paolo. She stopped in at neither at the prisoner of war camp nor at the emplacement, had her groceries delivered at home, and passed up meals at the diner. The routine continued without incident, though at any moment she expected to receive that final note from Old Man Gainor. *Turn in your badge*, it would instruct her, *hand over the keys to the coupe*. With the war winding down, there'd be plenty of veterans eager for a job with adequate pay and minimal responsibilities. After battling the Japanese and the Nazis, how challenging could Fourth Cliff be?

Evenings she spent at the lodge, trying to read *A Tree Grows in Brooklyn* but mostly staring into the empty fireplace. Once nightly, at least, she would fold and re-fold Archie's dress shirts and straighten his Sunday clothes in the armoire. Occasionally she would raise some garment to her face and inhale. Hints of his Lava soap might linger there, she imagined, of Burma-Shave and talc. Of skin and hair and breath. Other times she would venture to the shed outside and remove the tarp from his 1941 Harley. Run her hand over its cool black body and the squeaky sheen of chrome. The machine was fully oiled, she verified. Its key was still where Archie stashed it, in the rear of the shed, hidden in an old KC Baking Powder can.

How she had laughed, Mary Beth remembered, her arms locked around his waist as they churned across the dunes and splattered through moors—places that no car could pass, but an easy task for the Harley. How she'd laughed, sand and mud in her face, as he kicked the clutch and up-shifted the gear and twisted the gas handle to full. The Harley's roar, deeper and huskier than any Fourth Cliff engine, filled her ears.

Later, whether she liked it or not, Archie would test her on the parts: carburetor, distributor, voltage regulator, choke valve. And then, to her delight and horror, he would let her drive. Not far and usually on the road, but long enough for her to feel the 74 cubic inch motor pulsating between her legs, the savage power propelling her forward. Nothing, not even sex, was so exhilarating.

What in God's name would she do next, Mary Beth wondered. Go back to Boston, probably, stay for a while at the old Southie house and suffering her father's "I told you so"s. Later, she'd move out to Malden or Chelsea, get hired as a waitress at the L Street Tavern or as a shopgirl at Filene's—anything but police work. In time, she'd forget all about her time on the island. And though she'd never remarry, neither would she be unusual. Many a spinster and widow would be left by the war, and Mary Beth would merely be one of them.

She thought about all of this, but still, at the beginning and end of each day, she squinted down the potholed path and expected any second to see a ragged figure approach. Limping and wan, wide-eyed and scarred, he'd be recognizable solely by the boyishness of his smile and the way his thumb pumped in the direction of the lighthouse, up the spiral stairs she hadn't ascended since the day that telegram arrived.

Archie might yet come home, but the murders would never be solved. Many weeks had passed since the last one, of Fiorello the cook, and a certain calm had returned to the island. Though she continued to monitor Orson Pitt's movements and tried to get a glimpse of Grant's truck, a part of her said it was useless. Whoever was killing prisoners was most likely long gone, in a distant state perhaps, and seeking out other victims. There'd be no memorial for the dead Italians, not a single remnant of their camp. Only tales told to children around beach fires, spun with their marshmallows and weenies.

Nothing had happened and nothing would, Mary Beth assured herself as she sipped her Postum and wrapped herself in chenille. Outside, in front of the lodge, she took comfort in the plangent splash of breakers and in the stars overhead, stuck in the sky like pushpins. No bombers pierced the horizon or destroyers slit the sea. And for a moment she found some peace. But only for a moment.

Glancing in the direction of town, she saw a ghostly pink light flickering, licking the underside of the night. A strident cry reached her through the darkness, the wail of a distant siren.

*   *   *

Most of McQueen's was consumed by the time she got there. Bob Culliver in his turnout coat and leatherhead, his ancient fire truck laboring, hosed mightily, but without effect. The thick birch walls, while superb at suppressing the sound of moans and bouncing bedsprings, were simply no match for the flames. They devoured the first floor then fed on the second, the shingles glowing like hotplates. All Mary Beth could do was join with the rest of the townspeople, many in robes and nightshirts, and watch as the century-old boarding house collapsed.

Mary Beth's mind was racing. Was this Orson's revenge on Abigail? Did he strangle or bludgeon her before setting the establishment ablaze? If a little charred body was found inside, she wouldn't be the slightest astonished.

Just before dawn, Culliver stumbled out of the smoking wreck with a face that was equally ashen. Mary Beth didn't have to ask, only turned and suggested that someone go and wake up Doc Cunningham.

He arrived, groggy, frayed cuffs unbuttoned, an unlit Chesterfield on his lip. "This couldn't wait until morning?" he snarled. "The dead aren't going anywhere."

Culliver led him through the debris, to a place behind some charcoaled beams. Mary Beth chose to stay outside—she'd already seen one stiff too many—but didn't have to wait long before Cunningham emerged and limped toward her.

"Chalk up another," he said. "What's this make, five? Six?"

"Was it quick?"

"Quite, to tell from the hole in the back of the skull. That and the smell of gas."

Mary Beth looked stumped.

"It's everywhere, on the floorboards, in the soot. The deceased, it seems, was soaked in it."

"That poor, poor girl," she cried, but Cunningham merely struck a match. Holding it to the end of his cigarette illuminated his face.

The stained teeth and sallow skin, the hair thin and lifeless—a veritable death mask, all except for the smile.

"What could possibly be funny, Horace?"

"The corpse might indeed be poor, Mary Beth," he said. "But with the body of a bull and the wrong set of genitalia, I highly doubt it's a girl."

*   *   *

Though Abigail Pitt was not the body in the embers, Mary Beth was hardly shocked when she disappeared. One of the fishermen reported seeing her early that morning boarding the ferry, and another claimed she'd gotten hold of a motorized skiff and puttered off westward toward the coast. In both accounts, though, she was not alone but accompanied by a man whose name was unknown but whose handsome face seemed familiar. It belonged to one of the Italian prisoners, though he was no longer wearing his uniform. Dressed in an oversized suit that probably belonged to Orson, the man looked no different from the many veterans who returned from the war twenty pounds thinner and swam in their old civilian clothes. Strolling arm in arm, he and Abigail surely made quite the couple.

Mary Beth considered calling the Boston police, sending out an all-points alert. But back at the station, her cheeks and hands still blackened, she admitted it was probably too late. The culprits would be far inland already, avoiding major terminals, and quietly blending in. Soon, with peace restored, millions of people would once again be traveling. Nobody would notice a porcelain figurine of a woman and her taciturn husband moving into their modest new ranch house somewhere in the South or Midwest.

No use chasing them, she silently concluded, reluctant to admit the other reason for her inaction. Abigail had no choice. Remaining in Fourth Cliff with Orson nearby was a veritable death sentence, and fleeing him, especially with an escaped prisoner in tow, was futile. In her place, Mary Beth wondered, mightn't she'd have done the same?

Now, with Orson eliminated, there remained only one last principal suspect, Grant. All she had to do was return to the shipyard, check out the tires on his Bantam, and arrest him for multiple murders. All she had to do was to bring him to justice and declare the case closed. And she would do it, too, Mary Beth swore, once she mustered the energy.

All she felt, though, was exhaustion. A cumulative fatigue that built up ever since Archie left and, over the course of the past year, skyrocketed. Suddenly, they all weighed on her—the drowned and the stabbed, the dismembered, poisoned, and burnt—together with the backbiting of an entire island. *I need a vacation*, Mary Beth realized, someplace exotic or, better yet, anyplace dull. *But first I need sleep*, a deep and dreamless slumber.

Laying her head on the green blotter, that wish, at least, she got.

18.

She awoke to what sounded like a pistol shot. Her head jerked up from the desk, so fast it cramped her neck, and Mary Beth, whose father punished her for saying dang, let out a rare obscenity. But a coarser word, if she knew one, would have been flung when she noticed the broom handle rapping against the station's door.

"Go away!"

"But Mary Beth…"

"I said get out of here! Scram!"

Yet Paolo remained, in his streetsweeper's uniform and cap, streaming with sweat but nevertheless looking dignified.

"You have to come, Mary Beth."

"I don't have to do squat. And especially not for you."

"Not for me, Mary Beth." His broom at present arms, Paolo brought his heels together. "For my men. For justice."

"Justice," she spat, like another expletive. Still, groaning, she pushed herself up from her desk and managed to retrieve her hat. "Justice," she grunted several times more as she followed Paolo out of the station and headed toward the coupe.

"Really?" she snarled when he went to retrieve his borrowed bicycle. "Just get in and shut up."

They drove silently, never exchanging a word as the town faded behind them and the end of the island loomed. Well before reaching it, though, Mary Beth braked before a crowd of cheering prisoners. Though they mostly obscured her view, she thought she could see several men cowering between them, sobbing and shielding their heads.

To Paolo, she said, "Mind telling me what's going on?"

"The war is over. Our war. Mussolini is dead. Hung up by his feet and shot."

"So this is a celebration?"

"No," Paolo sighed. "Revenge."

The throng parted just long enough to give her a better view. That's when she saw it—the blood flowing from gruffly shaved scalps, the boiling hull pitch being slathered on them. Ripped-open pillowcases wagged in the air and clouds of goose feathers billowed.

"Fascists. The last of them. And these men want them to pay."

"So let them pay."

Paolo glared at her with a mixture of pity and shock. "They deserve it, yes, but this is no way to act. Not if my country is to heal itself. Not if we'll ever again be whole."

"And you expect me to…?"

"Stop them."

"Stop them how?" she asked.

His eyes lowered from her face to her duty belt, to the Colt holstered on her hip.

"No dice," Mary Beth said.

"Yes, dice. And I need you to roll them. Now."

What power did this man have over her, Mary Beth wondered, even as she slid out of the car. What combination of charisma and imperiousness had her approaching the mob with a hand on her pistol and shouting, "That'll do! Everybody back off!"

But they didn't back off. Instead, they merely seethed at her with their faces half-masked in feathers and their paintbrushes dripping tar. The only sound came from the victims, cringing and pressing their hands in prayer, begging her, "Avere pietà. Per favore. Avere pietà."

"That's it, I said. Back to the huts, all of you!"

She searched the crowd for anybody she recognized. But there was no one she knew by name or who even looked familiar. *If only Lorenzo were here*, she thought. *He would talk some sense into them.*

"Last chance! I mean it!" Her fingers closed on the pistol grip.

Paolo translated for her. The only reply was spits and curses. Suddenly, there was no other option. In a motion so fluid it surprised even her, Mary Beth drew out her revolver, pointed it skyward, and fired.

The report seemed to echo forever, rolling across Fourth Cliff. It faded, finally, and the only sounds were fascists still blubbering, "Per favore. Avere pietà."

Then, one by one, the prisoners peeled off and retreated to the camp. Soon, only the tar-singed men remained on the road, together with Mary Beth and Paolo.

"Tell them to head into town," she instructed him. "Find Doc Cunningham's office, right over the diner. He can patch them up."

Paolo did as he was told, and in English added, "Thank you."

"Don't thank me for anything," she snapped. "Just get your bunch of knuckleheads out of here. The minute the war's really over, go. Back to your boot or whatever it is you call your country. Out of my hair."

From soft with gratitude, his expression turned rock-like. "I assure you, Captain Swann, my men and I will leave this place as soon as humanly possible." Now he did click his heels and bowed. "And as for troubling your hair, please accept my apology."

She could have spit at him, slapped him and punched him and

maybe even shot him, but at the same time embraced him and kissed him again, this time without stopping. She was tired and frazzled, heartbroken and dazed. She needed to get back into her coupe and back to the station and the safety of her black ash desk.

Mary Beth threw herself inside the car and leaned out to slam the door. But another commotion stopped her. Not a sob this time, but a yawl such as she'd never heard. Frogs again in the cranberry bogs? Flocks of returning geese? No, she realized, these were human sounds, or just barely. The caterwaul of mourning men.

*   *   *

Designed for machine guns and searchlights, the four towers— one at each corner of the camp—were foreboding. Or at least they looked that way. In reality, none had ever been manned, much less armed, but rather stood like unused altars, relics of a religion in which no one any longer believed. High and surrounded by rusted wire, the structures were scarcely easy to access. A person would have to be determined enough to cut through the fence and get up the ladder that was missing some steps and climb through the dust and guano. A person would have to be strong—immensely so—to make that journey carrying another individual, who no doubt resisted fiercely. And a person would have to be bestially ill to put a noose around that individual's neck, tighten it, and cast him off the top.

Mary Beth, Paolo, and dozens of weeping prisoners gathered at the tower's base. The victim's shadow swept over them, stirred by a midmorning breeze. A minute or more passed before she finally removed her cap, lowered her head, and implored, "For God's sake, will somebody cut him down?"

This, too, wasn't easy. It took five men clambering and another five positioned underneath to sever the rope and delicately lower its load. Though short of stature and more bone than skin, the former quarryman was hefty. His body hit the ground with a thud. Next to the lifeless Lorenzo, Mary Beth knelt and lifted his icy hand. How could she have suspected him, this warm, lively man who wanted only to help? How could she have abandoned him to this horrific death?

Her rage soared. Looking into Lorenzo's bulging eyes, at the terror still frozen there, at the blue of his cheeks and swell of his tongue, she felt something inside her torquing. And inspecting the crime scene, observing the crosshatched footprints around the base of the tower and the bars-and-stripes tread marks beyond the fence, that something finally snapped.

"Grant," she murmured. "Grant," she growled and strode fuming past Paolo toward the coupe.

"Where are you going?" he called after her.

Mary Beth didn't turn. "To end this craziness once and for all."

*   *   *

She wouldn't remember driving there. The road was a blur to her, the moors on either side of it invisible. She wouldn't recall the cranberry bogs or the abandoned skiffs, the boarded-up summer homes or even the Flotsam Bar, only the spear of the car's speedometer jittering past ninety. Swerving, her tires made a sound like a flock of hungry gulls.

This time, she didn't brake but charged straight through the puddles, splattering mud and oil all over the freshly scraped hulls, and nearly ramming the Bantam. She flung open the door and propelled herself out, only to collide head on with Grant.

"Captain," he gasped, "Swann," the wind knocked out of him. "What…"

She tugged down her jacket and gripped the Colt handle and, mustering the remains of her breath, announced, "You're under arrest for murder."

"Murder? Me?" He swept off his woolen hat and mangled it between his hands.

"Of four Italian prisoners of war. Francesco Albertini, Antonio De Luca, Flavio…"

His child-like face suddenly looked terror-frozen, his gentle demeanor hard. "Stop it, Captain Swann," he seemed to order her, even as he added, "Please."

She tried to complete the list of the dead, to unhitch the handcuffs from her duty belt, but just then Grant bent over. A defouling rake lay near his feet, and she thought he was reaching for it, would bring it down on her with the force he had already used to kill. The gun was halfway out of her holster when the former pilot doubled over and screamed.

"We're hit! We're hit! We're going down!"

"Knock that off. Grant," she shouted, but he kept on howling, louder now.

"Mayday! Mayday!" His eyes rolled upward, his mouth bubbling with foam.

"Help!" Mary Beth heard herself call. "Somebody!" She took hold of his shoulders and tried to steady him, but he simply sank to her feet. Helplessly, she looked down at him, at the shocks of blond hair brushing her shoes, at the top of his head which bore no sign, not even a scab, from the blow of Paolo's broom handle.

"What in darnation is going on here!"

Glancing up from Grant, Mary Beth saw Old Man Gainor storming toward her. She had never stood so close to him and was surprised at his dimensions—tall, wide, compact beneath the bulk of his fisherman's sweater. His face looked sea-lashed; his hoary beard spumed.

"How dare you," he spat at her and shoved her away from Grant. "Hasn't he seen enough, suffered enough, without putting up with your poppycock?"

Mary Beth didn't answer. She merely stepped away until she backed up against the Bantam.

"It's all right, Grant," his great-uncle tried comforting him. "You're safe now." He glared at her. His urchin eyes seemed spined. "That's it, Swann. Your gangster friend's gone and you're through."

She gazed down at the bronze-star shield on her jacket and began to unpin it. While fumbling with the clasp, though, she also caught sight of the Bantam's rear tire. The tread was indeed distinctive, scored with deep horizontal bars. But they did not alternate and weren't linked by vertical stripes. The tracks she traced beside the cranberry bog where Antonio died, the marks she found not far from the tower and Lorenzo, must have belonged to some other vehicle. She'd put a man through hell for a question she could have solved with a little detective work.

"Take it," she said, tossing her badge in the dirt at Gainor's feet. The keys to the Mercury as well. "I don't deserve them anyway."

19.

Once a year, in honor of the first week of May, Pascal made his bouillabaisse. In addition to celery, onions, carrots, many tomatoes, and fennel, this contained a summary of the island's catches—scallops, clams, lobster, and fish. From a velvet pouch that he kept under lock and key, he added a pinch of saffron. The locals loved it, lining up at all hours, even breakfast, for a steaming portion of stew. Its aroma wafted across the docks, some said the entire town. A melee of flavors, a pandemonium of scents, enveloped all of Fourth Cliff.

But Mary Beth couldn't touch it. Rising to the surface, the ingredients reminded her of something painful, as if, rather than seafood, the bouillabaisse bobbed with the dead.

Fishermen came and ate, wiped their beards and donned their sou'westers, without so much as glancing at her. No one called her Black Bass. No one had to. Everyone knew she had failed. The Boston bigshot, the presumptuous snot who'd put on airs and her husband's insignia and may even have taken a foreigner to her bed, was defrocked. Pilloried in the way that Fourth Cliff's Puritan founders would have appreciated, her reputation, if not her head, placed in stocks.

Instead of Mary Beth or even the latest murder, conversation focused on the news from Europe, with Hitler's death only yesterday and Germany's surrender expected in a week. The word from the Pacific was less encouraging as American troops battled across yet another island, Okinawa. Its name all but eclipsed Iwo Jima and the thousands who'd fallen or gone missing there.

"Just one sip," Officer Hogan beseeched her. "It'll do you good, Captain."

"No, thank you, Lemuel. And please stop calling me Captain."

"Yes, ma'am. Captain."

She looked up at him, at the comically crossed eyes and bucked teeth. She saw his eyes, empty of everything except goodness.

"Don't worry about me, Lemuel. I'm fine."

"Yes, Captain."

He stood and did his best to salute and about-face. Mary Beth caught him by the back of his belt, turned him around, and adjusted his tie. She tightened his shoulder strap and straightened his high-peaked hat that hadn't been popular in decades. His holster seemed secure enough, along with the pistol he probably had no idea how to fire.

"There," she said. "You're in command now, Corporal Hogan. Do the police force proud."

He stiffened, he beamed, and once more before exiting, proclaimed, "Yes, ma'am, Captain Swann!"

Nobody else disturbed her. Only toward dusk did Doc Cunningham come down from his second-floor office, pull up a chair, and join her.

"Mumbo-jumbo's not to your taste, I see. You and me both." He leaned across the table with an anaemic smile. The stench of stale cigarettes wilted the soup's bouquet.

Mary Beth said nothing but watched as a lady crab claw rose groping to the bouillabaisse's surface.

Cunningham nevertheless went on. "I see you've gone civvie," he said, and pointed at the polo shirt she wore beneath her leather jacket, her work jeans and penny loafers.

Trudy came by, back bent and amicably homely, offering the doctor a mug. He shooed her away and waved off Pascal as well, who, in turn, flashed him a missing finger. Cunningham ignored him and turned once more to Mary Beth.

"Had a look at the Italian's body. Before they buried him, of course. Whatshisname."

She finally looked up. The smile was gone from Cunningham's face, though his cheeks and teeth remained sallow. "Lorenzo," she said.

"Lorenzo, yes. He was hanged, as you know. But before that he was stabbed."

"Stabbed?"

"In the spine. So there wasn't much blood."

Her expression was utterly dazed.

"A two-edged blade, about seven inches. Same as the one that did in that Antonio fellow, I expect. The same hilt bruise around the wound. And between the shoulder blades, the same four little holes."

She nodded.

"Made by some sharp, heavy object. A rake, I thought."

Mary Beth thought of Grant. "No, not a rake. Something else…"

"Well, whatever it was, it paralyzed that poor chap. He didn't climb up that tower, I'd wager. He was hauled."

"Hauled…By someone very strong."

"I'd say," Doc Cunningham replied and laughed morbidly. "A body builder."

Who would fit that description, Mary Beth wondered. Bill Hall or John Devereux? Another prisoner, perhaps, or even one of the GIs—Lieutenant Colburn, his way of finally getting into the war? She imagined him stabbing Lorenzo with his bayonet and clambering up with the body, looping a rope around its neck, and hurling it from the top.

Cunningham lit up a Chesterfield and exhaled a tower of his own. "That was it for me, Swann," he said.

Mary Beth, befuddled, blinked at him.

"One cadaver too many. I might have well been overseas, what with all the death I've seen around here. Time to say goodbye to Fourth Cliff." His voice, usually high, sounded strained, worn out.

"But where will you go?"

"Anywhere. Back to Newport, perhaps. Lawyers be damned." He offered her a cigarette. "And you?"

She declined. No longer gazing at her bouillabaisse or even at Cunningham, she stared at the dun-colored wall, empty except for the spindle-shaped knife slit she pictured projected there, the bruise of a hilt, and four little holes left by a weapon the likes of which she'd never before encountered.

✳   ✳   ✳

"Give it a break," Minnie said to her, but Mary Beth kept scribbling. On strips torn from the Barnstable Patriot, on empty liquor bills, and the back of her napkin, she doodled with her pencil again and again. Four round dots, filled in and evenly spaced.

"What could've made them?" she asked, though not necessarily of Minnie. "What poker?"

"No poker. They're too evenly spaced. More like brass knuckles. With tips." Minnie topped off her whiskey glass, lit a Viceroy, and sighed. "Enough, Mary Beth. You're making yourself bonkers."

"A spool of some kind. A sprocket."

"What difference does it make now? You're off the case. Off this crummy island soon, too, I bet." She lowered her face to where Mary Beth pored over her drawings, placed a pudgy finger under her chin and lifted. "Drink your booze. Smoke 'em if you got 'em."

"They're too perfect. Too…what's the word?"

"Symmetrical?"

"Yeah. They had to be made by a tool."

"Speaking of tools, why don't you take up gardening? Open a store or something. Doodads, whatnots. Anything but tackle."

"If I could've figured this out, I could've figured out everything."

"And if I was Greta Garbo, you could have been Katharine Hepburn." Minnie practically neighed. "I might have had you."

But Mary Beth didn't react. Since forfeiting her badge and the coupe a week ago, she'd wandered Fourth Cliff on foot, pacing the road she used to wend in her coupe, eyes sharp for any missed clues. Clearly, she had become obsessed, but that was better than confronting the reality of her dismissal, her failure to find the murderer, and Archie's missing-in-action. Leave, she told herself, reinvent yourself somewhere else.

And yet, for reasons inscrutable even to her, Mary Beth stayed.

"A spool," she said. "A sprocket, a hilt, and a knife."

"A vacation. A breather. A life." Minnie's hand again found Mary Beth's wrist. "Hang it up, sister. Go home."

Home? Mary Beth gaped at her as if she'd never heard the word. She swiveled off her stool and drifted toward the door.

"And button up," Minnie called after her. "They say there's a storm coming in."

*   *   *

A late-season nor'easter was indeed brewing, so the Coast Guard warned. But the people of Fourth Cliff simply ignored the forecast. Fishermen, dockworkers, merchants, and their wives—all came streaming toward the center of town. Reverend Miller and Viola emerged from the church, arm in arm, and Pascal held Trudy's hand. They crowded, they cheered and passed around bottles. Some went so far as to hug. Most unusual was Alva Fitch, in a threadbare gingham dress, warbling and dancing and even leaping on the stone inscribed with her lost loved ones' names. They celebrated under a roiling dark sky as Mary Beth Swann approached.

She knew perfectly well what was happening. The air had buzzed with it for several days now, as electrified as the tempest drawing near. The surrender of Nazi Germany. Mary Beth watched but didn't join in, stood apart even as others ran past her cheering. She scarcely reacted when suddenly the Italians appeared, clamoring and chanting, "È finite! Grazie Dio! È finite!" She observed, amazed, as the prisoners of a war that was finally over embraced their former captors and whirled. Somebody shot off a flare.

"Not joining in?" Doc Cunningham asked her.

"Get happy," Minnie Beaudet exhorted her. "It's peacetime."

But Mary Beth couldn't join them. Like Bill and Sarah Hall, whose son, Christopher, would not be coming home, she could not bring herself to rejoice. She could not forget the possibility that Archie would never return, not even after the Japanese surrendered. Nor could she escape the sense that somewhere among the celebrants, between the townspeople and the POWs, was a killer with the blood of four people on his hands. Somewhere there was a murderer who was reveling not just in the end of the war but in her ultimate failure to find him.

Fishing boats blasted their fog horns and the church bells reeled on their gudgeons. A string of firecrackers popped. Mary Beth turned and began climbing up the bluff, curious as to why some had not shown up, Lemuel Hogan, for one, and the soldiers from the emplacement. Most likely they were off getting blitzed on victory booze—which was a good thing, she thought. Who knew what a soused-up Falcone would've done, seeing all these liberated prisoners?

But Hogan and the soldiers weren't the only ones missing. Paolo was nowhere in sight. *Figures*, she said to herself. The killjoy preferred to stay alone in the camp.

Panting, Mary Beth trudged toward the intersection. Thunder was already rolling in from the sea, great unfolding peals of it, and another booming sound. The surf? No, too percussive, she thought, too sharp. Then, peering northward, she saw them: searing silver spangles, two every minute or so, backlighting the clouds. And she knew. Someone was firing the cannon.

*   *   *

Wind, like a riptide, rose. From a preternatural calm, a chilling breeze whipped the bangs from her forehead and slapped the lapels of her jacket, and within moments grew to a squall. Behind her, in town, the revelers scattered. Waves washed over docks, pitching the boats like bouncing balls in the matinee cartoon singalongs. Nighttime blew in before sundown.

Nearing the intersection, Mary Beth saw a pair of headlights closing in fast from the north. They didn't swing toward town but kept speeding, but to where? The only sites south were the police station, now manned by Hogan, and the lighthouse and the lodge.

She had to hurry there herself, before the downpour started. Bad enough being buffeted, worse getting drenched. And dangerous, the steeple above her already making ominous squeaking sounds and even seeming to sway. Though never much of a sprinter, she ran, loafers flopping, leaning into the squall.

Overhead, the first streak of lightning splayed. Mary Beth smelled it—a tart electrical scent—and felt it tingle her fingertips. The thunder pounded and the cannon boomed and yet somehow, through the clamor, she heard someone call out her name. She turned and squinted and made out a uniformed figure, hunched over, hatless, a receding hairline retreating in the gusts.

"Captain Swann!"

"Not captain anymore, Sergeant Perl, just Swann."

He was dressed for combat, complete with Sam Browne belt, bayonet, and sidearm. Water streamed from his helmet. But for once he didn't smile.

"You've got to help us, Captain," he hollered. "He's going to do it!"

"Who? Do what?"

"Colburn. The lieutenant. He's firing off six-inch shells!"

"He's happy," she shouted back at him. "He's free."

"Not happy, insane! He thinks we're under attack!"

"But the war's over...."

He put his face close to hers, his voice a rasp. "He says he'll die defending the bunker. Says he'll blow it up if he has to."

"And where are your men?"

"Gone. Ran off."

"Then call for help."

"Can't. The cable is down. Falcone drove off to fix it."

Mary Beth apologized as loud as she could. "Sorry, Sergeant. I'm out of action."

She left him on the road and resumed her jog, still trying to beat out the rain. But passing the road to the station, Mary Beth paused and cursed. "Goddamn you," she grunted, meaning herself, and detoured.

The station was already wobbling when she reached it, threatening to collapse or take flight. The door with the name CAPTAIN SWANN stenciled on it swung half-hinged. Inside, the ship wheel and whaler's portrait had fallen from the wall. Only the map remained hanging, just barely. The fan and the file cabinets rattled. Mary Beth sat behind the desk which was too heavy to budge, much less blow away, and tried to dial the phone. But the line was dead, just like

Perl reported, and the Philco broadcast only static. The two-way Motorola seemed to be working still, but who would possibly answer?

Nevertheless, "Calling all stations," she started to say. "Come in." She repeated it several times, receiving only static.

In theory, at least, Hogan now had the coupe, but he wouldn't have slightest notion how to drive it. Most likely, it was still at the shipyard, its bumper still pinned against the Bantam. No one would hear her distress signal. Still, she pressed down the lever and sent, "All stations, this is the Fourth Cliff police. This is an emergency. Over."

Silence. *How stupid*, she thought, as the ceiling began to creak. She had to get out of there now. But then, while hurrying toward the door, she heard someone calling her again.

"Mary Beth? Is that you?"

She practically dove at the Motorola, gripped it in her hands and, without thinking, cried, "Archie?"

"No, sorry," came the reply. "It's Grant."

"Grant. Grant," she echoed and tried to sound relieved. "Grant, listen to me. There's a situation out at the emplacement. Lieutenant Colburn. Somebody's liable to get hurt. Do you read me, Grant? Over."

But instead of a "roger," what she heard was a cuss. "You have no business being on this radio, Mary Beth. No business in the station." Old Man Gainor had pushed Grant aside and was barking at her. "Get it through your head, you're fired."

"And you're an old fool!" she snapped back at him. "You don't give a damn about this island!"

Slamming down the receiver, Mary Beth fled the station just as its roof gave in, folded loudly, and flew off. Bent against the gale, she hustled back to the road and continued south until she reached the trail to her home. The first drops of rain were falling. Not drops, really, but dollops, wind-lashed and flying sideways. There was no way she wouldn't get soaked. And no way the potholes wouldn't turn to quagmires, each one a loafer-sucking pit.

In seconds, the ground beneath her turned soupy, but not before she noticed some tracks. Three of them, two going in and one heading out again. A smooth thin line of bicycle treads and beside them the marks of a much larger vehicle. Alternating bars linked by vertical strips.

*   *   *

She was dripping by the time she reached the lodge. Hogan's bicycle was indeed parked where he peddled up, no doubt *brriinging* with the news of Colburn's rampage. Inside, the power was out, and it took a bolt of lightning to show that everything was in order—the armoire, the knickknacks. All except for the mantle. There were no more hydrangeas there, of course, and no fleur-de-lis of shells, but something else. Another streak revealed it: Hogan's high-peaked hat. And on the floor, a stippled line of blood.

She followed it out into the deluge. Wherever the trail led was long washed away, and there was no way of knowing who'd left it. She squinted and only belatedly thought to look up at the top of the lighthouse. Someone had lit her hurricane lamp.

Blackness encased the bottom of the stairway, but she knew each spiral by heart. Ascending, she came into the light and saw, once again, bloodstains. They were thicker now, puddled, and beyond them lay the mirror shattered, the gramophone bashed, the telescope with its legs in the air. Scattered around was evidence from her link chart—the sprig and the rubbing, Viola's note and the fascist ring—together with the photos of Francesco's family and of Archie in his various uniforms. Shreds of the Red Sox schedule blended with those of the map of the South Pacific. Pushpins littered the floor. And spread across the mattress, face up, the body of Lemuel Hogan.

Mary Beth dropped to her knees. "Oh, no," she cried, and continued sobbing even as she held up the lamp. His tie was still knotted as though she had just tightened it and his shoulder strap straight. Hogan looked much as he always did, except for the puncture wound, spindle-shaped and tapered, beneath his slackened jaw, and, in his forehead, four evenly-spaced holes.

"Oh, Lemuel," she wept and laid his arms straight at his side.

That's when she saw it. An M-1 Garand rifle, with blood on its stock and a bullet hole where the trigger used to be. It took her some seconds to make sense of it all. To find the pistol which had been knocked out of his hand and come to rest on the plinth. To flip open its barrel and see to her shock that one of the chambers was empty.

20.

Rain rang heavy on the shed's tin roof and weighed down the tarp, but Mary Beth flung it off effortlessly. Far in the back, from the old KC Baking Powder can, she extracted the key. She wasn't thinking, only moving, remembering how to retract the side stand and twist the ignition lock all the way to the right, which also turned on the headlights. To disengage the clutch and shift into low gear, to give it a little gas, and explode.

That's what it felt like, revving off into the night on Archie's motorcycle. Her hair plastered back, clothes sopping, and shivers drilling her body. Mary Beth felt none of it. She was deaf to the thunder and blind to the lightning. Her only awareness was of the engine's deep throaty roar, the motor racing between her legs and the wheels propelling her over potholes and patches of moraine. She felt at its mercy at first, fearful it would ditch her or send her plummeting over the handlebars. But then she remembered how Archie had mastered the machine, imagined herself acting as he would, and slowly gained control. By the time it reached the road, the Harley had become Mary Beth's servant. An angry, all-powerful steed.

She knew who she was chasing. A killer in a vehicle with all-terrain tires and a man without his military rifle but a bullet wound in his hand. But where to find him, in this maelstrom?

Regaining the road, Mary Beth swerved the bike northward, in the direction of town. All was darkness there, unbroken except for the lightning. She swung around in the opposite direction. There, too, fog and torrent enveloped the island's tip. Yet, for a moment, the gloom was pierced by twin shafts of light. Two quivering cones moving not toward but away from her, bounding south.

Wasn't that what Alva had warned her, *Watch out for the last cliff?* There was still time to heed her, Mary Beth thought. She tore as the nor'easter intensified, the wind screaming, the rain now laced with ice. Storm-boiled, the ocean rose and buckled, engulfed the shore and flooded parts of the road. She watched incredulously as a ten-foot wave came rolling up and broke across the pavement, depositing a skiff whose hull would rot and grow skeletal. Years later, people would wonder what unearthly quirk of nature had dropped it there.

Mary Beth didn't falter. Her face stinging with sleet, she tore to the point where the pavement ended. Beyond that was no path, no trail or even a crosscut, only marshland impenetrable to cars. But if all-terrain tires could traverse it, mightn't also a motorcycle's? Releasing the handbrake, kicking the clutch, and thrusting into high gear, Mary Beth gunned.

Into the swamp she splashed, grounding through the muck. Slime and rushes clung to her cheeks and clotted her eyes as she wrestled with the gyrating handlebars. The rain had softened to a piercing drizzle and the lightning had dwindled to faint flashes, but through it all she could still see the headlights intermittently bouncing. They stopped, finally, and disappeared, but closing in with her own high beams, Mary Beth saw what she'd already suspected: a helmeted soldier in a jeep.

Clearly, he had run out of island. There was nowhere to go but down forty feet onto jagged stones. This was the cliff that generations of sailors feared, but which also served as their landmark. The precipice, by all accounts the fourth, that had given the island its name.

Mary Beth killed the motor. A strange silence ensued, broken only by the smash of surf and the retreating thuds of thunder. Even the cannon had stopped firing. She kept her headlights on high and aimed at the soldier as he climbed out of the jeep and approached her, blinking. He tried to shield his one good eye, but there was no camouflaging the drooping one. One by one, they were illuminated: the narrow brow and knobby features, the chest and arms too thick for his uniform. The blood trickling from his fingertips.

"An accident?" Mary Beth spoke first, surprising herself.

"Cable snapped," he calmly explained and held up a gory palm. "Good thing it was only my hand."

"Good thing and how," she said. "And where's your weapon?"

"Gone," he admitted, "with the wind," but added with a laugh, "but who needs a rifle when I've got this." From his belt, he unsheathed a glimmering bayonet. A seven-inch, double-edged blade, a hilt, and a brass knuckle handle, and topping each finger hole, a dart. "A Mark 1 trench knife," he vaunted. "Ain't nothing like it."

In the grainy light, she could see something bulging in the back of the jeep, oddly shaped and blanketed.

"And what's that you got in there?"

"Tools," he responded, still matter of fact. "Extra wire." The communication lines to the emplacement were down, he explained, and he had to find the breakpoint fast. "Lieutenant Colburn's locked himself in the ammo bunker. God knows what he'll do. He's crackers."

"A real doozy base," she humored him.

Private Falcone smiled. "Doozy *bots*."

"And I guess that makes me the strunz."

"Hell no. I think you're one fine dame. I even left you some things, at home when you weren't there. Little stuff, just to show you."

"You showed me all right. That night in the parking lot."

He stopped, glowered, growled. "And you were enjoying it, too, weren't you? Until your lover boy showed up."

He started to turn back toward the jeep and the bundle that had strangely begun to stir. Mary Beth saw it and yet she could not take her eyes off the knife. Its blade would have left a wide spindled wound, tapered at the ends, and a bruise where the hilt hit the skin. The darts could have punched four even holes.

Swinging off the Harley, Mary Beth drew her Colt.

"Freeze, Falcone. You're under arrest."

But Falcone kept sauntering to his jeep. "Now, Mary Beth."

"Don't call me that," she ordered him. "Don't say anything." She released the safety. "Just put your hands in the air."

"Will do, Mary Beth, but first you'd better see this."

With a violent sweep, he whisked the blanket from the rear of the jeep and hauled up what lay beneath it. A person, uniformed, half-conscious and bloodied, not quite able to stand but lifted by the scruff to his feet. With Falcone's arm wrapped around his neck, his head lolled forward, hiding his face behind a black curtain of hair, and then side to side, exposing first a bat ear, a foxy nose, a moustache. Mary Beth gasped. Paolo.

"Found him on the road, all alone. Didn't want to celebrate their victory."

"Victory?" Mary Beth fought to restrain herself, to keep her pistol level. "I got news for you, buddy, they lost."

"That's what you think. You who didn't have to put up with being called a guinea, a wop, a dago all your life. Who didn't have to fight micks like you who blamed all your shit on us. And just when we were getting somewhere, these fascists showed up and ruined it." His lock on Paolo's throat tightened. "Because of them, you cops came and stole my family. Because of them, my mama died."

"Let him go, Falcone."

"Now they get to go back home like heroes while we get left with their crap." With his other hand, Falcone reached for his knife. "But some of 'em ain't going home. Not if it's up to me."

"Put it down." The revolver aimed higher, directly at Falcone's head. "Release him."

"Why? Because you're a khaki wacky and this bum's your boo?" He stepped away from her, dragging Paolo behind the jeep and right up to the cliff edge. "Some drop," he said, peering over.

"Last chance." Nine of her fingers encased the grip while a tenth curled steadily on the trigger. Here was not one of Archie's targets but a real human being—two of them, in fact, one of whom she could shoot by mistake or send them both plummeting. For a moment she pictured Paolo dashed on the rocks, shattered, sucked out to sea. She thought of all the mistakes she could conceivably make—that she'd already made—in the darkness and the rain and the uncertainty. And yet the gun remained stationary. The sights on its barrel didn't quiver, not even when Paolo groaned and blinked at her.

"Do it," he hissed. "Shoot." But a jerk of Falcone's arm silenced him.

"Forget about it, *jamoke*," he growled as he pushed the knife tip into Paolo's skin "A police captain," he snorted as the blood began to spurt. "Don't make me laugh," he snickered. His droopy lid seemed to dance.

Whatever sounds followed—the report, the gasp, the crack of bone on rocks below—were instantly squelched by a louder eruption. The earth shook and the sky combusted, or so it seemed to Mary Beth. As if all those years of war, the incalculable suffering, were condensed into one cataclysmic blast on the island's southern end. An inferno of ignited ammunition.

Epilogue: October, 1945

Just after daybreak, the Mercury coupe cruised through the town. It coasted in front of the stores that were still closed at this hour and the diner that wasn't. Inside, for the first time in years, Trudy was serving eggs that were no longer powdered and mugs of genuine joe. The aromas wafted seductively up to the second floor, though Doc Cunningham wasn't there to relish them. His office sat abandoned, empty except for the old examining table, the rusted sink, and the barren cabinets—that and a whiff of stale Chesterfields. A stench that not even Pascal's cooking could purge.

The docks, meanwhile, were teeming. Stevedores and fishermen, mongers, packers, and buyers all bustled. A month before, the Japanese had surrendered, giving in after two atomic blasts so bright that some of the local sailors claimed to have seen the glow. But now there was a nation to feed, a generation that returned hungry from afar and eager to produce hungrier mouths still.

The workers hardly paused for a smoke but ceased as the patrol car rolled by. They stood, ivy caps and helmet liners clutched in both hands. No one hissed or whispered the words Black Bass. No one grimaced. They merely watched stiff and silent as the old streetlamps while the coup made its usual loop around the memorial stone and began its uphill ascent.

It rose toward the intersection where the church spire also seemed to stand at attention, and from there, the coupe turned north. Past the shipyard, which Old Man Gainor announced was shutting down now that most of the boat-wrighting business had moved to the coast and Grant was transferred to a Minnesota facility. Past the Flotsam Bar, where the neon Schlitz had long stopped sputtering and the door was sealed with a handwritten FOR SALE sign.

"Time to amscray," Minnie Beaudet had told her. "Find me some zoot-suited crooner or, better yet, some Rosie the Riveter freshly out of a job. New York, Chicago, maybe even LA—anywhere but the Maritime and this rock."

She placed one of the rickety chairs atop a wobbly table and removed the dartboard from the wall. Holding it shield-like to her chest, Minnie whispered, "Come with me."

But Mary Beth merely shook her head. "My place is here now, Minnie. For better or worse. Here I'll serve and here I'll wait."

"For him."

"Yes, for him."

They stood there a moment, in the dark empty bar still smacking of beer, until finally Minnie smiled. "Dagnabbit, girl, I'm going to miss you," she wept and gave Mary Beth a parting squeeze.

Back in the Mercury, Mary Beth motored. She rolled across the hardscrabble landscape, past the faux rustic houses that were now reopened and the new ones being built next door. And though the skeletons of hulls remained by the road, someone had whitewashed them for the tourists. The moors were ablaze with seaside goldenrod, and ripened cranberries glittered crimson in the bogs. Ahead spread the camp, now deserted and soon to be demolished—so it was said— for a golf course. But the towers still loomed as reminders of those once imprisoned there. Silent witnesses of a war fought far abroad but also right here, at home.

Paolo had been one of the last to leave. He'd spent months re-
cuperating from his wounds, with dart dents in his skull and a knife
scar on his throat, and yet more material for his nightmares. Yet he
never lost his sense of dignity, his manners, and, especially, his patriotism. Which was why, he explained, he had to go back. To rebuild
and remind his people that a nation with so splendorous a past could
still seek an honorable future.

He professed this repeatedly, so often, it seemed, he needed to
convince himself. That while there might be love here, and more—
companionship and mutual respect—he would never fit in. That
somehow he would forever remain a prisoner, if not of war, than of
his emotions, his weakness for a woman who would always be waiting for another.

He knew it that night, with townspeople and his fellow POWs
celebrating, with the nor'easter blowing in, and yet he went in search
of her. The cannon was firing again and again, insanely, at nothing,
and the soldiers had all scattered. Only she could stop it, and perhaps
prevent even more people from getting killed. He searched through
the town and beyond and was about to take the path to her lodge
when Falcone found him.

Big, palsy Falcone, who spoke a bit of Italian and called him pai-
sano and threw his beefy arms around him before bashing him uncon-
scious and stuffing him in the back of the jeep. And Hogan had seen it
all. The poor boy was also looking for his old boss and just happened
to be nearby on his bicycle. He pedaled away as frantically as he could,
Paolo conjectured, to warn her. His heroism cost him his life.

Paolo was gone, Hogan was dead, and the Quonset huts stood
empty. The yard outside was already overgrown with beach grass, in-
terspersed with the purple flowers of the oregano plants. Their aroma
escaped the wire.

More desolate still was the emplacement, its bunkers reduced to shards of reenforced concrete, shattered ammo crates, and a cannon angled precariously down at the sea.

Perl had returned, smiling again, to Brooklyn. He planned to go into the carpet business—"After all this cold," he said, "people are going to want warm floors"—to get married and have three smiling kids. Dabrowski went back to the Pennsylvania mining town and the church where he'd indeed served as an altar boy. A lifetime of confessions would be needed, he told her, to atone for not seeing Falcone for the demon he was and for failing to stop him in time.

Of all the GIs, only Lieutenant Colburn remained—or rather, filaments of him sown among the debris. And his name. It was inscribed on a wall on his old college campus, together with the names of many young men who made the ultimate sacrifice.

The coupe reached the end of the road. Through the scraggly dunes, the Mercury toddled, until it reached the scarf. Below stretched the strand. Still barbed with pebbles and shells, the water too cold even for wading. And yet memories, both soft and torrid, abounded here, together with regrets and resentments and pain.

Recent weeks had seen a half-dozen letters in Mary Beth's mailbox. Postmarks from as far away as Kansas, as close as Scituate nearby. Handwritten, some barely legible, but all telling the same story. Of their commander's unfaltering courage under fire, his compassion for the wounded and even toward the enemy. His men spoke of their awe of him, their willingness to follow him anywhere. Survivors of some of the worst their war could give, they nevertheless wrote of their love. And of their sorrow, which had scarcely diminished ever since that night when, during a particularly horrific barrage, Major Archibald Swann disappeared.

She still kept his clothes in the armoire, his uniforms and Sunday best, and his Louis Armstrong records. The shed outside the lodge still contained his Harley-Davidson, covered with tarp again and fully oiled. The key remained in the rear, hidden in the rusty can.

Against all reason, she still half expected to climb to the top of the lighthouse one day and find him fixing the gramophone. He'd look up at her with his boyish smile, his pug nose and cleft chin.

"Mairzy Doats," he'd wink. "Might I have this dance?"

But that, she knew, was a fantasy. The reality was this, Fourth Cliff, the island on which she would spend the rest of her days, patrolling, keeping a peace that rarely needed preserving. Of the past, she would keep little. The wedding band on her finger, photos on the wall, and in her pocket, an ancient cranberry sprig. She'd grow old, she guessed, and someday hang up her uniform. On the wall peg would dangle the duty belt and the holster, the handcuffs and the eight-point hat. The black leather jacket with the silver captain's bars still pinned to its lapels. She would glance at them sometimes, not too frequently she hoped, and remember.

On the cliff—the third or the second, depending on who was asked—she watched as the sun rose before her in the east. Waves fell gracefully below her while, overhead, gulls and petrels shrieked. And from town, the distant clap of church bells tolling in celebration or, just as likely, warning. Mary Beth Swann saw and heard it all and tipped her cap brim in response. Then, turning away from the ocean, she went back to her black-and-white coupe.

But then came another sound. Deep-throated, lusty, unlike any other on the island. Mary Beth heard it, froze for a second, and ran. Across the sand she sprinted and onto the pavement heading south. Toward the roar of a 1941 Harley.

ACKNOWLEDGMENTS

WRITING A NOVEL ABOUT A POLICEWOMAN IN THE 1940S, ON A made-up Maritime island, and in the thick of a global war, would be challenge enough for any author, much less one who wasn't born yet and lived halfway around the world. I was grateful, therefore, to all the people who gave of their time and wisdom to bringing *Swann's War* and its intrepid heroine to life. I wish to thank Tammy Pechtold, Anne Dubitsky, Rachel Moore, Jeremy Herman, Huck Melnick, Aura and Fred Kuperberg, Paula Noah, Jason and Diana Perkins, Mike and Tziona Burstyn, Carrie-Keller Lynn, Michael Gordon, Stefanie Pearson, Charles and Ariella Zeelof, Jamie Gangel and Dan Silva, and Abbie Friedman Snyder.

I am especially indebted to my editor and friend, Pat Walsh, and his dedicated colleagues, Ingrid Lola Nilsson and Hannah Ogden. Michelle Dotter, editor-in-chief and publisher of Dzanc Books, could not have been more dedicated to this project. Nor could the team of Kim Dower, Tyson Cornell, Maria McCoy, and Dorothy Carico Smith, all of whom played a crucial role in delivering *Swann's War* to readers.

The island is imaginary but not so the name, Fourth Cliff, which is the site of a World War II coastal defense emplacement, now a recreational area, in Scituate, Massachusetts. I visited there with my father, a decorated veteran, twenty years ago. I called the island Fourth Cliff in respect to his memory and to the legacy of all who served there. Other aspects of the Fourth Cliff Island, from its flora, fishing, and cranberry farms, were culled from my experience on Nantucket, which I was privileged to visit during my diplomatic service in Washington.

Though entirely a work of fiction, *Swann's War* is based on numerous historical facts. Italian prisoners of war, some 51,000 of them, were interned in the United States during World War II. Considered more sympathetic to the Allied cause, they were kept separate from German POWs, placed in well-provisioned camps, and permitted to work. "Italian prisoners of war contributed one million hours of labor to the war effort," wrote Elizabeth Vallone in *Our World*. "They were farm workers, bakers, ditch diggers, dock workers, freight handlers for trucks, railcars, fulfilling the needs of the communities in which their camp was located."

While much has been written about President Roosevelt's appalling Executive Order 9066 for uprooting and imprisoning Japanese-Americans during World War II, relatively little notice has been given to the plight of Italian-Americans. Under that same Executive Order, 600,000 Italian-Americans, among them Joe DiMaggio's parents, were designated "enemy aliens." They were prohibited from almost all travel or from exiting their homes at night. Another 10,000 were forcibly relocated. J. Edgar Hoover's FBI relentlessly hounded them, confiscating their radios and occasionally detaining them without charge. These outrages took place while as many as 1.5 million Americans of Italian descent were fighting in the war. Fourteen of them received the Medal of Honor. Executive Order 9066 was only rescinded in 1976, but the record of its implementation remained secret until 2001. For furthering reading, see David A. Taylor's excellent article "During World War II, the U.S. Saw Italian-Americans as a Threat to Homeland Security" in the February 2017 edition of *Smithsonian Magazine*.

Several Italian-Americans contributed to the war in another way, however. Under Operation Underworld, the U.S. military employed the services of Charles "Lucky" Luciano and other mafia figures to help secure American ports from Axis sabotage. The mafia also proved instrumental in preventing dockworkers' strikes during the crucial stages of the war. Luciano's contacts facilitated the Allied invasion of Sicily and, later, of Italy itself. In return for his services, Luciano was freed from a fifty-year prison sentence and deported to Naples.

Oregano was virtually unknown in America before the Second World War. GIs brought it home with them from Italy and generously sprinkled it on their pizzas and spaghetti. Paralytic shellfish poisoning is, as Dr. Cunningham explained, a thousand times deadlier than cyanide. Metrazol (pentylenetrazol), the drug he used for treating battle fatigue, was popular in the 1940s but then discontinued. Injections of the drug were found to induce convulsions, coma, and death.

Though thousands of miles from the European front, America's East Coast was a prime target for German U-Boats. In early 1942 alone, they sank thirty-nine ships, many within sight of land. This prompted the United States to build twenty-one coastal defense installations, each armed with 16-inch guns and casemated against air attack. At the height of the war, in 1943, as many as 70,000 troops, including the U.S. Army Coast Artillery Units, were guarding America's shores. Together with sea and air patrols, they all but eliminated the enemy threat. Periodic attacks nevertheless continued. On April 16, 1944, U-550 was sunk near the shores of Nantucket, and the last U-Boat attack, near Rhode Island, occurred on May 5, 1945—three days before the end of the war.

Policewomen in the 1940s were generally confined to dealing with streetwalkers and urchins. They did not walk beats, drive vehicles, or carry guns. They were often called women policemen. Nevertheless, many strove to expand their roles, chasing down real criminals even if doing so meant hailing a cab. And apart from Francis

Lee, the pioneering forensics expert who received an honorary rank, there were no women police captains.

The Cocoanut Grove fire, which claimed 492 lives, indeed took place on November 28—the first Thanksgiving weekend of World War II—in Boston. It was the second deadliest building fire in United States history.

Swann's War required extensive historical research. I want to thank the many online sites that helped me get the language (https://grammar.yourdictionary.com/slang/1940s-slang.html) and clothing https://vintagedancer.com/1940s/1940s-fashion-history) right, and to understand life on the home front during World War II (https://www.history.com/topics/world-war-ii/us-home-front-during-world-war-ii). A special thanks must go to the Los Angeles Police Department, which posted a YouTube clip about the structure and function of a 1940 Harley-Davidson motorcycle (https://www.youtube.com/watch?v=hsDzISrncbg).

Special gratitude is due to Spencer Partrich whose generosity and vision helped make *Swann's War* a reality.

This book is dedicated to the late screenwriter and TV host Pola Miller. I met her when I was twenty-one and working as a window washer in Los Angeles. I overheard her discussing a vampire comedy script with her team; they were stuck on the title and I dared to suggest one: *Love at First Bite*. From then on, she took me under her wing and taught me lifelong lessons about writing. Number 285, for example, was that writers are indebted to even the most minor characters they create and duty-bound to give them the fullest possible characters. I hope I have lived up to that rule in this book and, by so doing, honored her memory.

As always, the deepest thanks go to my family—to my children, Noam, Lia, and Yoav, and my grandchildren, Romi, Mika, Matan, Alma, Ariel, and Tamir. They are, by far, my greatest story.